Also by Steve Brown

Black Fire
Radio Secrets
Of Love and War
America Strikes Back
Woman Against Herself

The Susan Chase® Mysteries
Color Her Dead
Stripped To Kill
Dead Kids Tell No Tales
When Dead Is Not Enough
Hurricane Party
Sanctuary of Evil

The James Stewart® Adventures
Fallen Stars
River of Diamonds
Rescue!

Read the first chapter of any
Steve Brown novel at
www.chicksprings.com

At this web site you can also
download a free novella:
In the Fast Lane

The Belles of
Charleston

The Belles of Charleston

STEVE BROWN

Chick Springs Publishing
Taylors, SC

First published in the USA in 2005 by
Chick Springs Publishing
PO Box 1130, Taylors, SC 29687
e-mail: ChickSprgs@aol.com
web site: www.chicksprings.com

Library of Congress Control Number: 2005902855
Library of Congress Data Available

ISBN: 0-9712521-3-0

10   9   8   7   6   5   4   3   2   1

Author's Note

This is a work of fiction. Names, characters, places, and incidents are products of the author's imagination or are used fictitiously. Any resemblance to actual events, specific locales, organizations, or persons, living or dead, is entirely coincidental and beyond the intent of either the author or the publisher.

Acknowledgments

For their assistance in preparing this story, I would like to thank Mark Brown, Sonya Caldwell, Missy Johnson, Kate Lehman, Jennifer McCurry, Kimberly Medgyesy, Ann Patterson, Ellen Smith, Susan Snowden, Dwight Watt, and the helpful people at the South Carolina Cotton Museum, and, of course, Mary Ella.

Dedication

*When writing about the past, it's always hard to keep modern-day sensibilities out of the text. **Margaret Mitchell** was probably the best at this, and that's why this book is dedicated to her.*

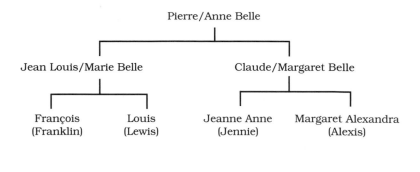

Pierre/Anne Belle

Jean Louis/Marie Belle — Claude/Margaret Belle

François (Franklin)   Louis (Lewis)   Jeanne Anne (Jennie)   Margaret Alexandra (Alexis)

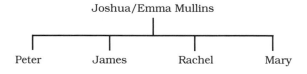

Joshua/Emma Mullins

Peter   James   Rachel   Mary

Other characters:
Burke Randolph of Richmond, Virginia
Nicholas Eaton of Lowell, Massachusetts
Colin Murphy of County Cork, Ireland

And in Charleston:
Abraham Marcus, Factor
Susannah Chase, Baker's Daughter
Virginia Hampton, Debutant Queen
Sidney Craven, Cad
Ella Mae, Servant
Homer, Servant

"South Carolina is too small for a republic and too large for an insane asylum."

¬James L. Petigru

Chapter One

In the year of 1842 the General Assembly of the State of South Carolina created the Citadel to keep the peace and prevent slave rebellions. That same year Margaret Belle gave birth to twins, and the fate of that military institution, the city of Charleston, and her daughters would be forever entwined.

The day of the twins' birth, Margaret labored in an upstairs bedroom at Cooper Hill, the Belle family plantation. At Cooper Hill, Jeanne Anne, called "Jennie" at the insistence of her uncle who doted on her, and Margaret Alexandra, designated "Alexis" to avoid confusion with her mother, spent the early years of their lives, except for summers when the air was so poisonous that it drove the family from Cooper Hill into town. As Low Country wags said: "In the spring Charleston is a paradise, in the summer it becomes a hell, and in the winter, a hospital."

On that evening in March, the two brothers sat in the study of the plantation house and listened to the screams of the new addition to the Belle family. The screaming was good news. It meant a healthy baby, and shortly the nurse would be down to tell Claude Belle that he had a son. Of course, if it were a girl, the nanny would probably take longer since there was no similar urgency for such trivial information.

Claude Belle and his brother, Jean Louis, were sixth generation Belles, descendants of Huguenots driven from France when Louis XIV, commonly called the Sun King, revoked the Edict of Nantes in 1685. After the Edict was revoked, which meant Protestants would no longer be tolerated in France, several of the Belle family were burned at the stake; some fled to other parts of Europe, many to America. Claude and Jean Louis' branch ended up in the Low Country, and though many Huguenots spent most of their fortune escaping from France, the ancestors of Claude and Jean Louis Belle arrived in America with considerable gold and silver in their purses. Now, six generations removed from that family disaster in France, the Belles of Charleston were known for their spendthrift ways, a tendency toward tuberculosis, and an uncanny ability to produce twins, many of them girls who left the family with dowries large enough to impress any fellow Charlestonian.

On this night Claude Belle waited in the study of the plantation house with his brother, who reclined on a settee across the room. Jean Louis Belle, Claude's junior by less than one year, spent his time in the city playing cards, shooting billiards, or in his cups. Once his allowance was expended, Jean Louis would fling himself on horseback and ride inland to Cooper Hill, where he would run roughshod over the field hands and those working in the plantation house. In contrast to his brother, Jean Louis *had* produced sons, and *his* set of twins had survived their mother's death and bouts of typhoid and yellow fever that struck down hundreds of Low Country residents each year.

At the unmistaken sound of two babies being birthed upstairs, Claude crossed the study and opened the door. Perhaps his luck had indeed changed and he would be able to match his brother's offspring. Jean Louis, deep in his cups because of the long delivery, struggled off the settee, walked to the sideboard, and poured yet another drink. Once fortified, he followed his brother to the foot of the grand staircase, and the longer it took for the nurse to appear at the head of those stairs, the longer became the look on Claude Belle's face.

"Cheer up, brother. They can't both be girls."

Turned out they were, and when this was announced, Jean Louis convulsed with laughter, spilling much of his drink on the hardwood floor. Regaining control of himself, he lifted his glass in salute. "To girls and the dowries they bring with them."

"Daughters," replied Claude with a sneer, "the curse of this family."

"Your side of the family perhaps," said Jean Louis, continuing to smile, "but not mine."

Chapter Two

In March of 1850, when the twins were eight years old and their boy cousins fifteen, John C. Calhoun died. A former United States senator, secretary of war, and two-term vice-president of the United States, John C. Calhoun had realized which way the winds were blowing in South Carolina and become the leading proponent of Nullification, a theory proposing that because the separate states had joined the union as sovereigns they could void any federal law deemed dangerous to a state's existence.

Calhoun's comrades acknowledged the great man as being the premier political thinker of the age. His enemies whispered behind his back that on everything concerning the Negro race, John C. was absolutely deranged. And this was the man who would cast his shadow across the South, especially Charleston, and at a time when Jennie and Alexis Belle began attending Madam Ann Marsan Talvande's French School for Young Ladies.

Jean Louis' sons, François, who had recently begun to ask family and friends to call him "Franklin," and Louis, had attended one of the city's premier boarding schools and would continue their education at South Carolina College in Columbia, where low country and upcountry gentry, educated together, were beginning to think as one about the politics of the day. François, however, had come up with an alternate plan. He would emulate their grandfather who had followed Andrew Jackson, the hero of the Battle of New Orleans, to the Florida Territory where, unfortunately, Pierre Belle had fallen during the First Seminole War. Louis thought his brother a fool and said no less.

"You'll get yourself killed like Grandfather, or worse, stationed out west where some Indian will lift your hair." Louis glanced at his brother in the adjoining rocker. "What little there is left to lift."

François' long black hair was no longer tied back with a colorful ribbon, and Louis had been puzzled as to why François' hair had been cropped so short, that is, until his brother made the announcement that he had secured the appointment to West Point. Louis and François differed in their views over the usefulness of the Union, and Louis wondered if this might be why his brother preferred to attend school with a bunch of abolitionists.

"It's better than suffering the slings and arrows of neighbors," countered François.

The two young men sat in rocking chairs on the veranda of Cooper Hill, drinking lemonade and watching two field hands saunter across the crushed shell turnaround and head toward the river, fishing poles over their shoulders and shaded by the cedars flanking both sides of the road.

François pointed them out. "They do that earlier and earlier and there's nothing you nor I can do to stop them."

Louis rose from his chair behind which a small black girl swished away flies with a fan. "I can do something and I'll do it now."

There was a gasp from the little black girl and the fan stopped its swishing. François put a hand on Louis' arm, pulling him down in the rocker. To the little black girl, François said, "Tammy, why don't you fetch us another lemonade."

Though their glasses weren't half empty, and he was truly upset at his brother for rebuking him, Louis knew better than to quarrel in front of the servants. With François it was an obsession, along with his brother's tendency to downplay their French heritage, which made little sense to Louis. Everyone knew the Belles were distantly related to the Marquis de Lafayette, who had stayed overnight at Cooper Hill during his final visit to the United States in 1825.

Louis gulped down the remainder of his lemonade and gave the glass to Tammy, who put down her fan and hurried off into the house.

Once she had disappeared, Louis said, "François, I know you don't want the servants gossiping about the family, but don't you think what you just did will set tongues wagging and we'll have more displays of ill-humor from the Negroes?" Settling back in his chair and looking in the direction of the river, he added, "Speaking for myself, I don't remember a time when the Negroes weren't surly."

"Because neither you nor I were old enough to re-member such a time. You know, Louis, at one time our family used to summer at Newport, Rhode Island."

Louis didn't follow and said as much. But when François' answer came, it was even more oblique. "We have a problem and it concerns Father."

"We've always had a problem with Father," said Louis. "What whorehouse did you have to pull him from this time?"

François leaned back in his chair and stretched out his long legs. His and his brother's legs were booted to the knee, their breeches mustard-colored; François' jacket blue, Louis' red. Only fifteen years of age, they were already six feet tall; faces sunburned and bodies tough from long hours of riding, and both young men had the rich black hair and pale blue eyes that pro-claimed to all that they were Belles of Charleston.

"It's a wonder Father hasn't caught the pox," Louis chuckled. "Always lie down with virgins is my motto."

"Don't you think it's rather odd that our father still patronizes whorehouses instead of having an octoroon of his own as many men of his age and position do?"

"A practice that is occurring less and less with the slings and arrows *we* suffer from the abolitionists." Louis smiled. "But to consider one's own father in the act of love—"

"Louis, don't be frivolous. I won't be here much longer to reason things out for you." François uttered this remark so loudly that anyone inside could hear what he had said through the windows over the veranda. Lowering his voice, François added: "You've noticed the surliness of the Negroes, but have you noticed the run-down appearance of Cooper Hill, the buildings in need of repair, the march of weeds across our property? Have you ever wondered why there are no grand parties or picnics held here as there are on other plantations? Or failed to notice the growing social isolation experienced by our family?"

Louis could only stare at his brother.

"Perhaps it's because you run with a crowd that only cares about the next card game, the next horse race, the next girl."

"You know I don't like it when you take such a high-and-mighty manner toward my friends."

"What I'm trying to tell you, dear brother, is that the Belles have shot their bolt, and you and I, in a few short years, are to be driven into the streets. You should make plans for the future, as I have by accepting an appointment to West Point."

"I'm the one being frivolous? The Belle family has lived in the Low Country for almost two centuries, and our grandfather, whom you want to emulate, fought not only Indians, but the British on more than one occasion."

His brother said nothing, only stared across the crushed shell turnaround and beyond, down the lane sheltered by cedars and leading to the Cooper River. As they watched, the field hands threw their lines into the water.

"Explain yourself, François."

"You know I prefer to be called 'Franklin.'"

"And I certainly don't understand why. 'François' was good enough in the past, why not now?"

"Because I believe people will accept my penniless state much easier as an American than as a Frenchman."

Louis sighed. "If you continue to speak in riddles, perhaps I should've been the one to fetch the lemonade." He glanced toward the double doors leading to the Big House. "Tammy will take forever."

Louis was more than a little irritated with their young servant, a flat-chested and sourly disposed girl if there ever was one. For some reason, their uncle had recently sold one of the most voluptuous and winsome slaves Louis had ever bedded, and this contributed to his foul humor. And for good measure, François had finally bested him in their latest horse race from Charleston to Cooper Hill.

"Exactly my point."

"You haven't made a point, as far as I can tell."

"My point is that very soon our family will no longer own Cooper Hill."

"Don't talk nonsense. Father would never consent to such a sale." In the Low Country, the law of primogeniture, or the right for the eldest son to inherit all real property, had been revoked in 1791. Still, it was always prudent to make out a will, and that's what Pierre Belle had done before decamping for Florida, passing along his estate to all his sons. "Rarely are Father and our uncle ever in agreement about anything."

François rolled his head across the back of the rocker and looked in his brother's direction. "Oh, as if you and I could ever agree on anything."

"I guess there is a similarity, but no one's selling Cooper Hill."

"It must be done, to cover the family's indebtedness. It's just that no one's told us, and they don't have to. Being fifteen, we're minors."

Louis looked over the rice fields stretching for miles alongside the river, finally returning his attention to the veranda and the columns supporting the overhead roof. "Debts? What debts?"

"Where do I start?"

"François, if you're toying with me—"

"I told you I prefer to be called 'Franklin.'"

"Well, Mister Benjamin Franklin, you're not making yourself much clearer than when you were called 'François.' Perhaps we should step down into the turn-around where I can clear your head of some of its feathers."

"That's always been your way of settling everything. You think you can support yourself with those fists of yours?"

"François," said Louis, after reclining in his rocker and uttering a very long sigh, "I simply said you're not making sense."

"And you should learn to listen, even at keyholes. Our family has lost our home though indebtedness, and I don't know how much longer we can afford the town house."

Tammy returned with the lemonade, handed the two young gentlemen their glasses, and picked up her fan.

"Thank you, Tammy," said François. "You're free to return to the kitchen. Louis and I will stroll down to the river now."

Tammy nodded and, fan in hand, scampered inside,

revealing her first enthusiasm for any instructions given to her that day.

Louis said it was too hot for a walk, but when his brother put down his glass, Louis did the same and trailed him across the veranda and down the steps. "I was much more comfortable on the porch," he groused.

"And you're the one wanting to pick a fight. But I'm not going to talk where the servants can hear me. It would amuse them greatly that you and I were the last to know."

Louis followed his brother across the crushed shell turnaround, skirting weeds sprouting here and there. It was the first time Louis had noticed the weeds. "See here," he said, but his heart wasn't in it. Of the two, François was the clearer thinker, "You can't be right about Cooper Hill."

"Ask Father," said his brother as he started down the sheltered road to the wharf where visitors disembarked. The road from Charleston to Cooper Hill was much too long and winding, only suitable for racing. "You and I are descendants of wastrels, Father and uncle included."

Louis gripped François' arm and held him up. "I know Father has his faults, but Mother died giving us life, and I don't like your name-calling of the only parent I've ever known."

François glanced at the hand on his arm. "And I grow weary of you putting your hands on me. As for believing me or not, it's not just the signs of decay that you've missed, but what I've overheard in conversations between our father and *his* brother. I, for one, decided to listen for a change."

Louis released his brother's arm. It had always been like this. If the brothers disagreed, Louis was willing to fight, but now, it suddenly occurred to Louis that he'd always let François, or Franklin, take the lead when it came to matters of some importance. Of his father, he asked nothing. "Then we won't fight, but I won't tolerate any more of your riddles."

"Come on, Louis, even you should be able to understand that because of our family's spendthrift ways, we will inherit nothing, unless you want to count the house in the city, and as I said, it may be mortgaged to the hilt."

"And that's why you must go north for schooling?"

François stared down the sheltered lane leading to the wharf. Two black men were preparing to tie up the boat; the boat that brought supplies to Cooper Hill, a run usually handled by their factor. That is, if Abraham Marcus was still in the employ of the Belles. A rich man now, the Jew no longer had to suffer fools. François suddenly realized this matter was no longer his concern and it filled him with sadness.

He said: "I don't see I have any choice. I've always had a head for numbers and West Point turns out some of the best engineers."

"But to attend school with abolitionists—"

"Actually, that worked in my favor. Very few Charlestonians want those appointments. Many of our crowd will attend the Citadel, and I'd recommend you consider the Citadel instead of the state college. What they teach you in the militia may become more important than anything you could learn in Columbia, especially if South Carolina leaves the Union."

"You believe there will be war?"

This was hardly news. People had been discussing the possibility of secession ever since Louis could remember, but it did come as somewhat of a surprise to hear it from his brother. Because he was a staunch Union man, François scrupulously avoided such discussions. Nowadays there were fewer and fewer Unionists in the city of Charleston.

François nodded as he looked back at the Big House atop the slight hill. "And in the service of South Carolina, all debts will be forgiven and prior service will not be ignored. " He smiled and clapped his brother on the shoulder. "Imagine, Louis, you may become governor, and think of all the money that could spill into your pockets from such connections."

Louis was thrilled, and it had nothing to do with becoming the next governor. His crowd practiced their jumps with the coming war on their minds, raced against each other as they hoped one day they would ride against the Yankees, actually kept their pistols primed for that day, but anytime he broached the subject with his brother, François shushed him into silence. Slaves could not compete with mass production, said his brother, as the cotton gin had proved, and mass production was the future of their country, whether it remained one country or split into two. And that was where François lost him. Others said that the cotton gin was the most important advance for the South's economy since the introduction of slavery.

People would look down their noses at them?

Louis' fists became balls at his hands. It wouldn't be the first time he'd used his fists to silence an opponent, and images of several young men flashed through his mind. But François was speaking of a day when fists wouldn't be enough, against locals or abolitionists.

Louis could remember families who'd lost everything and how their children had, slowly but surely, been excluded from their crowd. For those boys there had been no money for boarding school and their sisters had to settle for less prosperous beaus. Merchant houses now employed those young men, and they never had the time to ride, gamble, or pursue women.

How much longer would their money last? And what would become of his cousins, especially sweet Alexis. "What will happen to Alexis and Jennie?"

François looked at his brother with great sadness. He knew the affection in which Louis held his twin cousins. "For them, one can only hope they are fortunate enough to marry well."

Chapter Three

In March of 1852 *Uncle Tom's Cabin* was published in book form (previously serialized), and by 1853 the novel had sold over one million copies. And just as the book's readership was getting a shocking view of slave life on Southern plantations, Jennie Belle learned that girls who were about to turn eleven, whether residing up north or down south, weren't supposed to be so clever.

Sister Alexis was upstairs, sick again—she had always been a sickly child—and this time the family feared the family curse: tuberculosis. But when both children were well, their cheeks glowed pink, their hair was rich and shiny black, and those pale blue eyes could disarm you—everyone, that is, but their father.

So, Jennie, who always snapped back from one disease after another, was left to her own devices, but forbidden to go into the city as she might spread her sister's infection. For this reason, and the fact that her personal servant and companion had recently been sold, an inconsolable Jennie wandered the plantation house, disturbing the servants and annoying those from the "yard" who had snuck inside and wanted to socialize with the household help, but without some little white girl underfoot.

Jennie finally ended up in her father's study, guarded by the imposing portrait of Pierre Belle. Over the fireplace hung a portrait of the founding Belle, Antoine, who had arrived in this country with gold and silver coins in a money belt and quite a few British banknotes sewn into his wife's petticoats. Antoine had a square head and a great deal of black hair and a pair of pale blue eyes. In contrast, Pierre Belle had a round face, tufts of gray over each ear of his bald head, and the family's light blue eyes. And where Antoine had sat for his portrait in a plain business suit, his grandson wore Revolutionary blues with medals over a breast pocket, military shoulder straps, a high collar, and the French-style cocked hat.

On one side of the room was Pierre's rather large and ornate desk with an enormous upholstered chair behind it, a layer of dust on both, and opposite it, a fireplace with a small fire to chase away the chill, in front of it a woven, circular throw rug. The windows were closed and shuttered, and the wall behind the desk packed with books. Indeed, it had been the third generation of Belles who had purchased those books that filled the huge bookcase occupying one wall of their new plantation study.

Jennie could read quite well for a ten-year-old, though she'd been warned not to read too much, for books could fill her head with nonsense. She should stick to romances, such as *The Pickwick Papers.* Bored beyond belief, and overcoming her fear of the imposing portraits, Jennie began to walk back and forth in front of the rows of books, running her fingers over the spines until her fingers bumped into one title taller than the others and jutting out from the lowest rows. Prying the book loose and pulling it out, Jennie discovered it bore some rather odd and intriguing drawings burned into the cover. So she lugged the volume over to her grandfather's desk, and unable to maneuver the unwieldy book onto the desktop, slumped to the floor and began to turn the pages, but only after brushing her hands against her gingham dress and sneezing more than once. And wherever she opened this amazing book, she found points, lines, and angles described in drawings, numbers, and words that intrigued her, but in such detail that it took a great deal of concentration for her to understand. So absorbed in the book's pages, Jennie never heard her father, her uncle, and their factor enter the study.

Both brothers were the older version of the young men who had conversed on the veranda the year before, but where François and Louis were muscular young animals, Claude and Jean Louis were heavy around the middle but concealed it by the cut of their jackets. The third man wore a black suit, dark tie, and white shirt with a heavily starched collar.

The third man was Abraham Marcus, a Sephardic Jew whose family had been in Charleston since the 1740s when Jewish immigrants from London and Amsterdam began arriving in the Low Country to work in the indigo trade. Abraham Marcus handled all the family business, what little of it there was, and fought diligently against any and all attempts by these two middle-aged fools to bankrupt the Belle family estate. Marcus's hands were large and stubby, he had a pock-marked face from a youthful bout of chickenpox, and there was always a leather notebook in his hands, a record of all transactions made for the families by whom he was employed.

Jennie's father wore a pair of tan trousers and a blue cutaway coat with a ruffled white linen shirt. In his hand was a tall gray hat he placed on the corner of his father's desk on his way over to the card table on the far side of the room. He said, "It's a remarkable idea, but who shall we get to build the boat?"

"Ship, brother, ship," said his brother, coming through the door behind him. "Boats are craft you and I could master, but to ship cotton overseas, we'll need a packet. We shall be rich beyond our dreams, and instead of having to depend on Cooper Hill, we'll have people coming to us to ship their cotton overseas."

Jennie's uncle, Jean Louis, wore fawn-colored trousers and a rich green cutaway coat. A pearl stickpin held together the tan silk fabric around his neck and set off his light, grayish brown suit. Before joining his brother at the card table, he also set his hat on the desk beside his brother's. Early on the brothers had agreed that, because only a year separated their births, it would be improper for one of them to occupy the chair behind the desk, and now that François had chosen a career in the military, it seemed even more so. Sooner or later the affairs of Cooper Hill would rest on the shoulders of Louis, and it was important that these two brothers put on a united front. The fact that Louis now studied at the Citadel gave them a sense of relief, but there was no relief from the increasing debt eating into the family estate.

Older brother Claude had decorated the Big House with elegant furniture, tables covered with the finest Egyptian marble, and gorgeous curtains and sparkling mirrors shipped all the way from New York, and he entertained accordingly. The same could be said for Jean Louis' bachelor quarters in the city and was to be expected. A planter's status was for naught if his home failed to measure up to his neighbors', which meant the house in the city couldn't be any less stylish.

So, as if it made any difference, neither brother took a seat behind their father's desk but sat in straight-back chairs at a former whist table. The game of poker had become all the rage while the brothers had been growing up—several games were played weekly at the Charleston home of Jean Louis—and both Claude and Jean Louis owed large sums to their fellow Low Country neighbors, who, in the most tactful manner, pressed them for payment. Another reason for the shipbuilding scheme.

Abraham Marcus took his customary seat between the two brothers in a futile gesture to split their power. Overhead, from the expensive oil painting, Pierre Belle stared down at them.

"And who shall pilot this ship?" asked their factor. "You, yourself, Jean Louis, have admitted such a craft would be beyond either of you."

"Beyond me to build and navigate, but not to own," said the brother who usually came up with these crazy schemes.

"Yes, yes," said Claude. "We would simply wait until the ship returns and pocket our fortune. You yourself, Abraham, must agree that the returns on shipping have been far out of proportion for the risk."

"But in that case the Belle family was not responsible for the return of the ship, only the return *on* the cargo."

"Abraham, these are packets, not clipper ships, and would be able to carry tons of cotton."

"And passengers!" said Jean Louis. "You've repeatedly counseled us to spend wisely the capital left to us by our father, and in the past we've listened to your advice, but now that the economy's on a solid footing once again, this is our family's hour, our generation's opportunity."

"And it certainly won't be as boring as raising crops." Claude was the brother who resided at Cooper Hill, the family's gentleman farmer.

A servant entered the room, passed around glasses of Madeira, and added a log to the fire before leaving and closing the door behind him. During this brief interlude, Abraham wondered if he could talk these two fools out of this latest venture. Railroads, canals, or breeding horses. None of them had paid off, but all had become a constant drain on the Belle's family resources. Unfortunately, Abraham knew he'd probably lose this battle, as Claude, the usually sensible one, had come up with this particular scheme, overheard while attending Race Week.

Jean Louis held up his cup in toast. "To *The Belle of Charleston*."

Claude had not heard this before, but quickly warmed

to the ship's name. Over the course of a lifetime he and his brother had been the butt of more than one humorous remark because of their surname. "Yes," he said, raising his cup. "To *The Belle of Charleston.*"

Abraham did not raise his cup. He hadn't even touched his drink. Instead, he opened his journal and asked, "How much cotton will this ship carry?"

The two brothers looked at each other. "Tons!" they shouted and toasted *The Belle of Charleston* once again.

"Yes, yes, I understand," said their factor. "A long ton is two thousand, two hundred, and forty pounds, but what is the weight of a bale of cotton these days?"

"Long ton, short ton, what does it matter?" asked Jean Louis. "It all shall be weighed before being put aboard."

Abraham thumbed to a well-used page. "At last count a bale of cotton . . . with the new methods of baling was . . . four-hundred fifty pounds. So what will be the registered tonnage of this . . . *Belle of Charleston?*"

"And passengers," added Jean Louis. "Don't forget that packets carry passengers and make regular runs despite the weather."

"Yes," joined in Claude after putting down his glass. "And weather always affects crop production."

Abraham stared at Claude as the fire hissed and crackled behind him, a piece of unseasoned wood having been added to the fire by the departing servant. Bankruptcy was the only thing that could bring these two fools to their senses. Still, it was his responsibility to hold the line until the money ran out.

Abraham could remember Pierre Belle imploring him to see that his family was cared for, saying his widow would be alone in the world with small sons to raise. Abraham had done that, comforting the widow beyond the intent of the deathbed utterance, but never marrying her, as she was a Christian and he a Jew. And the commercial contacts this lowly Jew had made from being named the Belle family's factor and protector, you couldn't put a price on that.

"Plant more cotton!" was the command of the family banker once Abraham had shown him the letter from Pierre Belle and convinced the banker that he, a Jew, was to control the Belle family estate. "And buy more slaves," added the banker.

Which was the reason why Pierre and Abraham had set out for Florida in 1818. Slaves from Georgia and South Carolina were making their way into Florida Territory, much easier than the arduous trip north. Pierre Belle had gone there to locate several missing slaves and to assist Old Hickory in bringing Spanish Florida under American control. That would end any temptation for Low Country slaves to run off to Florida.

Abraham Marcus had gone along to capture a few runaways and return them to Charleston, as was his due under the Fugitive Slave Law of 1793. But marching through an East Florida swamp, Abraham had become mired in quicksand and was fortunate that Pierre Belle had been there to throw him a rope. Later, struggling to reach Chief Billy Bowlegs' encampment on the Suwannee River (present day Gainesville), Pierre had been grievously wounded, one of the few casualties of the First Seminole War, and this was where the deathbed utterance had been made.

Abraham turned to a new page in his journal as the

fire bit into the unseasoned wood. "Let's say this *Belle of Charleston* has a thousand ton capacity . . . and if a long ton is two thousand two hundred and forty pounds and you divide that number by a bale of cotton that weighs four hundred and fifty pounds, then you would have . . ."

"Four point nine seven, or five bales of cotton," said a small voice from under the desk.

After writing down the number, Marcus continued: "And five bales of cotton times a one-thousand-ton-capacity ship would be five thousand bales of cotton."

"That much?" said Jean Louis, amazed.

Enthralled by the large number, the timbre of the voice did not register with Jean Louis. Abraham, under the same spell, had simply written down the number. But Jennie's father was on his feet, chair screeching back, and looking for the source of that voice. He found Jennie in the kneehole of his father's desk, feet scooted up and the oversized book opened against her knees.

"What are you doing there, child?"

Jennie closed the book. "Reading, sir."

"I've told you that you're not to enter this room. This is a room for adults, not children."

Jennie scrambled from under the desk, dropping the book where it came to rest against the base of her grandfather's chair. Though Jennie loved books and would never dishonor them, she knew from past experience that she'd need both hands free to protect her bottom.

"I'm sorry, Papa, but I was lonely." Backing away, she tried to round the desk and reach the door.

Her father came after her, and with one of his boots, kicked the book across the floor where it slammed into the baseboard. By this time his brother was on his feet. Jean Louis had seen his brother's rages before, and usually they were directed not only at his daughters and wife but any female members of the household staff.

"Claude!"

His brother pressed on, berating his daughter and taking her by the hand. "Loneliness isn't an excuse for using the materials of others. You must have permission to enter this room. No telling what mischief you might get into."

Jennie backed up to the door, and when she reached behind her to grab the knob, her father seized her arm. Jennie cried out as she was whipped around where her father's hand could reach her bottom. There was no switch nearby; more's the pity.

"Claude!" said Jean Louis again, raising his voice.

Claude looked at his brother.

"Would you please stop playing with Jennie and return to the table?" Jean Louis inclined his head toward their factor.

Claude took a breath, and his hand shot past his daughter's head—Jennie cowed; she'd been smacked over the head before—and yanked a velvet cord. When Claude opened the study door, someone was already hurrying down the hallway.

"Yes, sir, Mister Claude?" The young Negro wore a dress and blouse, her hair in a white wrap.

"Hattie, please find some way to usefully employ my daughter. Preferably in the kitchen."

"Yes, sir, Mister Claude." Hattie took Jennie by the arm and marched her down the hall toward the rear of the Big House.

After closing the door, Claude turned around to find his brother standing behind their father's desk and examining the oversized book. Jennie Belle was Jean Louis' favorite. The girl had perfect pitch and could recite nursery rhymes from memory, making a joyful noise in an old widower's life.

Holding out the book, Jean Louis asked, "Do you suppose Jennie was actually reading this?"

"Nonsense," said Claude, glancing at the title: *The Elements of Basic Geometry.* "Jennie merely said that to avoid being disciplined." He glanced at the door again. "Discipline that should make it very difficult for her to sit down at supper for this and several other evenings."

"I'm sure she meant no harm." Jean Louis walked over to the poker table, put down the book, and opened it. He flipped through the pages.

Claude joined him, returning to his seat. Behind him the fire flared up as the older logs bit into the greener one. "Now where were we?"

Abraham looked up from his journal. "But the number is correct."

"Pardon me?" said Claude. Sometimes their factor would refer to his journal but fail to note where the particular information belonged in the current discussion.

"The number Miss Jennie gave me."

"The number . . . Jennie gave you?"

"Four point nine seven, or five bales of cotton per long ton."

Claude was still trying to understand, and making plans for a more severe punishment for his daughter. Embarrassing him in front of his factor . . . . Jennie would regret the day she'd entered this room. "What number?" he asked.

"The number used for calculating the bales of cotton to be shipped on *The Belle of Charleston*."

The Belle of Charleston?

Oh, yes, the name Jean Louis wanted to christen their ship. His brother pushed the open geometry book across the table, but when Claude looked at any page, all he saw were incomprehensible points, lines, and angles.

Jean Louis asked, "Didn't Jennie's mother say the girl was advanced in performing her sums?"

Abraham was staring at his notes. He'd divided the number three times; Abraham being from the school that said it was better to be slow and sure. But the child had simply told them the answer. Remarkable.

Jean Louis had left the poker table and was looking under the desk, pulling back their father's chair and examining the floor. "I don't see a pencil under here."

"Pencil?" asked Claude. Why would Jean Louis need a pencil?

Abraham scooted around in his chair to examine the floor behind him. He saw nothing. "No pencil. No paper. The child simply did the sum in her head."

Jean Louis glanced at the floor on the far side of the desk, then pushed the chair back into the kneehole and returned to the poker table to stand beside Claude. He thumbed through the front and the back of the text as if searching for something.

Claude glanced up, looking from one man to the other. "May I ask what in the devil the two of you are talking about?"

Abraham closed his journal and placed it on the table. "What I believe Jean Louis is saying is that your daughter calculated the answer without the use of a pencil or pen. No paper, and if I don't miss my guess"— he gestured at the geometry book—"there are no tables of division in that book."

"None whatsoever," said Jean Louis, leaving the book open in front of his brother, "and nothing that would assist in dividing such a sum. Claude, I've never seen anyone who could do large sums in their head. I've heard such people exist, such as those who can count cards, but I've never met one."

"Nor have I," said Abraham, nodding.

Claude stared at the two men, the knowledge of what they were saying, finally sinking in. "Are we sure that Jennie did the calculations in her head . . . and arrived at the correct figure?" Claude directed this question to their factor.

Abraham nodded, as did his brother.

Claude flipped through the pages of the geometry book. Behind him a log broke in half, fell from the grate, and the fire spit and hissed as the newer log found its place on the grate.

Claude closed the book and looked up. "None of this is to leave this room. If it became common knowledge that my daughter can do sums in her head, she would never find a suitable husband."

Franklin

Chapter Four

Franklin Belle arrived at the United States Military Academy for the summer term, or encampment, by taking a paddle steamer up the Hudson River to the wharf below West Point. The docks, along with the academy, were surrounded by the Hudson Highlands and jutted into the broad expanse of the river.

As the steamer closed with the docks, it paddled past Constitution Island, where Revolutionary soldiers had strung a boom and chain to hamper navigation by the British into what was considered the gateway to upstate New York. Franklin knew this, and quite a few other useless facts, because he had studied like a madman the preceding year. Never an assiduous student, Franklin had won his appointment in a rage—at himself for his past study habits. Only the math had come easily.

The gangplank was lowered and the departing passengers faced a surly soldier, along with his partner, a larger thug who wore no stripes but the same worn blue uniform. Both uniforms needed a good cleaning, noted Franklin, as did their white gloves. On the soldiers' heads were flat hats with some kind of decoration that flashed in the sunlight.

Roger Custis, who had joined Franklin and James Mullins in New York City for the trip upstream, felt it his due to disembark at the head of their small contingent. After all, Roger Custis was related to the widow who had married George Washington, and before stepping onto the gangplank, the Virginian doffed his hat toward the bow and the young woman standing there. An older woman, the young woman's companion, frowned, took the young woman's arm, and turned her to face upriver.

Moments later their baggage was dropped unceremoniously to the deck, the gangway raised, and the steamer's paddles dug into the water. At the sound of the whistle, the young woman on the bow glanced over her shoulder and smiled in the direction of the three young men. Again the young woman's arm was seized and she was forced to face upriver.

The smaller of the soldiers, a sallow-faced man with one hand on a cutlass, asked a question that was becoming more commonplace since Franklin had crossed the Mason-Dixon Line.

"Where are you young men from?" The soldier sounded Irish, as if he had just gotten off a boat himself.

"Boston," said the blond young man to Franklin's left.

Franklin said he was "from Charleston." Both voices were drowned out by Roger Custis announcing that he was from "the Commonwealth of Virginia, which had provided the Republic with more than its share of illustrious presidents."

The soldier's eyes narrowed as he studied Custis, then the belongings at their feet. Franklin and James both had a chest. Roger had the same, plus two carpetbags; and the Virginian wore a cape, though Franklin couldn't see how he could stand it. Today was as warm as any Low Country summer.

The sallow-faced soldier jerked a thumb over his shoulder. "Take the path to the top of the hill and report to the adjutant."

"To the what?" asked the blond young man.

James Mullins was a city boy, and in truth, he had just returned from Washington and his interview with the secretary of war. Mullins was the son of a manager of a New England textile mill and he had little interest in following his father and an older brother into the textile trade. James had won his appointment when the previous appointee, after spending only one night at the summer encampment, quickly bowed out. Mullins had been the next name on the list, and he had been rushed to Washington for his appointment with the secretary of war.

"And you'll see to our luggage?" asked Custis of the short, sallow-faced soldier.

"Not likely. You want your belongings taken up the hill, you'll do it yourself."

All three young men looked at the path winding up the hill and disappearing into the foliage.

"Sir . . ." started Custis.

"Corporal, Mister. I'm Provost of the Post."

"Very well, Corporal," said Custis, noticing a cart at the beginning of a rutted-out road that wound, like the path, up the side of the hill. "Then we shall require the use of your cart and mule."

"Sorry, Mister," said the corporal, sharing a smile with his thuggish-looking companion, "the mule's gone lame."

All three young men, including the larger of the two soldiers, stared at the animal.

"He doesn't appear lame," offered Custis.

Gripping the handle of his cutlass, the corporal said, "Mister, did anyone brief you that personnel at this post would test you?"

"Of course," said Custis, straightening up to his full height. "And I welcome the challenge."

"Well, Mister, I'm one of those personnel." He gestured toward the dusty trail leading up the hill. "And that path is your first test."

Custis and Mullins returned their gaze to the path, but Franklin only picked up his chest and hoisted it over his shoulder. He made it look easy, as was his intention. Bullies are more easily cowed by a show of force. Still, Franklin wondered if he'd strained something with his bravado and didn't think he'd feel so clever the following morning.

A moment later, James Mullins, the more slender of the three, began dragging his chest up the hill. Ahead of him, Franklin put one foot in front of the other and leaned into the hill, knowing full well that a stray root could bring him down as quickly as hubris. One root did just that to Mullins, and Franklin stopped, shifted around slowly, and faced downhill.

"Going to need a hand?" he asked, knowing that if the New Englander required help, Franklin, with the pain radiating through his shoulder, would be incapable of providing assistance.

Mullins was on his feet, brushing off the dust with his hat. "I'll make it."

Franklin smiled down at him. "Came ashore with the wrong party, didn't you?"

James stopped brushing and looked up. "Pardon?"

"Custis and I are from the South."

James looked at the dock where the two soldiers were watching Roger Custis try to figure out how he was going to move the chest, two carpetbags, and his cape up the path.

James faced uphill, wiped the sweat away, and smiled. "Next time I'll fall in with more worthy companions."

Franklin smiled, and after steadying himself, turned around, and started up the hill again.

From below, James called out, "How did you do that anyway?"

Franklin shuffled around and faced downhill. Again the chest dug into his shoulder. "How did I . . . do what?" He had to get moving or he was going to collapse—with his trunk on top of him.

"Swing that chest up on your shoulder?"

"Easy," said Franklin, forcing a smile. "By jerking my arm out of joint."

And to the sound of the New Englander's laughter, Franklin trudged up the dusty path to the flat, open area called the Plain, where more suffering was in store for those who made it to the top of the hill.

Chapter Five

During the five years that Franklin Belle and James Mullins attended West Point, and poor Roger Custis finally dropped out, the crisis in the Kansas-Nebraska Territories came to a head. The pro-slavery forces were happy to let the Nebraska Territory enter the Union as a "free" state, but they drew the line at Kansas, and many members of the government, including the president, thought it only fair that Kansas join the Union as a slave state. It did not matter what the people of Kansas desired, what was important was that the crucial balance of "slave" and "free" states be maintained.

This was why the American government turned a blind eye to adventurers who sought to overthrow governments in Central America or buy the island of Cuba and bring those countries into the Union. Everyone knew the "slave" state faction was running out of territories and that the "free-soilers" had plans to split the Oregon Territory into more than one "free" state.

During this volatile time in the Republic's history, a

new senator appeared on the national scene: Charles Sumner of Massachusetts. And during his service in the Senate, Sumner repeatedly attacked the institution of slavery. One of those attacks would almost get him killed. In Kansas, people *were* being killed. The people of New England supported their citizens moving to Kansas and had financed such moves, while in Missouri "border ruffians" rode into Kansas and acted in support of any government that included slavery in its state constitution. And each time the pro-slavery faction in Kansas proposed a state constitution or elected delegates to Congress, the federal government recognized them. At all costs the Union must be preserved, and the only way this generation saw that could be done was to maintain the balance of "free" and "slave" states.

It wasn't only the federal government and the states entangled in slavery. An uneasy alliance had sprung up between slaveholders in the South and the textile industry in New England. This was what emboldened Southerners to later proclaim: "Cotton is king," or all those spinning bobbins in Massachusetts would come to a stop.

For this reason James Mullins tempered his remarks about slavery during the years he roomed with Franklin Belle and this was why Franklin thought nothing of accepting an invitation to dinner during their final term at West Point. All the Mullinses tempered their remarks, including James's sister, Rachel, a stunning blonde, attractive enough to make any man forget the belles back home. Cordial at the table, Rachel declined any overtures made by Franklin Belle, and before dessert was served, she had retired to her room.

James had warned his friend that there was only one type of person his sister despised more than slaveholders and that would be anyone in uniform.

Over cigars on the veranda of the hotel, Franklin said, "Well, that pretty much leaves you and me out, doesn't it?"

Though Franklin was making an attempt at humor, James could see the pain on his friend's face. James was familiar with that pain. He'd seen his sister break more than one heart, many of those hearts belonging to his friends.

After a puff on his own cigar, James said, "Then take comfort in the fact that you belong to a large army of disappointed suitors."

Before leaving his family, James complained to his mother. "It's as though Rachel turns to ice." James was pacing back and forth in the parlor between two bedrooms rented for the night and trying to keep his voice down. "The one time Rachel condescends to attend one of my functions, she freezes out my best friend, perhaps my only friend at West Point with all the arguments and fights I've seen in this place during the last five years."

James's mother, a beauty herself even in middle age had asked, "You believe an attractive woman owes an explanation to every young man who pursues her?"

"Well, you'd think she would be more considerate to one of my friends."

"Oh, you mean encourage him."

"I don't mean that . . . just be more . . . considerate."

"And why is that? You think Franklin Belle and your sister could possibly have something in common?"

James had to admit that they probably did not.

"Then perhaps the fault is with your friend, that he shouldn't have tried to make such an impression on my daughter. You did tell Cadet Belle about Rachel's feelings toward soldiers and slaveholders, immature and unrealistic as they might be."

James admitted that he had warned Franklin that his sister held some very silly ideas.

"Then what did you expect to come of this meeting?"

James could not say. Franklin Belle was educated, handsome, and the best friend a man could have. Franklin had tutored him on more than one occasion; math came easy to his friend, and he spoke French like a native. When it came down to it, West Point was about the math and the languages, and personal responsibility, but the tales civilians insisted on hearing were the ones about the harassment every plebe learns to survive his very first year at West Point.

"Perhaps," added his mother, "you thought you might be able to spend more time with Franklin if he were courting your sister."

James had to concede his mother might have a point. He and Franklin had just concluded five productive years together and now that time was coming to an end.

"Or it's possible you're concerned that once Cadet Belle is exposed to others who hold the same opinions as your sister, he'll wonder if your friendship was a sham. Really, James, your father and I thought you would be able to stand on your own two feet by now."

"Of course I can, Mother." James drew himself up tall in his bright blue uniform. "I'm about to graduate from West Point."

"Well, all I can see is the same little boy who always wanted everyone to like him."

"Mother, do we have to have this talk again?"

His mother smiled. "Do you remember the last time we had this little talk?"

Five years ago, confessed James, before he came to West Point. Was it true he wanted people to like him? Then he'd make a lousy field officer and could only hope he'd rate an appointment as an army engineer.

Still, for the first time in his life his father was proud of him and actually listened to what he had to say. His father could picture him managing a New England textile mill and not some child who'd once talked earnestly about becoming a poet.

As a child James had been the one in the family who was quick to laugh or sing, and he could carry a tune. He could also play the piano and was the apple of his mother's eye for his concertos. Unfortunately James also discovered songs that could be played on upright pianos in dance halls and taverns, and those songs impressed girls and many of his friends.

When his mother caught James playing a beer parlor song, she had upbraided him for wasting his talent on such foolishness, and soon after that his father had him tested for West Point. Though James outwardly resisted the appointment, he secretly welcomed the examination, and when he became first runner-up, it was the first time his parents seemed to approve of anything he'd accomplished.

Now, with a great deal of help from Franklin Belle, in a few months he'd win his gold bars. Still, his mother was sitting in this parlor and reminding him that it was the women who did the choosing, and if his sister hadn't chosen someone of James's liking, that was none of his business. It would come as a complete surprise to James, and even his mother, that in the adjoining room, his sister had become entranced with Franklin Belle, even more so than her brother.

Rachel sat in a chair near a lamp and tried to concentrate on *Uncle Tom's Cabin*, the very book she'd brought along in the event she should run into Cadet Belle. It was true Rachel hated slavery, but she did not hate Franklin Belle. She'd tried to hate him, but from the very moment she'd met the tall cadet with the wide shoulders, dark hair, and pale blue eyes who not only was pleasing to gaze upon but whose words fell so pleasantly on the ear . . . .

Rachel slammed her book shut. Franklin Belle was nothing like Simon Legree, and when she thought of Franklin, her breathing became difficult and she considered throwing open a window to lower the temperature in the room. Problems with breathing, the rising temperature, all made it impossible for Rachel to remain at dinner. So, as soon as the meal was over, she fled upstairs to the safety of her room. Never in her life had she felt this way, and from the romances she'd read, Rachel knew there was only one reason why a lady's legs might weaken in the presence of a man she'd never met before.

When first seated beside Franklin, she'd wanted to announce that she wanted nothing to do with him or his kind. But by the time dinner was over, Rachel knew that anything she shouted, anything she said, would not be heard by her heart. And thinking of the tall cadet with the black hair and pale blue eyes, tears formed in the corners of her eyes.

Why was God doing this to her? Was this some sort of test?

Rachel sighed. Franklin was such a manly name, and Rachel wished he'd simply scooped her up and carried her away. Spirited her away to where, Rachel did not know, but from her reading of poetry, Rachel knew there was a place where dissimilar souls could dwell in peace and joy.

A knock at the parlor door caused Rachel to snatch up her book and open it in her lap. "Yes?"

Emma Mullins came in, closing the door behind her. She saw her daughter sitting in the glow of the oil lamp, the open book in her lap. "Are you all right, my dear?"

"Of course, Mother."

"Well, you did leave before dessert was served. It had the appearance of being rude."

"I wasn't trying to be rude. I wasn't all that hungry." One of Rachel's hands involuntarily rose to her eye where a traitorous tear had appeared. She jerked the hand down and returned it to the book.

Her mother crossed the room and took a seat on the edge of the bed, a bed large enough to sleep Rachel and her two younger sisters, who had demanded to be brought along to see their brother strut and march. At the moment, the two younger girls were in their parents' bedroom with their father, reading their nightly devotionals and saying their prayers.

Once she was seated on the bed, Emma said, "I think Cadet Belle is one of the most charming young men I've ever met."

"He's a Southerner, Mother. They're known for their manners." Rachel's hands turned white as she gripped her book.

Her mother could see her daughter's hands in the light from the lamp. She could also see that her daughter held her book upside down, and a look of concern appeared on her face. "You've met other young men, especially in Boston. Many of them just as gracious."

"Those young men were more our kind."

"But, my dear, you did not treat those other young men as you did Cadet Belle. You practically ignored him."

"I don't want to see him again, Mother."

"My dear, I haven't asked you to see him. I just came in to see if you were well or not. You did leave before dessert."

"And I'm telling you that I'm perfectly fine."

Emma stared at her daughter before finally getting to her feet and heading toward the adjoining door. At the door she faced her daughter again. "You know, your father and I want you to make up your own mind about your beaus."

"Yes," said Rachel, finally closing the book, "until you and he become impatient. After all, I am almost seventeen."

"You can understand our concern. I was engaged by the time I was your age."

"That was back in ye olden days. These days women can take more time selecting a husband, and they certainly don't need the advice of their parents."

"Oh, and do you think I made the wrong choice?"

"Of course not. I think you and father suit each other quite well."

"And Cadet Belle does not suit you?"

"He does not!"

"How could you possibly know? You didn't draw him out, and that embarrassed your brother because James had asked your father if he might seat Cadet Belle at your side."

"And I don't need any help from my brother." Rachel returned to the book in her lap, suddenly realized the volume was upside down, and quickly righted it. Red spots appeared on her cheeks and she glanced at the windows across the room. It was certainly becoming warm in here.

"Are you sure there's nothing else, my dear?" asked her mother as she opened the door to the parlor.

Rachel looked at her, this time her eyes filling with tears. "Oh, Mother, what's the use of becoming better acquainted with Cadet Belle? Everyone knows as soon as the Southern states leave the Union, their officers will resign their commissions, and how could anyone live down there with those people?"

Her mother stared at her daughter for a very long time; then, without saying a word, she left the room.

Chapter Six

The following spring, when her family was preparing for James's graduation from West Point, Rachel's father called her into his study, a wooden-panel room with several windows and the curtains pulled back to allow in the spring sunshine. The study was Rachel's favorite room, or so she thought. She'd read many of the books found there and considered the sofa the most comfortable piece of furniture in the house—that is, besides her own bed. Sometimes she'd lie on her bed, romantic novel at hand, and dream up scenarios about what life would be like married to a man such as Franklin Belle, the problems that would come from such a union, and how the two of them would work out their differences.

She'd been imaging such a scenario when summoned to her father's study. It was her father's habit of taking Saturday evenings to review the deportment of his children, and the following day, which was the Sabbath, would be the proper day for them to repent.

And this was late Saturday afternoon.

Rachel entered the study and found her father running a pencil down columns in a ledger. It was also her father's habit to review the mill's business, and as Rachel grew older and her interest in the outside world increased, she could not understand why this had not become a vexation for her mother.

Wouldn't any sort of social gathering be preferable to whiling away another evening at home? Her mother hinted she'd been quite sought after as a girl and could've had her pick of beaus. But her mother's heart had been won by this stern, serious man several years her senior.

Joshua Mullins was the product of a devout family and had been recommended as a bookkeeper to Simon Eaton, one of several New Englanders building textile mills along the lines of Nicholas Cabot Lowell's innovation. Nicholas Cabot Lowell had built the first factory that could take raw cotton and turn it into finished cloth, all in the same building. The cloth could be dyed there, too. But at the conclusion of the War of 1812, when trade reopened with Great Britain, the British began dumping cheap English linen in the United States to revive its own sagging textile industry.

Lowell, Eaton, and others went to Washington, in one of the first, and definitely not the last attempt to persuade legislators to see the country's economic picture their way. The result of this "lobbying"—it would not be called that for another generation—was a 25-cent-a-yard duty on cloth, the first protective tariff.

In the South tariffs were considered an abomination because its residents depended on exports, not only to Great Britain, but, increasingly, to France. What if Europe should retaliate with a tariff of its own? And wasn't the New Englanders' tariff nothing more than a way for northern industrialists to gouge their southern customers by selling them cloth at higher prices? And with the distain gentlemen planters had for the merchant class, it would be years before South Carolina would have its own textile mill, and that mill, built in Graniteville, would not be built by a Southerner, but a Yankee from Pennsylvania.

Northern pressure on Washington kept the tariff rising until 1828 when Congress passed what the South called the Tariff of Abomination. It was then that John C. Calhoun proclaimed that the individual states had the power to rule federal laws unconstitutional. Firing back, Andrew Jackson made it clear that he would send in troops to enforce any federal law. The secessionist threat ended when a new tariff bill was passed, and it would be another generation before "King Cotton" spread throughout the South and these secessionists would be joined by more sympathetic states.

During this time of increasing sectional strife, Joshua Mullins rose from bookkeeper to head bookkeeper and finally to factory manager, and along the way he acquired a social climbing wife, several children, and one of the nicest homes in Lowell, Massachusetts. He also developed a ledger system for correcting his children.

Joshua looked up from his figures as his daughter entered the study. "Please close the door and take a seat."

Rachel did, sitting across from her father.

"My dear, your mother has asked me to speak to you about a rather delicate matter."

"My beaus."

Joshua stared at his daughter, the same blond beauty as her mother, but a girl with many more opportunities than those to be found in a textile mill.

The beauty that had entranced Joshua Mullins had been working on the floor of Simon Eaton's factory when he'd first met her. Joshua had openly stared at her until Emma told him to close his mouth and return to his ledgers. Flushing, Joshua carefully avoided the spinning room for several days, but the image of the blond beauty remained in his head.

Emma was working in the mill because her father had died and her two brothers had gone west, as had most young men who'd given up farming the rocky soil of western Massachusetts. When her mother decided to join her sons in Ohio, Emma moved to Lowell, found a job and a home in one of the dormitories provided for single women who wanted to escape the drudgery of farm life, whether in Ohio or western Massachusetts. Now Emma set her sights on Joshua Mullins, who not only had graduated from college but aspired to be more than a bookkeeper.

Joshua was hardworking, frugal, and appeared to have few interests outside the mill beyond his church. Of course, it came as somewhat of a surprise when Emma discovered her husband keeping a ledger on each of their children's deportment. He'd kept one on his wife until Emma learned of it, tore up the ledger in his presence, and threw it out.

And, thought Joshua, as he stared across the desk

at his oldest daughter, Rachel has her mother's spark and her tongue. Perhaps that's why his wife had asked him to speak to her so there'd be no doubt that they were of like mind about the issue at hand.

"May I be direct?" asked her father.

"I think it's best." Rachel began patting down her dress around her. Better to finish this and quick, and get back to her novel.

"We're returning to West Point for your brother's graduation and James has asked that you not accompany us."

Rachel's head snapped around from where she was patting down her dress. "But—but I must go. I have a right to go."

"Not if you upset everyone."

A pain cut through Rachel like a knife. Actually, Rachel had no idea what a knife would feel like, but it felt like James—her own flesh and blood!—was cutting out her heart. "Father . . . ."

He raised a hand. "You may not care for the pleasure of someone's company, but it is your Christian duty to accept people as they are."

"Father, you may accept slavery, but my generation will rid our country of this blot on its virtue."

"Rachel, I'm not accustomed to being interrupted when I speak."

His daughter closed her mouth, but when she did, she felt her heart breaking. Oh, how could James do this to her? Her father was speaking. She should be listening, but that was impossible. She wanted to leap from her chair—though that might be quite unladylike—and rush out of the room . . . and do what?

A letter! Perhaps a letter to James could undo this misunderstanding.

That's it! She'd write her brother that very day and see that the letter was posted.

Today was Saturday. How long would it take for the letter to arrive at West Point, and could she compose a letter on the Sabbath?

Even if she did write the letter, as she'd written Franklin previously—why was he not returning her correspondence! The West Point headmaster had to be intercepting her letters—what good would it do to send another letter? And the family was due to leave next week for James's graduation.

Oh, Lord, what would she do? And immediately she was ashamed of taking the Lord's name in vain.

There was a tapping sound.

Rachel blinked and looked at her father. He sat there, patiently tapping his pencil on the desktop.

"My dear, are you listening?"

"Of course, Father."

"It doesn't appear that you were." Her father put down the pencil, but only after making a note in her ledger. "Well, that is quite enough about Cadet Belle."

Cadet Belle? Her father had been speaking of Franklin while she'd been anguishing over how to find some way to contact him.

Oh, Lord, what had she done?

"Your mother and I have agreed that you are to re-main here while the family visits your brother, and to drive home this discourtesy toward your brother's friend, the headmistress of your school has agreed, for an extra sum, to accompany you home each day and attend to your school lessons and your practicing of the piano." Her father arched an eyebrow. "Do not waste your time nor my money. Is that understood?"

"Yes, Father, but I did wonder as to what was my transgression. The Sabbath is tomorrow and I'd like to appeal to my Lord for his forgiveness."

"Rachel, don't blaspheme. I doubt you've heard a word I said."

"No, sir, that's not true. I simply wanted to know which one of the Lord's commandments I'd broken. You covered so many transgressions. On which one would you prefer I concentrate?"

Joshua sighed. Perhaps it was like his wife said, that he was becoming quite wordy in his old age. Or the girl could simply be confused. It wasn't like he was talking to one of his sons, though James's mind did have a tendency to wander, and this was why he and his wife would not allow Rachel's rudeness to come between their son and his newfound friend. Franklin Belle appeared to have been given a solid foundation by his family, something that had gone terribly amiss with his own son but had been corrected at West Point.

Their firstborn had done well, but James had been headed down the road to becoming a wastrel when the Lord had interceded with the congressional appointment. The Lord did move in mysterious ways, testing the secretary of war's first choice and finding him lacking for the rigorousness instruction at West Point. And now it fell to him, and the Lord, to make sure his daughter would accept one of her beaus.

"Your transgression was your rudeness, which means you dishonored your parents."

Staring into her lap, his daughter said, "You've always taught me to honor you and mother, so if I've wronged you, I apologize."

"Thank you, but my ruling about your traveling to West Point stands."

Rachel looked up. "I understand, Father, but I'm confused."

"What are you confused about, my dear? You know I'm always here if you need guidance."

"Well, I do hate to bother you, but I believe this goes to the very foundation of myself as a person." Her father was very strong on building solid foundations, and one of the very reasons he was so dreary. Oh, my, what it would be like to be whisked away by a Southern cavalier. The dances, the parties, the . . . slaves.

She shuddered.

"Rachel?"

"Sir," she said, focusing on her father again.

"I'm waiting."

"Forgive me, Father. I was organizing my thoughts."

Joshua nodded. He'd made his ruling, and now he could be more lenient. After all, in the future his children would come to him for advice. There was just so much a mother could teach them.

"If I was rude to Cadet Belle, that was not my intention. The man comes from a family of slaveholders, and I did my best not to rebuke him. So that my heart would not run away with my mouth"—that was an understatement if there ever was one!—"I chose silence over discourse. In this, I believed I wouldn't dishonor our family. You know of my feelings about such issues. I believe they are stronger than anyone's in this family."

"Judge not, Rachel, less you be judged." Joshua's textile mill purchased a great deal of cotton from slaveholders.

"Father, I did not come in here to discuss slavery but my penitence."

"Daughter, watch your tongue!"

Rachel stared into her lap again and allowed her father's wrath to wash over her. When he had finished, and he had made a note in her journal, she said she'd be more careful in how she phrased her statements.

"Father, if I were to accompany the family to West Point and engage Cadet Belle in a discussion about the immorality of slaveholding, I wouldn't want anyone to think I was being rude."

"Well," said Joshua, leaning back in his chair, "that issue's been settled. You are not to travel with us."

"Yes, sir, and I accept your decision. Still, you've told us that what people think of you is most important, and that is why we should all strive to be upright and virtuous."

"That is correct."

"Have I ever given you cause to think you could not trust me?"

Actually, Joshua couldn't think of a time when he had not thought of his daughter as reliable, and that brought him to the second point on his agenda.

"Yes, Rachel, I believe you are quite dependable and trustworthy."

"Then if I promise not to be rude, why should I not travel to West Point?"

Joshua smiled. "And you have always known how to argue a point. But your mother and I are determined to support James's relationship with Franklin Belle." He raised a hand to cut off any further protests by his daughter. "You, who've complained about your brother's foolishness in the past, should understand most of all."

"And I have no say in our family's plans?"

"Rachel, I'm not prepared to discuss the rights of women anymore than you were prepared to discuss the rights of slaves."

Tears formed at the corners of her eyes, but Rachel would not wipe them away. Franklin was gone . . . gone forever. If she could not see him . . . if he would not answer her letters . . .

Finally, she was able to say, "I assume in the future Cadet Belle will visit us in Boston."

"I very much doubt it, seeing that when some of our fellow New Englanders hear such an accent, they forget all sense of propriety and attack such visitors in the most vicious manner." Joshua sat up. "But that is no longer your concern. Your mother and I want to know where you stand with Nicholas Eaton."

"Nicholas is as against slavery as I am. We have often discussed the issue, as well as women's equality."

"I'm not interested in his political views, my dear. I want to know if you've encouraged him?"

"I really don't care for him, Father, except that we share similar views." And Nicholas helps me escape from this dreary house from time to time. How her mother could stand being here, day and night . . . . There was more to life than church socials.

"I was told you and Nicholas have been intimate."

The sides of Rachel's neck began to heat up. She didn't know quite what to say. Discussing romance with her father . . . it was unseemly.

"Rachel, everyone knows a woman's intentions . . . if she allows one of her beaus to kiss her."

"Father, I have no intention of marrying Nicholas Eaton."

"But you did kiss him."

"I did not kiss him. Nicholas kissed me."

"Are you saying he took advantage of you?" Joshua leaned forward on his desk. He had to be careful here. Nicholas Eaton was the son of his boss and such a relationship would be fraught with danger.

Rachel's hands nervously washed each other in her lap. "It was nothing. The last time he was here, when Nicholas left, he kissed me on the cheek. That was over a week ago."

"Are you sure you did not encourage him? You must have; otherwise, a son of such a prominent family wouldn't have taken such a risk. The Eaton family knows what this means to a young woman's reputation."

"It was nothing, really. We're just friends."

"Young people are sometimes rash, and their actions can lead to . . . more indiscreet behavior. That's when the parents of the couple must step in. I have spoken with the young man's parents, and when we return from West Point, Nicholas will again press his attentions on you, but this time he has my blessing."

Rachel stopped washing her hands and gripped the arms of her chair. "But I have no interest in becoming engaged to Nicholas Eaton."

"Young women don't know what's best for them these days. Together your mother and I, and the young man's parents, will see this relationship through to its logical conclusion. Our family is not to be shamed."

"And I have no say in this matter?"

"The young man has family, fortune, social standing, and most important, he is devout—what else would you want?"

Rachel slid forward in her chair. "But I don't love him!"

"You can learn to love him. It's been done before."

Now Rachel was on her feet. "Father, I can't believe you'd do this to me. Why, you're treating me like . . . like a slave!"

"Rachel, remember who you're speaking to, and don't compare your standing to a Negro. You are free to come and go."

"But only if I marry Nicholas Eaton."

Joshua sat back in his chair. "I wouldn't allow you to leave this house without a suitable escort. Your husband will do the same."

"Father, you can't do this to me." Tears began to run down her cheeks. "Please don't do this to me!"

"Rachel, you act as if your life would be over."

"It would be!"

"Nonsense. It is your duty to marry and bear children."

"But bear the children of a man I love."

"Rachel, you've been reading far too many romances."

"Then I have that advantage over a Negro. At least I can imagine myself living with someone other than a man I do not love." And she turned on her heel and hurried out of the study.

Her father sighed and then carefully entered his daughter's transgressions in the family journal.

A couple of days before the Mullins were to arrive at West Point, James broke the news to Franklin that his sister would not be accompanying his family. James thought this would relax his friend, who had seemed rather edgy of late. Instead, the news appeared to set off Franklin, like the new types of artillery rounds James had been studying.

"Then she is a damn coward!"

"Who? What?" asked James, confused. His friend sat across the room from him composing yet another letter. Southerners wrote more letters than politicians.

Franklin took the letter and ripped it to pieces, scattering those pieces across the floor. The company commander, upon hearing Franklin's slur on someone's honor, glanced in the door and spied the litter on the floor. Cadet Belle was immediately written up, and now Franklin would be marching a punishment tour while James dined with his family.

Oddly enough Franklin was able to steal away, and he apologized to the family for not being available for dinner. He also pressed a note into Mrs. Mullins's hand. Another thank-you or apology, James imagined. Southerners always had to get the last word in, even when they no longer had an audience.

And Franklin Belle had few friends at West Point. The more heated the exchanges became between the cadets from the North and those from the South, the more distant his friend became. Wags, on both sides of the slavery issue, believed Franklin Belle wanted his commission so badly that he would actually remain at West Point even if South Carolina left the Union.

Chapter Seven

When the Mullins family returned from West Point, Rachel's younger sister, Mary, blurted out that Cadet Belle had asked for her. Mary was twelve and old enough to enjoy a good intrigue.

"What did he say?" asked Rachel, looking up from her book. She glanced at her bedroom door to make sure it was closed.

"That he was sorry you had not made the trip." Mary threw herself across the far end of her sister's four-poster bed and flashed a big grin. "He looked very sad, if I say so myself."

Rachel's chin quivered. "I'm—I'm sure that's due to the difficulty of the curriculum at West Point."

"Oh, yes, that must've been it." Smirking, she added, "Or could it be that Franklin Belle is sweet on you?"

"Mary, don't be silly." Despite what she said, her heart soared, the room swam, and for a moment Rachel thought she just might swoon. She gripped the nearest post of the four-poster bed. When her sister had burst in, Rachel had been absorbed by the impassioned poetry of Walt Whitman. "You're much to young to know anything about love."

Mary rose up on her arms. "I'm older than you think."

Rachel closed her book and stared at her sister. Was it possible that Mary could keep a confidence? Being the older of the two younger girls, Mary constantly bothered her about how to apply makeup and which dress to wear, a far cry from playing dress up and smearing makeup all over her face.

Franklin Belle sweet on her! Rachel glanced at the door. If this were true, at any moment, Franklin might burst in her room, sweep her up in his arms, and . . .

She must remain composed. She couldn't let herself be carried away. After all, this was a child stoking the fires of her passion. "Mary, please go to your room and speak no more of this. I'm betrothed."

Mary leaped off her sister's bed. "Engaged to a man you don't love!"

"Mary, watch your tongue!"

"If you were looking forward to marriage, then why do you cry so much?"

"That . . . that is none of your business." Rachel gripped her book. "Now, would you please leave?"

Mary sauntered over to the door. "Then I take it Mother didn't give you the note?"

"What note?" Rachel put down her book and swung her legs off the bed. After all the letters she'd written, there was finally a reply from Franklin?

"The note from the man you prefer to your betrothed." At the door Mary turned around, and the look on her sister's face told her all she needed to know. "No. I didn't think she would."

Rachel was on her feet now, crossing the room. "Mary, if you're teasing—"

"I am not! There was a note from Cadet Belle. For you." Her sister opened the door and turned to go. "Ask Mother if you don't believe me."

Rachel did, and within earshot of the servant girl and the family cook.

"Where is my note from Cadet Belle?" she demanded.

Her mother glanced at the two women, and then took her daughter's arm and escorted her from the kitchen and into the dining room. Between the two rooms was an adjoining door and Emma closed it behind her.

"Rachel, I've told you before that family business is not something you want the servants to hear."

"I want that letter!"

"It wasn't a letter. It was a note."

"I still want it." Out came Rachel's hand, palm up.

"I'm sorry, my dear, but I no longer have it."

"You . . . don't . . . have it." Rachel's arm sagged. "What—what did you do with it?"

"I tore it up."

"You tore it up?" Rachel stepped back. How could her mother have done this to her?

"I'm sure Cadet Belle meant well. He had no way of knowing you were engaged when he gave that note to me."

"Is this why you insisted on my engagement being announced before you made your trip to West Point? What did the note say?"

"Rachel, that is no longer important."

"How do you know what's important and what's not important? To me?"

"A mother knows best."

Rachel didn't know what to do or say. Her hand searched for something to hold onto and found one of the chairs around the dining room table.

"You'll just have to trust me, my dear. Mothers do know what's best for their daughters."

"I . . . I . . . I demand the right to my correspondence."

Emma reached out to take her daughter's arm, but Rachel backed away, bumping into the dining room table.

"Mother, I can't believe you'd do this. You're treating me like a child."

"You're betrothed, Rachel."

There was that word again. She'd never thought marriage could be such a prison, but it appeared that it was, and the doors to that prison locked behind you the moment you became engaged.

The room began to swim, her chest tightened, and Rachel had a hard time catching her breath. What was she to do? She had no more freedom than some damn slave. Her hand left the chair and rose to her mouth. Had she just cursed in front of her mother?

"Rachel, it's entirely inappropriate for you to correspond with another man now that your engagement has been announced. Cadet Belle should not have been so bold."

"You don't trust me."

"With you making this scene, I certainly don't."

Rachel's mind was whirling, not with the usual romantic notions about Franklin sweeping her away, but questioning the odd manner in which he'd chosen to correspond: a note given to her mother.

"Mother, have there been other letters?"

Her mother glanced at the floor.

"Oh, Mother," said Rachel, gripping a chair again. "Franklin has written before, hasn't he?" There was such a pressure on her eyes. At any moment she would burst into tears. "You intercepted all of them, didn't you, even the ones before I became engaged? Where are they? I want to see them."

"Really, my dear, you shouldn't use another man's name with such familiarity."

Rachel let go of the chair and held out her hand. "Give me the letters."

"Would you listen to what you're saying? You want to know what another man thinks of you when the only opinion that counts is the opinion of your betrothed."

The hand remained out, palm up. "Either give me the letters or I might have to travel to West Point and learn what Franklin Belle really thinks of me."

Now it was her mother's turn to draw back. "Rachel, think of what you're saying. Young women don't travel unescorted."

There was a knock at the door, and both women looked in that direction. The servant girl hurried down the hallway, and as she did, flashed an embarrassed smile passing the dining room.

It was her fiancé. Rachel had completely forgotten Nicholas would be calling today. She'd been dressing when Mary had come to her with the news about the note, and now Nicholas would see her without her makeup properly applied.

Her hair! What did her hair look like? Cowed, she remained hidden in the dining room while her mother went to the door.

"It's Nicholas, dear. Here with your newspaper."

Nicholas was there to drop off the *Liberator*, which detailed the latest misdeeds by Southern slaveholders. Later her fiancé would return for the dinner honoring James's graduation from West Point. Early on Rachel had told Nicholas that other young men had kept her in the dark about the changes occurring in the world, but if Nicholas really cared for her, he would not hold onto the latest news but share it with her immediately, and as equals.

"Here's something for you to read," said her mother, returning to the dining room and thrusting the paper at her daughter.

Rachel brushed past her and rushed upstairs. She had plenty to think about and she didn't need a damned newspaper to sort out the difference between slavery and equality.

When her brother returned from swaggering around Lowell in his uniform with its shiny new bars, Rachel was waiting for him, and she showed no respect for his rank. James, though, was full of himself and strutted into the parlor like a peacock.

"I understand you wished to see me, sister dear. Though I would've expected an engaged woman to be in a happier frame of mind." James stared at his sister, taken aback by what she wore.

"You put me in this mood," said his sister from the settee. She wore a jacket and knee-length skirt of navy blue and, underneath, men's trousers of the same material, gathered at the ankle, not an outfit she'd be allowed to wear outside the confines of her own home.

"Er—are those bloomers?" asked her brother.

"They are. I made them myself."

"Well, yes, I see." James had come to stand in front of his sister, hands behind his back, at parade rest. "Nicholas is a wonderful choice for a husband, though a bit bookish for my taste."

"James, I want to talk to you about Franklin."

"Franklin? I can tell you that Franklin doesn't want to hear your abolitionist ranting. Of course, slavery's not the sort of issue he and I discuss, and that's how we've remained friends, right through graduation. No small accomplishment, if I must say so myself."

"Then how would you know his opinion?"

"I know his opinion of you."

"And that would be?"

"Rachel, Mother said you might try to engage me in conversation about this subject, and I agreed with her that this is not an appropriate subject for the two of us to discuss."

Rachel sat up. Her eyes narrowed. "Mother said what?"

"She—er . . ." James's hands came out from behind his back. "She said I wasn't to discuss—"

"Discuss what?"

"Why Franklin Belle, of course, and you can understand. It's not proper."

"Everyone in this house seems to think they know what's best for me."

"My dear, we only have your best interest at heart." James crossed his hands behind his backside again and spoke over her head. "In the future, you'll be happily married, and I'll be a brevet lieutenant in the United States Army, stationed where, I really don't know, though I hope for a posting in New England."

"Must I remind you that when we were children, you hated the army."

"Sooner or later we must put away childish things."

Rachel's hand reached out, clutching the hem of his military blouse. "James, please tell me what Franklin said and I'll never mention his name again."

Her brother looked down, pity in his eyes. "My dear, a relationship between the two of you wasn't meant to be. You're from different parts of the country. Different worlds."

Rachel released his tunic, uttered a sob, and held her head in her hands.

James didn't know what to do. He looked toward the hallway. Should he call his mother?

No. He should be able to comfort his own sister.

Kneeling in front of her, he took her chin in his hand and raised it. "Rachel, everything's going to be all right."

His sister uttered a sick little laugh. Now the tears were really pouring, and that made it the absolutely worst time for Nicholas to return for dinner. And standing on the stoop beside him was Lieutenant Franklin Belle.

Rachel gasped and gripped the sides of the settee to remain upright.

"Franklin," asked James, leaping to his feet as his friend was ushered into the parlor, "what on earth are you doing here?"

The servant girl made herself scarce, after hanging up the men's cloaks.

Rachel's fiancé entered the parlor, smiling. Nicholas Eaton was a brown-haired, round-faced young man who could afford the latest fashion and always wore it. Today, besides the cloak handed off to the servant girl, his attire was a jacket, silk shirt, snug trousers, and Wellington boots.

"Hello, everyone. Hello, James. Good to see you again. My, my, but you do fill out that uniform quite well." He extended his hand to his future brother-in-law.

But James's attention was riveted on his best friend. What was Franklin doing here?

"Your sister and I have a difference of opinion," explained his friend, "and I'm here to settle it once and for all."

"Why, Franklin," said James, glancing at Nicholas, who stood beside the South Carolinian, still offering his hand, "I'm not sure this is totally appropriate."

Franklin had posted himself as James had done, hands behind his back, practically at parade rest. He gave a short bow to Rachel, who remained seated on the settee.

My God, the love of her life was here and she was wearing bloomers!

Franklin didn't appear to notice. "Miss Mullins, if I understand correctly, in this part of the country women meet men as equals and thrash out their differences face to face." There was no humor in his voice when he said this.

Rachel was dumbstruck. Franklin was in her home, and much more handsome than she'd remembered. Talk about filling out a uniform. And that black hair, pale blue eyes, and sunburned face. After all these years, her knight in shining armor had come to rescue her! And her fiancé was standing right beside him!

With a cry, Rachel leaped to her feet and bolted from the room. Her fiancé withdrew the hand he had offered James, stepped back, and watched her race up the stairs to the second floor.

As Rachel disappeared, slamming her bedroom door behind her, her mother came down the hall with cups of hot tea and freshly baked biscuits. This should hold everyone until her husband arrived, thought Emma. After all, when you had two growing sons, rather a son and future son-in-law, there was nothing like showing the personal touch.

"Oh, there you are, Nicholas. So very good to see you again."

Emma came around the corner, saw Franklin Belle standing in the parlor, and dropped her tray.

Chapter Eight

At the sound of broken crockery, the cook and servant girl rushed out of the kitchen, down the hall, and into the parlor. The older woman took the time to bring along a broom and a dustpan. With only a glance at the three young men, they immediately set about cleaning up the mess. On their way down the hall, they passed their matron, who was going upstairs and leaving Franklin Belle with her son and her daughter's fiancé.

Upstairs, Emma rapped on Rachel's door. It was closed but not locked, and the girl had thrown herself across her bed. She was sobbing violently. Emma's stomach knotted up as she stood over her daughter. Her best-laid plans were going awry, but she would have the truth.

"Why is Franklin Belle here?"

Behind her, Mary sidled into the room. When her sister continued to give no answer but simply bawl, the younger girl said, "No one knew he was coming to Lowell, Mother."

"What's he doing here?" Emma asked her daughter, the one lying across the bed.

"He's in love with Rachel. Why else would he be here?"

"Mary, don't talk such nonsense. Rachel, you must answer me. I want to know what's going on."

"I don't know why he's here," moaned her eldest daughter, and Emma had to listen closely to hear what her daughter said as Rachel's face remained firmly stuck in her pillows. "I didn't know he was coming. I promise. Oh, God, I promise."

"Rachel, don't blaspheme. Are you telling me the truth? How did you correspond with Cadet Belle?"

When there was no answer, the younger daughter said, "I really don't think Rachel would be in such a state if she'd known Lieutenant Belle would appear at our door."

Rachel would be in such a state? For the first time Emma looked at the younger girl, the one with the reputation for listening at doors. "Mary, what do you know about this affair?"

"Nothing," said Mary. "But I do know when someone's in love, and I certainly know the difference between a cadet and an officer."

"Mary, return to your room."

"I wasn't in my room."

"Then return to somewhere. I must talk with your sister."

"I believe I'll go downstairs," said the girl, opening the door. "We can't leave Lieutenant Belle unattended. One of the women in this family should be with him."

Rachel's head jerked out of the pillows and whipped around. "Mother, don't you dare let her go downstairs!"

"Mary, go to your room. I'm talking with your sister."

Mary sniffed. "You think this is none of my affair, but even I know when a girl needs to be rescued from this house."

In the parlor, James said, "Franklin, you didn't tell me you were coming to Lowell."

Watching the cook and the servant girl clear away the biscuits and the tea, Nicholas Eaton asked, "Why did Rachel rush upstairs? Is she ill?" Eaton appeared more puzzled than outraged. Of course, women sometimes did the strangest things.

Franklin pulled several sheets of paper from inside his tunic. To James those sheets appeared to be one of his friend's many letters home.

Franklin handed them to him. "These were returned from your sister. Refused." He produced the envelopes with "Refused" scrawled across them, and then pulled from his tunic other letters, those with a feminine script. "And these were from your sister."

James opened one of the letters with the feminine scrawl. "Rachel's letters?"

Nicholas Eaton wasn't sure he'd heard correctly. "Whose letters?" Nicholas had only received one letter from his fiancée, and that was when he'd been in Liverpool, learning his father's business.

"These are to you?" asked James. "I thought they were from your family in Charleston. I thought *you* were in Charleston."

"And I will be, once I conclude my business with your sister."

"Business . . . with Rachel?" Nicholas glanced at the

letters held by his future brother-in-law. "James, what in the world is this man talking about?"

James was scanning one letter after another. "But these are nothing more than abolitionists' tracts . . . apparently copied by my sister."

"And she refuses to answer my rebuttal, preferring to lecture me about my family's way of life. I simply won't have it. You and I have labored mightily to maintain our friendship. I, myself, have kept this issue from you because it opens a discussion that could destroy our friendship. But if our friendship is to continue, there must be a resolution to this matter. At the least, your sister must hear me out."

"Look," Nicholas said, "I don't understand anything you've said, but if you've been corresponding with—"

Franklin wheeled on him. "I'd hardly call it a correspondence. For that it would take two."

"Really, Franklin," said James, "you mustn't allow these people's raving and ranting to come between us."

"James," asked Nicholas, "who is this person?"

"My apologies. Nicholas, this is Franklin Belle, my roommate at West Point. Franklin, Nicholas Eaton."

The two men shook hands as the servants beat a hasty retreat to the kitchen. It was turning out to be an interesting day, and in a household known for its dull predictability.

Nicholas Eaton gestured for the letters, and James turned them over to him. After looking over a page or two, he asked, "You wrote these letters to Rachel?"

"That is correct," Franklin said.

"And she to you?"

"Yes." To James, Franklin said, "I don't mean to

harass your sister in the privacy of her home, but I'm not leaving Lowell without a full airing of my complaint."

"Complaint? Against Rachel?" Nicholas returned the letters to Franklin who slid them inside his military blouse. "Sir, I really don't think Rachel has to answer to you."

"Franklin," pleaded James, "you can't let some girl's foolishness come between us."

"I'm sorry, but either I'm granted an opportunity to have a free and open discussion with your sister, as she believes women should be permitted, or you can consider our friendship at an end."

"See here, sir," said Nicholas, moving to stand beside James, "if Rachel doesn't care to speak with you, then she will not. With that accent of yours, I would assume you had better manners."

Franklin looked at him. "Sir, do not involve yourself in matters that are not your business."

"Sir, the woman is my fiancée. What concerns her, or any threats made toward her, *are* my business."

Franklin stepped back as if struck. He looked at his friend. "Is this true? Your sister is betrothed?"

"Yes," said Nicholas Eaton, puffing up considerably. "And I'm her intended."

Franklin bowed curtly to him. "Then I hope you'll accept my apology. I had no intention of pressing myself on any woman who was spoken for."

"Apology accepted," said James with an obvious sigh of relief.

"James, I'm not sure an apology is enough. Perhaps your friend should make one to the young lady. After all, she was here when—"

"That won't be necessary. Franklin, I'm sorry you

came all this way for nothing." He cut in front of his sister's fiancé, taking Franklin's arm. "Let me see you to the door."

"James," said Nicholas, following them. "I insist on a personal apology to your sister."

"Nicholas, please. The last thing my sister needs is more unpleasantness."

"More unpleasantness? Has this man been rude to your sister in the past? If so, I insist on knowing the details. As a Southerner, he'd certainly understand the consequences."

"Nicholas," said James, as he handed Franklin his cloak and opened the door, "only twice has my sister met my friend: tonight, which he has apologized for, and a dinner at the military academy, which was before the two of you became engaged."

Nicholas Eaton reached past James and grasped Franklin's arm as he went out the door. "Sir, I must insist."

James said, "Nicholas, please don't . . . ."

After being so thoroughly embarrassed, Franklin would not be manhandled. That would be too much. First he was being ignored by James's high-handed sister, then learning of her recent engagement, and now this fool wanted to fight. Very well, there would be a fight, and he would welcome it.

Franklin glanced at the hand on his arm. "Unhand me, sir, or suffer the consequences."

"I will, sir, if you reconsider your decision."

"Nicholas, let's not have anymore unpleasantness."

"No, James. He must remain here." Gripping Franklin's arm tighter, Eaton added, "At least until he has apologized to the lady."

James took Nicholas's hand where it grasped Franklin's arm. "He won't see the lady again; isn't that enough?"

"James, I cannot understand your feelings on this matter. You might want to reconsider your friendship with this coward."

Franklin's hand came up, knocking away both hands. "Sir, watch your tongue. Where I come from those are fighting words."

"Sir, I'm not afraid of you, but you, you appear to be afraid to apologize to a woman."

"Nicholas," pleaded James, "there's no point of honor here."

"I disagree," said his friend from the South. "Your sister's fiancé has insulted me, and if I'm correct, by the pallor of his skin, he appears to have spent far too much time in his father's counting house. That, sir, you should consider before proceeding."

"I, sir, have insulted no one. I've only insisted on you honoring my fiancée. Certainly that doesn't offend your Southern sensibilities."

Franklin was reaching back to bring his hand forward to slap this fool when Rachel Mullins came downstairs. Behind her was her mother, and upstairs, peering between the balusters, younger sister Mary.

"Gentlemen, please," said Emma from the stairs. "My daughter has an apology to make."

The young men faced the stairs, but all eyes were on the daughter. Hands fell away from each other and brushed down tunics and shirts.

"Cadet Belle," continued Emma, "I mean, Lieutenant Belle, you've been such a good friend to James, we

should've made you feel more comfortable in our home."
She gestured at her daughter and her son. "If I understand the situation correctly, my daughter was
disagreeing with her brother and was embarrassed to
be caught in the middle of an argument. That's why
she left the room."

"But," said Rachel, "I'm here now, and I apologize
for any rudeness." The girl's cheeks were still pink,
but her voice level. "If you don't mind, Lieutenant Belle,
please close the door and return with us to the parlor."

But it was James who closed the door and ushered
the other two men back inside.

"Miss," said Franklin, bowing, "I apologize for my
earlier comments and actions. I did not know that you
were betrothed."

"And what would that have to do with our argument
over the merits of slavery?"

"Lieutenant Belle," explained Emma, "my daughter
is prepared to answer any charges to her beliefs and
put this whole matter behind us." Emma gestured at
the parlor before heading down the hall again. "If you
would only take a seat while I do something about the
tea and biscuits."

Franklin glanced at Nicholas Eaton. "Miss Mullins,
I don't wish to upset you again."

"You did so, sir, when you wrote those letters." Rachel
glanced down the hall where her mother had disappeared. "Letters I never received." She saw the three of
them didn't understand so she rushed on. "They were
intercepted by my mother . . . because, at that point, I
was engaged. In that action, I agree. So, Lieutenant
Belle, what we have here is a misunderstanding about

some letters that went astray, and, for that, I truly apologize. But not about the information contained in those letters. I will not now, nor anytime in the future, condone the practice of slavery. It is a sin in the eyes of God and should be against the law of man." Rachel glanced at James. "And those who build their lives on such a vicious practice could never have a place in my life, even as a friend of my brother."

"And you think, Miss Mullins, that I will stand here and take your insults?"

"Sir, I said I would answer any challenge."

"We shall soon see about that. You presume to know me, but you know nothing. Still, I understand you and your kind. People such as you are disciples of Satan, bent on destroying the South and our culture."

James gasped. He couldn't believe what he was hearing. Thank God slavery had not been discussed in their quarters at West Point.

Hands on hips and eyes flashing, Rachel shot back: "Sir, I'm not the least bit surprised that you don't understand the opinions of us north of the Mason-Dixon Line. It's common knowledge that Southern women are forbidden to speak their mind."

Nicholas was speechless. He was getting a preview of what his mother had warned him about if he should proceed with his marriage to "that Mullins girl."

The two combatants were now face-to-face, the taller South Carolinian bending down in the face of the New England girl who jutted out her chin. Franklin was close enough to smell her perfume; Rachel able to smell the peppermint on Franklin's breath, peppermint taken to hide the liquor he'd drunk to gain the courage to make the journey north. And after seeing this woman once again, he could understand why he hadn't been able to get her out his thoughts: blond hair, blue eyes, and an hourglass figure.

"Miss, only my friendship with your brother has kept me from detailing the natural arrogance of you New Englanders."

"Sir, since you call Charleston home, that would be the kettle calling the pot black."

"Miss, if there's one thing that can be said for Southern ladies, it's that they know when to curb their enthusiasm."

"Oh, I'm not to speak my mind, is that what you're saying, Lieutenant Belle."

"Miss Mullins," said Franklin, face flushed and only inches from her, "you have the same problem quite a few Yankees have: you can't hear anyone else's opinion because you're in love with the sound of your own voice."

"And who are you in love with, Cadet Belle?"

"You!" shouted Franklin, and he scooped Rachel up in his arms and kissed her.

James and Nicholas's mouths fell open, as did Emma's when she came down the hall, saw what was happening, and dropped a second tray of tea and biscuits.

Chapter Nine

Rachel couldn't keep still. She lay on the bed or she sat on the edge of the bed or she got up and wandered around her room.

"Please sit down," said her mother from a chair near the window. "You're working yourself into a dither."

Instead, her daughter flung herself across the bed. "But, Mother, I don't know what's to become of me."

"Oh, Rachel, don't be so melodramatic. The same will come of you as does most young women, if they're fortunate. Some man will propose, you'll marry, and settle into family life. That's where the real sacrifices will be made."

"But I'm not in love with Nicholas. I never was."

"Rachel," said her mother, letting out a long sigh, "if there's one thing I've learned from James' ordeal at West Point, it's that your father and I didn't know how fortunate we were with Peter."

"Mother!"

"Rachel, please don't interrupt, and try to remember

that much of what you believe people want to hear from you, they're really not interested in, whether it be something from one of those abolitionist newspapers or one of the many romances you read. Perish the thought you'd have to find your own way in the world. I had to find a job and a husband, and I wouldn't wish that on anyone."

"I could've done it, too, Mother."

"Oh, I'm sure you think you could."

"Mother, I'm not helpless."

"You may not think so, but—"

"You think I'm one of those Southern belles who has to be waited on hand and foot?"

"I think you're helpless in another way. Sometimes I wish I hadn't told you how difficult my life has been. You've come to believe you could emulate me."

"Well, I could!"

"If that's so, why do we have such a calamity downstairs?"

Rachel stared at her mother and then burst into tears and buried her face in the pillows once again.

Her mother left the chair by the window and moved to the bed. There she began to stroke her daughter's head. "Your life of privilege has allowed you these flights of fancy. You believe Franklin Belle is some sort of knight in shining armor who will spirit you way to some idyllic place where you'll live happily ever after. For that to happen, my dear, you'd have to be waited on . . . hand and foot. By slaves. You know, my dear, by your age most young women have learned that every bride resides in the domicile provided by her husband, and most of them look forward to that. Or they become spinsters and live with their parents, caring for them well before their parents have entered their dotage."

Rachel looked up and made a face.

"I didn't think so. You've already suffered enough at your parents' hands, haven't you?"

"Mother," said Rachel, sitting up, "I've said no such thing."

"Of course you have. Every time you spurn my advice. This is why you must marry a suitable young man and make your home in Massachusetts."

"You mean Nicholas."

"If Nicholas will have you."

"But I won't have him."

"Then you quite possibly may become a spinster, and that's not going to please your family, especially those who will have to care for you."

"No one will ever have to care for me."

"Oh, and what particular skills do you have?"

"I can sew!"

"You certainly can, and if you couldn't, we might need one of those dormitory rooms where I once lived. Remember, my dear, it wasn't your father or I who stopped your beaus from calling." Emma paused. "Is it really so important to let every young man know what you think about every subject under the sun?"

"Oh, Mother, you've been listening to those society ladies too much."

Emma leaned against one of the posts of the four-poster bed. "Cleverest thing I ever did was to join their church and take part in their charity work. They may not accept me as an equal or want me in their circle, but those women talk, especially when they're together, and a person like me, someone from the country, can learn how to speak, what's expected of my family, and how to elevate this family's position in society. I kept my mouth shut and my ears open, and you're going to throw away all that effort."

"Mother, you're not being fair. I don't love Nicholas."

"You think I loved your father when we married?"

"Mother, what are you saying? I often suspected . . . ."

"Still, I grew to love your father." Emma smiled again. "Probably because you weren't there to recommend someone else to be the provider for our family, or do you ever consider your future?"

"I consider the future. I consider the future quite a bit. That's why I have opinions you don't think ladies should have. And that's why I don't want to marry Nicholas."

Emma sat up, coming off the post she'd been leaning against. "But that makes absolutely no sense. Nicholas tolerates your opinions and even encourages you to speak out." She raised a hand when Rachel tried to interrupt her. "My dear, you simply cannot live in the South, nor can Cadet—I mean, Lieutenant Belle live in the North. Did you not hear what happened in Congress? Your father says the day's coming when neither North nor South will be able to speak to each other."

Rachel had read about the beating that Charles Sumner had taken on the floor of the Senate, and on this point, she and her father were in total agreement. One day, neither North nor South would be able to tolerate each other and must go their separate ways. The Union, said her father, will be torn asunder and Northern businessmen will have to explore other avenues of doing business with the slaveholders.

That wasn't what young people thought. They believed that . . . oh, my, her mother was correct. There was a disaster downstairs and she was discussing politics.

"So I should marry Nicholas?"

"Why not? He's a very devout, agreeable young man who comes from a good family."

"Mother, I've heard this before."

"Oh, I'm sure you have, and one day, if you're truly fortunate, you'll have these same quarrels with your own daughter."

"And I hope I can encourage her to follow her heart."

Emma laughed. "Oh, my dear, but you are young. I had other beaus, but could any of them have ever provided for this family as well as your father?" Emma shook her head. "They could not. Actually, they did not."

Rachel swung her feet over the side of the bed and sat up. "How do you know this, Mother?"

"I just know."

"You've . . . kept in touch?"

"Of course not. That would be inappropriate. One simply hears . . . things."

"Such as?" asked Rachel, leaning forward.

Emma glanced at the bedcovers. "Oh, this is silly."

"Not to me, it's not."

"Oh, all right then. One of the men who courted me died in a drunken brawl, leaving a wife and a child. The other was scalped by Indians on his way to prospect for gold in California." Emma smiled. "I'm certainly glad I didn't accompany him west."

"But we live in different times. Nowadays we have steamboats, trains, and instant communications with the telegraph. Even women are accomplishing more than they have in the past."

"And what kind of women are these? Those without prospects?"

Rachel didn't know what to say. She'd heard of women speaking before crowds of men and demanding not only an end to slavery but the emancipation of women. Still, she'd never considered who these women were or where they came from or if they had families.

How would Franklin feel about her speaking before crowds of men and demanding the right to vote? What did Franklin believe when it came to women's suffrage?

Oh, God, she knew what Franklin thought. She'd read about Southern girls. When those girls weren't attending balls, they were waited on hand and foot—by slaves! And they led a life of leisure. They did little or no work. Southern women didn't read; their men read poetry to them. Southern women didn't think, and if they did, their thoughts were what their husbands told them to think.

Oh, my, but she knew what it would be like to be the wife of Franklin Belle, even more than her heart could ever understand.

"Rachel?" asked her mother.

Rachel blinked. "Yes?"

"What are you thinking, child?"

Her daughter reached out and took her mother's hand. "How do you grow to love someone? How long does it take?"

Chapter Ten

In the study downstairs Joshua handled the meeting between the two aggrieved parties as he would in his book-keeping office. His son was told to keep his opinions to himself, as only Franklin Belle and Nicholas Eaton had a vested interest in the outcome of this discussion.

"But, Father, Rachel is my sister—"

"And soon to be one of these men's wife."

Franklin blanched at this comment, but Nicholas Eaton nodded enthusiastically.

"If you can't let this be, James, perhaps you should leave the room. I'm sure there are women in this house in need of comfort."

James stiffened at the rebuke, but he had been trained well at West Point. "Then I will keep my thoughts to myself."

"Very well." Joshua turned his attention to the young men in the straight-back chairs. On his desk lay the letters that had prompted the duel. "Now, gentlemen, and we are all gentlemen in this room, as Lieutenant

Belle is from Charleston and Nicholas from one of the finest families in Massachusetts."

Both young men nodded in agreement but did not look at each other.

"I point this out because duels are fought between gentlemen. Gentlemen can also work out their disagreements, and one would think if either of your families heard of this incident that they would wish to hear that you had accorded yourselves with the greatest amount of dignity and decorum.

"Now, on the point of the duel, there's plenty of time to spill blood, but before any duels are fought, seconds are to be chosen and it is their responsibility to work out the details. It is also the seconds' responsibility to find a common ground, if there is one."

Joshua had never fought a duel, didn't even know anyone who had, but the rules were so inbred in the fabric of his world that he could address the issue as an expert. Twenty years ago, the governor of South Carolina had codified the rules of combat, but much earlier, the first duel had been fought, in the state of Massachusetts.

He looked from one young man to the other. "Are we in agreement about this?"

Both young men nodded.

A half-hour had passed since Joshua had arrived home and had been told of the affront to his daughter's honor. Joshua hoped tempers had cooled and both men had had ample opportunity to regret their actions. Still, even if all went well, that did not mean Joshua would not have Franklin Belle arrested. For assault. Still, that would lead to even more notoriety.

Ignoring James who shifted around in his chair, and having sent Peter's family away, he would now try to mediate this rivalry. "Lieutenant Belle, you've made your intentions known in regard to my daughter, and in quite an unacceptable manner."

"Hear, hear," muttered Nicholas.

"Nicholas, please. My rights precede yours; that is, until I give my daughter away."

"Er—yes, sir."

"You understand your affront?" he asked Franklin.

"Yes, sir, and I apologize."

"Lieutenant, you should be apologizing to Nicholas."

"We're too far along for that," Nicholas said.

Joshua waved this off. "Can we take this one step at a time?"

Nicholas nodded.

Turning his attention to Franklin, he said, "Unless you're considering shaming my family further by eloping with my daughter."

"Eloping?" asked Nicholas. "Impossible. Rachel and I are kindred spirits."

"Nicholas, please . . . ."

"No, sir," said Franklin, shaking his head.

"I would hope not. Now, tell me what claim you have on my daughter."

Franklin's face flushed. "Well, I . . . I love her."

Nicholas turned to object, but Joshua silenced him with an upraised hand. "Infatuation. Nothing more."

Franklin was willing to entertain the idea. His ardor *had* cooled since the kiss. Still, there was Rachel's upturned head, the soft lips of that small, delicate mouth. Had she embraced him when he'd put his arms around her? Franklin didn't remember.

"Has my daughter encouraged you in any way?" asked Joshua, breaking into his thoughts.

"Sir?"

"A simple question, Lieutenant. Has my daughter encouraged you in any way?"

Franklin had to agree that she had not. "But I must point out that I did not receive all of her letters."

Joshua gestured at the stack of envelopes on his desk. "These letters my wife intercepted since our daughter's engagement."

"There were letters before then. Sir."

"Yes, and if my information is correct, they, too, were intercepted." He pointed at an envelope beside the stack of other envelopes. "And the letter my daughter wrote contained nothing more than points any abolitionist would make against the practice of slavery, something that could be easily dismissed by any gentleman."

Franklin could see what Rachel's father was driving at. Nicholas, however, took every pause as a signal to jump into the conversation.

"Which makes the lieutenant's affront even more despicable."

Joshua ignored him. "Do you really think you have grounds to upset this engagement, Lieutenant? You don't actually know what my daughter thinks of you, do you?"

Franklin had to admit Rachel's father was correct. Still, there was that kiss . . . Rachel had returned his kiss, hadn't she? Hadn't her lips parted to . . . ?

"So, based on one meeting with my daughter, the dinner at West Point, where you were invited as a friend of James, not my daughter, you presumed that her silence toward you meant that she was interested in you courting her?"

"I thought—"

"And I propose that you didn't think. Matter of fact, I believe both you and James have been at West Point far too long and the first pretty girl you see, you swoon like schoolgirls."

Reluctantly, Franklin had to agree. This man's daughter had done nothing to encourage him, and he stood before God and man charged with a severe case of puppy love. The sides of his neck began to heat up.

Joshua looked from one young man to the other. "Has either of you heard of 'turning the other cheek,' as our Master says?"

That brought him nothing but cold stares.

"I take it neither of you has asked what advantage it is to my family for either one of you to die or to become grievously wounded."

"There remains a point of honor," Nicholas said.

"So, with the exception of my family, who have little to gain by retelling this incident, you insist on pressing this issue?"

Nicholas slid forward in his chair. "Are you saying your daughter wasn't insulted?"

"I said nothing of the kind. Though I would've thought such a poor excuse for redress would be far more common in other parts of the country."

"Sir," Franklin said, straightening up in his chair, "I must protest this slight."

"What slight?" asked Joshua. "You take offense too easily, Lieutenant. Could I've not as well meant the western portions of our country?"

"Yes, sir. You are right. I stand corrected."

"And I take no offense. Sometimes, in our youth, we infuse too much passion into positions we later lose interest in."

"Sir," interjected Nicholas, "as you said, you were not here, but I was. Your daughter was molested right in front of me."

"Nicholas, choose your words carefully. I don't think you want me prejudiced against your engagement."

"Then you are content with a simple apology?"

"There are few things with which I'm content. I'm not content with the effort given by my employees nor my lack of perfection when it comes to the example set by our Lord, but I have learned to let things go. It comes with age."

"I'm not sure . . ." started Nicholas.

"Sure of what?" Joshua gestured at Franklin. "That you would prefer to meet this man on some fog-shrouded morning and attempt to kill him?"

"Attempt?" Nicholas glanced at Franklin. "I assure you that I would make more than an attempt."

Franklin turned on him. "And you, sir, are welcome to try."

Joshua waved them both off. "Nicholas, you're soon to be my son-in-law, and that means a part of this family. I owe you the opportunity to remedy this situation before it leads to tragedy, and please remember I have much more at stake. Rachel cannot marry a dead man, nor would I allow her to marry a cripple."

"Sir, I cannot believe—"

"Nicholas, perhaps you should wait to pass judgment until you have daughters of your own who depend on the good health of their husbands."

"But my family would—"

"You don't know what your family will do once you are dead."

"I don't plan on being killed."

"Yes, yes," said Joshua, nodding his head. "Another illusion of youth."

Nicholas opened his mouth to say something, but Joshua silenced him with another upraised hand.

"Still, I must ask a question I'm certain that your second, or your father, would certainly ask. Are you sure you've thought this through? Not only is Lieutenant Belle familiar with firearms from his experience at the military academy . . ." Joshua glanced at Franklin. "And I mean this as no slight . . ." Once Franklin nodded, Joshua turned back to Nicholas. "But you're challenging a man from a part of our country where duels are commonplace."

Nicholas leaped to his feet. "So I'm to live with this black mark on my reputation? I'm to take a woman in marriage who is so casual with her affections?"

Franklin, too, was on his feet. He would not listen to Rachel being slandered. He would not allow any woman to be slandered.

But it was James who issued a warning from his chair. "Watch your language, Nicholas. I'm not going to sit here and listen to you slander my sister."

"Then it's acceptable to you that this man took liberties with your sister."

"Nicholas, please . . ." pleaded Joshua from behind the desk.

"You take back what you said about the lady," said

Franklin, "or you'll have that match that you so much desire."

Nicholas looked from one man to the other. "I'm the one who's wronged Rachel? I've besmirched her honor?"

"You certainly have," said James, leaving his chair to stand shoulder to shoulder with his friend, "and if Franklin doesn't put a bullet through your black heart, then I will have that honor."

"James, please . . ." pleaded Joshua once again.

Nicholas looked from one man to the other. "I can't believe what I'm hearing. I was told to expect such from a family of bumpkins, still I was willing to overlook—"

He fell back. Struck in the face by James.

Nicholas caught himself against the wall. Dazed, he touched his jaw, saw the blood, and glared at them. When he was able to regain his footing, he said, "Now I will have satisfaction."

"Then don't dawdle," said James, stepping forward. "Have your second call on me tomorrow."

Nicholas looked at Rachel's father who was on his feet behind his desk. "Sir, is this the way you wish this to end?"

"If you think so, son, then you haven't heard a word I've said."

Chapter Eleven

Outside the study, Nicholas met Rachel coming downstairs. Behind his fiancée came her mother, and watching through the upstairs balusters, the three younger children.

"Nicholas," said Rachel, "I'm glad you haven't left. I have something to say to you." Out of the study trooped her brother, her father, and, oh, God, Franklin was still here! Still, she had to say what she must. She had a responsibility to her family.

Nicholas beat her to it. "There's nothing to say. I've spoken to your father and the engagement is off." And Nicholas snatched his cloak from the hook near the door, lifted his head, and after opening the front door, marched out of the house.

Rachel took the last steps without realizing she'd done so. She didn't see her father, her brother, anyone. All she saw was her future disappearing through the door. The Eaton family had done so much for her family, the least Rachel could do was marry their son.

She must apologize. She must go after him.

"No, Nicholas! Please come back."

James grabbed her arm before she reached the door. "I will not have my sister chasing after that man. He's not worth it."

Emma Mullins finished the stairs, black rage in her face. "What has happened here? What have you done?"

"I've done as much as any man could do," said her husband, his shoulders slumping.

"What do you mean: you've done as much as any man could do? This is more than Rachel's future walking out that door. Go after him! Apologize! Make amends. Do whatever men do to make things right."

Joshua only shook his head.

His wife was beside herself. "I cannot believe you're helpless in this matter. There must be more you can do, or am I to scheme further to ensure our daughter's future?"

"Emma, don't speak to me in that tone."

"Oh, you've heard this tone before, years ago when you weren't sure if you should take responsibility for the factory, and you'll hear it again now."

James and Rachel gaped at their mother. Never in their lives had they seen their mother speak to their father in this manner. Franklin wished he could disappear into the woodwork. He couldn't. Emma saw him and turned her wrath on him.

"What right do you have to come into my home and cause such pain? No one invited you here, and for that reason you had no right to show up unannounced and declare your love for my daughter."

Rachel protested. "Mother, please—"

"Close your mouth, girl, and learn a thing or two." Emma glanced at James but continued to speak to Franklin. "You had no right to form a relationship with anyone in this family. You're not our kin, not even a citizen of this state. Of the Eatons we know much; of your family we know nothing."

"Mother, Franklin is my dearest—"

"Oh, James do close your foolish mouth. Franklin Belle is your friend only because I've done nothing to discourage it, hoping the longer you remained at West Point, the experience might give you a moral compass. Or did you think all those lewd songs you play on the piano would help you acquire a proper wife?"

Seeing the shocked look on his face, she added, "Oh don't bleat. Consider instead why you might've been chosen for such treatment by your family? Perhaps, like your father believes, you needed to learn how to make the proper decisions."

"Emma, please . . . ."

She crossed the foyer to her husband. "Come on, Joshua, don't you think it's time the children learned the sacrifices that were made to live in this house? I married you because you were smart enough to be head bookkeeper and clever enough to speak for Mister Eaton when he wasn't in the plant. Now look at you. You're what they call a 'manager,' when all you ever wanted was to be a simple bookkeeper." She cupped the side of his face and her own face softened. "Without me, dear, you could have never seen that future."

She dropped her hand and looked from one young person to another. "None of you knows what it's like to be raised on a farm, certainly not Lieutenant Belle with all those servants at his beck and call, and even if a simple farm girl does what's considered proper, that doesn't mean there'll be someone around to court you. They may've gone west to Ohio. Oh, damn those newspapers and their 'Go west, young man!'"

"Emma, please watch your language."

His wife ignored him. "What does that leave for a woman left behind on those worthless New England rock farms? I'll tell you. Nothing. Absolutely no one. If Mister Eaton hadn't built that dormitory where young women could live unmolested until we could find a husband—"

"Emma, please stop. You're frightening the children." This was true. The ones peering through the railings had tears running down their cheeks.

"The children should be frightened, especially since their father doesn't understand this incident will have ramifications for our other two daughters."

"Emma, these issues do not concern them at their age, and it's best if they don't—"

"And when was the last time you knew what was best for this family? Why don't you tell the children who actually runs that factory where you work: a foulmouthed Irishman who does your dirty work and a disappointed spinster in charge of a dormitory where our daughters will have to live if Mister Eaton turns us out."

"Emma, that is not going to happen."

"You're damned right, especially if I have anything to say about it." She looked at Rachel and shook her head. "A match I've engineered for years . . . ."

"Mother, you didn't have to do anything on my behalf."

"Of course I did. Like James, you've always had your head in the clouds." From the rear of the house came the creak of a door. Emma turned her wrath in that direction. "Out of this house! Leave right now! Go to the market and take the girl with you."

In seconds the cook and the servant girl had grabbed their coats, with the cook bringing along a basket, and were heading out the front door.

The last thing they heard was: "I want a first-class meal tonight." Emma's mind was racing, planning for any and all eventualities. She would not be turned out again. She would not be laughed at for rising above her station, and most of all she would not be at the mercy of strangers. "Do you understand?"

Without looking at her, the cook nodded, closed the door, and was gone.

This interlude gave everyone a chance to recover. It also gave Franklin an opportunity to slink toward the door.

"I'm not through with you yet, Lieutenant."

And because women of all ages, races, and kin had been telling this Southern boy how to act, Franklin stopped at the door.

Emma looked upstairs to the younger children, all three with plenty of tears running down their cheeks. "Children, return to your rooms and dress in your Sunday best. I'll be upstairs to check on your progress."

"But, Mama," said Mary, wiping away the tears as she got to her feet. "There's no church. It's Saturday night."

"There still may be a service," said their mother, glancing at Franklin and Rachel. "Once you're dressed, begin your lessons. If you don't learn your lessons, you could be turned out of this house and forced to work in Mister Eaton's mill."

"Emma, please . . . ."

As the younger children scurried to their rooms, Emma took her husband's cloak from the wall and held it out. "James, you and Franklin go with your father, as you two probably know haunts my husband has, thankfully, never seen. Check the taverns. I've heard Nicholas likes a drink from time to time."

"Mother!" Rachel said.

Ignoring her daughter, she pressed on. "If we're lucky he might've gone there instead of to see his father."

Joshua went to stand where his wife could cloak him. "This isn't going to work. You can't make over the world to suit you."

"You'd better hope I can, my dear," said his wife, handing him his hat. "Or you might not be employed Monday morning."

"Emma, I will not have you speaking to me like this in front of the children. After all, I'm their father."

"Yes, and our family appreciates your contribution to that effort, but this is not a problem to be solved in the solitude of your office. So either you go after Nicholas and repair the damage or bring the minister home. In that event, James, you'll be best man."

"Best man?"

"The minister?" asked Joshua. "Why the minister?"

"Well," said Emma, finally looking at her daughter, "you wouldn't want us to send Rachel away without a wedding band on her finger, would you?"

Lewis

Chapter Twelve

The history of the South Carolina military academy goes back as far as 1783 when the state ceded to the city sections of land now known as the Citadel. This land included the remnants of fortifications from the Revolutionary War and was intended for a warehouse to inspect and store tobacco.

Here, too, was to be the city police station, and later the municipal guard inspired by the ill-fated slave rebellion in 1822 led by Denmark Vesey, a free black man. The tobacco warehouse was also found to be an excellent place to store arms, and there was enough room for a guardhouse. The name "Citadel" did not appear in common usage until 1826; the building known as "The Citadel" was not completed until 1829.

In 1832, when John C. Calhoun insisted that the individual states had a right to nullify any federal law considered grievous to the individual states, the state took over the operation of the Citadel, stashing away arms in the event South Carolina should have to go to war against the other states. Still, it wasn't until 1842, the same year Jennie and Alexis were born, that it occurred to the governor that there were a good many indigent males who might benefit from a liberal arts and military education. And who knows, perhaps South Carolina would need a few trained officers if it should ever cross swords with the other states.

So, when Louis Belle applied for entrance to the military college of South Carolina, he was sure he'd be accepted. After all, he was no pig farmer from the upcountry.

He was not. Louis simply didn't have the background for the demands of the curriculum, not to mention the inclination. Anyone who knew Louis knew it was the other Belle brother who was the serious candidate for entrance to a military school, and François had proved that by gaining an appointment to the United States Military Academy. The Citadel and the VMI always know what's going on at West Point.

So, when Louis recovered from his funk and realized his brother would soon return wearing a brand new uniform, Louis bore down on his studies, and when brother François returned home on his first leave, Louis wore a uniform similar to his brother's.

Not that it was always easy. Most of Louis' life had been taken up with cards, billiards, drinking, horse racing, and the occasional well-turned ankle, so Louis took poorly to discipline. But that did not mean the young man was not clever.

When the adjutant, the staff officer that handles correspondence for a commanding officer, asked Louis if he wanted to continue using his name, Louis said,

"Of course." Then added, "Sir."

The adjutant looked up at this handsome, well-turned-out young man with the long black hair, pale blue eyes, and tanned face. He was dressed in the latest fashion, and pretty enough to get in trouble with the wrong element—there were always a few odd ducks in any exclusive men's club—and the adjutant had just such a difficulty in mind.

The adjutant was a young man himself, as were all who did the actual work around this place. The general assembly wasn't about to fund another West Point where rich men's sons were coddled and spoiled.

The very idea that they were coddled and spoiled would amuse the cadets at West Point, the Citadel, and the Virginia Military Institute. Their beds were hard, their covers thin, and the uniforms what any soldier would expect during peacetime. And the discipline sometimes perverse.

"Your name is 'Belle,'" asked the adjutant from the other side of the desk, "as in 'Southern belle?'"

Louis drew himself up to his full six feet. "I don't care for such observations. Sir." Louis could've added that he'd called out many a young man or received an apology when his name was used with derision. But this was the Citadel and the man behind the desk probably expected some sort of explanation. "In France, sir, 'Belle' is a well-known and respected name." Louis had no idea whether this was true or not, but it was part of the family folklore no one dared to question, or even think about.

"But we're not in France, are we?"

"Er—no, sir. We are not."

"Mister Belle, you, sir, have a French name, both surname and given name, and your family is well known in this state, which is where the other members of the cadet corps originate."

The adjutant gestured at the paperwork on the desk in front of him. "To some cadets, that might be two black marks against you, and I wouldn't want any marks against me if I were planning to subject myself to the discipline of the cadet corps."

"It was my understanding . . . sir, that the Citadel took both the rich and the ordinary into its ranks, without differentiation."

"That's true, Mister Belle, but you, sir, are bringing that differentiation with you through the front gate. Try as we might, not every cadet is able to park his pride outside, so what kind of torments would you think some of our cadets would enjoy parceling out to someone of your class and breeding, especially if those cadets were not Charleston born?"

Louis remembered how François had demanded that people call him "Franklin" instead of "François." This, even a year before he departed for West Point.

"You think I should change my name. Sir."

"That decision is not mine to make. I, sir, am not so burdened."

"Yes, sir, I understand, and make that 'Lewis,' sir. Lewis Belle." If François could steal his name from Benjamin Franklin, then he'd take his name from the explorers Lewis and Clark.

The adjutant picked up his pencil and wrote out the name, spelling it as he did, to make sure there was no question. And with the completion of the paperwork,

Louis Belle became Lewis Belle and just another plebe at the Citadel. Now, six generations after arriving in Charleston, the Belle family was finally being Americanized, and their name Anglicized.

A sergeant sitting at a desk outside the adjutant's office also had words for Lewis. "Young man, mark this day because what the adjutant said are certainly the kindest words you'll ever hear at this post."

This was true, and the unkind words began as soon as Lewis left the building. And with the often and derogatory use of the word "plebe," Lewis would've been surprised to learn the word hadn't been in existence as little as a generation before. "Knob" would come into general usage much later, as more and more hair was shorn from a cadet's head.

Chapter Thirteen

For as long as Lewis could remember the world had bent to his will, and where his brother had a degree of humility, Lewis had none. Members of the cadet corps, quick to note any flaw in a plebe's character, and how that cadet's failing might reflect on their institution, focused on Lewis, stripping him down to a raging animal who finally had had enough.

If it hadn't been for the letters from his cousin, not Alexis, the sweet one, but Jennie who, at eleven years of age(!) wanted to know how he was adjusting to life as a cadet. Cousin Jennie made him out to be such a hero, and perhaps he was . . . to a lonely girl living on a rice plantation.

Lewis felt compelled to write back and explain that not everyone should be a soldier, that the curriculum was very different from what he'd expected, and she shouldn't be disappointed if he left the Citadel and read for the law.

In the return mail Jennie asked why some of the

nice boys from Charleston weren't assisting him with his studies as Jennie did her sister Alexis. It was only right. And a few days later, upperclassmen began to appear at the door of his barracks room asking if they could help him with mathematics, science, or drawing. Not only could his cousin read minds; she could perform miracles. The girl was a witch!

And since the Citadel was part of Charleston, there would eventually spring up a secret society within its ranks, and that's when Lewis realized, during his senior year, that he hadn't been fully accepted by the leadership corps.

Lewis had grown up in Charleston and he knew about clubs. His father belonged to the Ugly Club, the Golf Club, Three Pace Club, for duels, and then there was the South Carolina Jockey Club, the first jockey club in the United States. True, Lewis had more demerits than many, walked more punishment tours than others, but there were worse cadets, some of them members of the leadership corps. If the cadet leadership was so accepting of him in every other aspect of his studies, why had they not accepted him into their secret group?

Simple enough to learn why. All Lewis had to do was be in obvious deficiency regarding his uniform, and in plain view of someone Lewis was sure belonged to that particular society. And there couldn't be anyone around to overhear their conversation. When this opportunity availed itself to Lewis, he demanded to know what his shortcoming was or his representative (second) would soon call on this cadet.

"Cadet Belle, might I remind you that although dueling is winked at in the city of your birth, it would be a violation of the honor code."

"Very well, sir," said Lewis, "but if I were you, I would not tarry long in any dark alleys."

"Cadet Belle, is that a threat?"

"Of course not. I would never threaten a gentleman."

The other cadet's eyes narrowed. "Meaning you don't consider me a gentleman because I won't meet you on the field of honor?"

"Sir, that is your interpretation of what has been said. I simply asked for an explanation for why I cannot be a member of your select group."

"And I say again that there is no such group."

"Then, sir, since you dishonor this school by lying, I will have my second call upon you." Lewis smiled. "My second is not a member of the corps, but will appear tomorrow at the gate and ask to see you. Please see that he's admitted."

Which meant word of this duel would spread, not only through the cadet corps but the officer staff, possibly even reaching the ear of one of the Board of Visitors. Off in the distance came the crackle of lightning as a storm approached Charleston.

The other cadet studied Lewis. "And this foolishness will end? Between you and me"—he glanced around—"between my friends and you . . . and their supposed association, if I give you an explanation as to why you have not been issued an invitation to join our, er—group?"

"Yes, sir. May I remind you that it was only a week ago that I bested everyone in horsemanship."

"Which is the very reason for your exclusion. You are haughty, proud, and very loud. You might consider yourself a gentleman, but others do not."

"Sir, my family can trace its lineage back to France, while yours only goes back as far as some back country pig farmers."

The older cadet's face reddened, but he was still able to get out: "And you, sir, believe the ownership of horses and a few slaves means you are superior to others?"

"No, sir," said Lewis, shaking his head. "I believe I'm superior because my family never raised pigs."

"You, sir, are a disgrace to your uniform, passing judgment on your betters."

"And you believe that my betters reside in the upper part of the state?"

"Quite often that is the case, and I can assure you that's the very reason some of us pig farmers attend this institution. We plan on upsetting your little Charleston applecart."

"Sir, my family has survived epidemics, hurricanes, and the harassment of the British twice; certainly your betters."

"We shall see about that. There may be tasks my fellow cadets and I have to perform in your service, but we will never accept you into our group." The cadet drew himself into the position of attention. "And if that means your second will call on me, do your worst. You are dismissed."

Instead of Lewis taking his leave, the other cadet did, leaving Lewis standing in the middle of the parade field to fathom what the older cadet had meant: "There may be tasks my fellow cadets and I have to perform in your service . . ."

But Lewis knew very well what it meant when the cadet said: ". . . but we will never accept you into our society."

These people dared pass judgment on him! A bunch of pig farmers!

Still, giving the matter considerable thought after lights out, Lewis knew a bunch of poor boys couldn't be the ones opposing him. Someone was providing the backbone for these pig farmers, and Lewis could only deduce it had to be someone who knew him, one of those boys who couldn't ride, shoot, or bed women as well as he. But in this line of thought, he'd get nowhere. These days too many Charlestonians attended the Citadel, and it could be a younger cadet as well as an older one. Respect, or fear, knew no age limit.

Who might he contact to redress this grievance? Certainly not his father. His father still chastised him for not reading for the law.

The law was boring, as were most of his classes, and where was that war he'd been promised? When he'd entered the Citadel, war had been just over the horizon. At least, that's the conclusion you'd draw reading the *Mercury,* and entering a military academy had appealed to Lewis because he might learn a trick or two, not to mention acquiring the lingo.

Maybe it was true. Maybe the abolitionists would allow South Carolina to leave the Union peacefully.

If so, why were those people from Beaufort after him to enlist in their cause? Now there was an exclusive group! The Bloodhounds were off to Kansas to defend the rights of slaveholders in the territories.

Lewis slammed his fists into the bed beside him, and in the bunk across the room his roommate snorted and resumed snoring.

So much for being elected governor! After graduating

what would he have? He'd still be penniless, or so said that Jew in the employ of the family.

It wasn't fair, simply wasn't fair, and when situations arose that confounded Lewis, his first instinct was to run. But not tonight. Outside it was pouring.

But wasn't that the best time to leave? Remember the women who'd received him during such storms, and once much of his clothing hung in front of their fireplace, those women had taken him to their bed. And that created another pressure on Lewis, and it wasn't long before that pressure, mixed with his frustration over being blackballed, caused him to leave the grounds of the Citadel without permission.

Using his one exceptional talent, stealth, Lewis snuck out of the barracks, avoiding the barracks guards and those walking the perimeter. Taking nothing but the uniform on his back, and wearing a heavy cloak to avoid being soaked, he returned to the house on High Battery. Even his father would have to agree there was no reason for a member of the Belle family to suffer such degradation at the hands of a bunch of pig farmers.

Despite his cloak, Lewis was soaked by the time he reached home, and as he clamored up on the porch, one of the slave patrols appeared out of the darkness, guided their horses in Lewis's direction, and demanded that he identify himself. Once Lewis had done so, the riders tipped their hats and rode off into the wind and rain. The storm had to be the reason the slave patrol hadn't heard the woman's screams coming from inside the house.

Chapter Fourteen

"No, no! Don't do it!" cried out the girl.

The protest came from the parlor where his father often entertained his women. Of course, none of this was his business, but since Lewis had just deserted, there was an empty place in his heart, a void he'd fill with action, or at least righteous indignation.

Lewis threw open the parlor door and saw the girl sitting in his father's lap. In the lamplight, and under a very thin nightgown, he could make out pert breasts and some very nice hips. Her feet were white and bare.

What was she doing here? And what kind of a man kept a woman in the house when one of his young cousins might arrive anytime to escape the boredom of plantation life?

Two quick steps across the room and Lewis pulled the girl from his father's grasp. Forgetting about the storm, he shoved her toward the door.

"Get your clothes on and leave this house!"

"But I live here," said the girl.

She lived here?

Impossible.

In the lamplight and the light from a dying fire, Lewis thought he recognized her. "Alexis?"

"Jennie," said the girl.

Lewis glanced at his father, who was fumbling with—what was that?

A pistol!

"He's trying to kill himself!" shouted his cousin. "Oh, Lewis, take the pistol away. I almost had it when you interrupted us."

Interrupted us? Interrupted you doing what?

Lewis reached down and snatched the pistol from his father's hand. Jerking the weapon away, the pistol went off, throwing a ball into the wall over the girl's head.

Jennie screamed.

Lewis looked at her—she was all right—and then glanced at his father before holding out the weapon to examine it.

One of his grandfather's dueling pistols. He glanced at the wall, saw where the pair had been taken down; its twin lay on the desk. Lewis placed the weapon beside its twin, but only after checking to see if the second pistol was loaded. It was not.

Jennie now clutched him, and it only took seconds for Lewis to become aware that he was holding a full-grown woman in his arms, not some rail-thin youngster. It was a woman who trembled in his arms.

"Do you mind telling me what in Sam Hill is going on here?"

"Watch your tongue, son." The dumpy middle-aged man righted himself in his chair.

Lewis glared at him. "Oh, yes, Father, let's mind our manners when it comes to murder, molestation, or suicide."

"Son, I will not be spoken to in that tone."

"And I will not be lectured to by some lecherous old man who uses pity to seduce one of his nieces."

"I did nothing improper."

Lewis held his cousin out where he could see her. The girl continued to tremble, tears ran down her cheeks, and she would not meet his gaze. In a similar nightgown, would Alexis be just as desirable, the bare shoulders, the maturing breasts, and the swelling hips?

Homer, the gray-haired house servant, came to the door. "Mister Lewis, is there anything I can do for you?"

Lewis told him to leave, and he wasn't polite about it.

"What are you doing here?" demanded his father. "Do you have a pass?" The Citadel was worse than any slaveholder when it came to granting passes.

Lewis wasn't listening. He had his arms around his cousin again, trying to stop her trembling. God but it was good to hold a woman again. The pressure in his loins increased to such a degree that he turned his hips away. After all, she was his cousin.

Lewis remembered the nights when he'd needed a woman more than he was willing to admit. Those nights, he simply drank more wine and groped the nearest woman. Which appeared to be what his father had been doing.

Lewis released his cousin, and the frightened girl found her dressing gown on the floor and quickly slipped into it. Lewis watched Jennie cover herself. The whole scene was simply too grotesque to comprehend. His father and his cousin . . .

"My God, Father, what have you done?"

"I did nothing improper."

"Jennie?" asked Lewis.

His cousin wrapped her arms around herself, hugging herself, and looked away. As she did, she stepped toward the small fire in the grate.

Lewis reached down, snatched the front of his father's shirt, and pulled him out of the chair. "I want to know what you did!"

Jean Louis came out of the chair easily; Lewis's rage was that intense.

"Unhand me!"

Instead, Lewis slapped him and let his father fall back into his seat. Just turned twenty and already slapping his father. What kind of son was he?

Lewis knew the answer. The kind who loved his wine and his women, even when that woman might be his kin. The thought sickened him, and Lewis wondered when a man crossed over from being a blade to a lech.

"You ungrateful lout!" screamed his father. "What have you done to make a father proud? And now you want to fight. Perhaps you and I should settle this at dawn." Jean Louis struggled out of the chair. "That's what duels are for, to settle who's the better man."

Jennie stepped between the two of them and eased the older man back into his chair. "There will be no more fighting. We're family and should know better."

"Jennie, I want to know what happened here. I have a right to know what happened."

"It's none of your business," said his father. "As I

115

asked before: Do you have a pass to be off the grounds?"

"For someone who shows little interest in the scope of my education, you appear to know a good bit about the rules of the institution."

"Rich boys' club, that's what they call it."

Lewis laughed, and he laughed loudly. At this moment his complaint about the upcountry pig farmers lording over him seemed rather farfetched. At a sideboard he found the wine and poured a drink. He swallowed the Madeira and poured another. Lord how he'd missed that taste.

"I assume this is what I have to look forward to when I'm old and fat and can't pay an octoroon to spend the night with me."

"Lewis, don't be so crude."

Lewis turned on Jennie. "And what do you have to say for yourself? You must've encouraged him."

"Lewis, what an outrageous thought."

"Is that so? I come home and find you in the arms of my father." He smiled wickedly. "You know there are men in this family much closer to your age."

Jennie slapped him.

Lewis looked her up and down, and so much so that Jennie clutched the top of her dressing gown, drawing it together.

"I'd watch who you slap, cousin. Not all men will be so tolerant."

From behind his niece, Jean Louis lurched out of his chair once again. "You, sir, have more than enough rudeness to answer for, and it shall be on the field of honor tomorrow."

"Don't insult me with a challenge," said Lewis. "The

two of you make me wish I'd changed more than my given name."

And Lewis shoved his father back into his chair. Jean Louis fell back with such momentum that he flipped over, landed on his back, and slammed into the baseboard.

Jennie's hand was at her throat again. "My goodness, Lewis, what have you done?"

Jennie rushed around the overturned chair and knelt beside him. Thankfully her uncle's breath was hot and sweet in her face. She looked up at Lewis, who remained on the other side of the chair.

"Take him upstairs and put him to the bed. I'll heat some coffee; then I want to know what you're doing here."

"And I the same of you, dear cousin."

Chapter Fifteen

When Lewis returned from putting his father to bed, he found the overturned chair righted and Jennie sitting in it. Her feet were pulled up, her dressing gown hung from her knees, and it covered her feet. In her hands was a cup of coffee, held with both hands as though she was warming herself.

She gestured at another cup on the desk. "Get out of those clothes. You're soaking wet."

Lewis shook his head. "I don't think you need another member of this family stripping in front of you tonight." Still, Lewis took the coffee and went to stand in front of the fireplace. His cloak he threw over a chair in front of it.

"He didn't do anything, Lewis, but one day he will."

He eyed his cousin over his cup as he sipped the coffee. "Do what?" He was almost afraid to ask.

"Kill himself."

"*Kill himself.*" Lewis coughed up his coffee, strangling himself. Once he had control of his breathing, he asked, "Why would he do that?"

"Cooper Hill has been sold. To Yankees. My parents will be moving in, like we have during the summers."

"Everyone will live here? Permanently?"

"Until the money runs out. We might survive if we're frugal. But when was the last time you heard of a Belle economizing?"

The word stopped him. Not that he hadn't heard the word "economizing" before, but to hear it come from the mouth of this child. Actually, Jennie was no longer a child, not the way he'd ogled her earlier in the night.

How old was she? Thirteen? Fourteen? What did it matter? She looked, and acted, much older.

"I'm not sure I follow."

"Alexis will marry, and my parents can live with her. I'm the problem. I don't have a proper beau. That's why we're here, to attend the fall balls, and hope for the best."

"Certainly people don't believe that bewitched foolishness."

"Children carry tales, and I was a showoff at school doing my sums. It went past the point of being unladylike. Now I'm paying the piper."

"I didn't think you had to learn your sums. I thought they came naturally."

"One must understand a number before they can use it." Jennie shrugged off his interest in her bizarre ability. "Anyone who didn't know me might think I'm qualified to be a seamstress or a tutor. But what family would want their children taught by a witch, or wear clothing that might fall to pieces in the middle of a grand ball?" Jennie's face colored and she looked into her cup.

The Belles of Charleston

"That's why it doesn't matter whose lap I sit in."

Lewis put his cup on the mantle. "Jennie, I want to know what happened here tonight. Perhaps there's something I can do."

"It doesn't matter. When Mother and Father move in, all of this unpleasantness will pass." She looked up. "Speaking of that, why are you here?"

"I left the Citadel."

"And why is that?"

"It didn't suit me."

"Oh, and being a pauper does?"

"Jennie, I don't think we're to be paupers."

"And I think you should reconsider the attraction a uniform will have for a girl of means. Our fathers have bankrupted the Belle estate. It was all explained to me by Abraham Marcus."

"That Jew? Why were you talking to him?"

Jennie almost told him that she had had Homer take her to the factor's office but decided that fell in the realm of showing off. Instead, she upbraided him. "Marcus said he explained all this to you and Franklin years ago. Why did you not tell Alexis and me?"

"No reason to worry you. Besides, by the time the money ran out, I assumed you and Alexis would be married."

"Assume again. I have no beaus, but, because of my peculiarity, I've attracted the perverse attention of some of your more disgusting friends."

Lewis stepped away from the fire. "Name them, and I promise they'll never dare whisper your name again."

"Oh, you're going to give up your uniform all for the sake of poor little ol' me?"

"If that's what it takes."

"What it requires is money, and our family has none. Oh, they have the dowry for Alexis, but why would they keep anything for me? I'll never make use of it, and a larger dowry makes my sister much more attractive."

"Jennie, you mustn't speak of yourself this way."

His cousin tossed her head and her long black hair shimmered in the firelight. "I'm not sure what I'm to do." She placed her cup on the table. "But I do know this: Abraham Marcus told me every business arrangement our fathers have involved themselves in has turned as sour as a pitcher of day-old milk. And there's the expense of keeping up Cooper Hill, which, by itself, is enough to keep us, like Sisyphus, rolling a rock up the mountain, only to have it tumble down on us again. As for Mother, she's so worried—Father finally had to tell her he was selling Cooper Hill—that she's taken to bed, and that's why she couldn't accompany us to town." Jennie paused. "Alexis sometimes nurses her, and it's the first time I can remember my sister making an effort for anyone other than herself."

Lewis tried to object, but she cut him off. "Besides Homer and Ella Mae, there are no servants in the house. All were sold long ago; the rest go with Cooper Hill. And you want to quit your studies, something that might make it possible for your family to hold their heads up in Charleston."

Lewis stared into the dying fire.

Jennie left the chair and joined him. Reaching up to brush his wet hair back, she asked, "What's the matter, Lewis? Did they hurt your feelings? Leave you out of their group again?"

Lewis jerked back. He'd left the Citadel because he

didn't belong, only to return to a world that no longer existed. Actually, after finding his father with his cousin, he wondered if that world had ever existed.

"I'm sorry if I hurt your feelings, Lewis, but what *are* you doing here?"

What was he doing here?

"Your brother never comes home, even when he's offered leave. He remains at West Point tutoring underclassmen. Evidently having a head for numbers is all right when it comes to being a boy."

Lewis put his arm around her. The girl was so beautiful, and a similar copy, without the mental defect, probably slept upstairs. Alexis and Jennie didn't go anywhere without each other.

Lewis cleared his throat. "Alexis is here, you say?"

Jennie frowned as she left his embrace. "I didn't say, but she's upstairs. Alexis can sleep through the bells of St. Michael's. Tell me, Lewis, who are these young men who're mistreating you?"

Lewis muttered a few names.

"But I don't understand. Some of those cadets are from the finest families in Charleston."

"They aren't so fine once they're on the grounds of the Citadel."

"But, Lewis, if you would only—"

"Please don't reproach me. I'm not in the mood. I received a severe soaking while walking over here."

Jennie returned to her chair and said nothing. This came as no surprise to Lewis. His cousin could sit for hours, and when you asked what she was thinking, she'd simply say: "Just thinking." It was enough to make anyone nervous.

Jennie and Alexis of the rich black hair, pale blue eyes, and porcelain skin. Why wouldn't his father be attracted? Lewis was, but that was different. Belles had been marrying their cousins for generations. Some said it strengthened the line; some said such intermingling weakened it.

Without preamble or explanation, he asked, "Jennie, what do you think of me?"

The girl's face broke into a quick smile. "Why I love you, Lewis. After all, you're my cousin." She paused. "Can I tell you a secret?"

"Of course."

"When I was younger, I was greatly infatuated. You were so tall and handsome." Her hand trailed an uneven line through the air. "And you could ride and ride all day and never tire. You were my hero, my cavalier. And you taught me how to ride."

"I thought that was Franklin."

"It was you, but I pretended it was Franklin so as not to disappoint him. Father wasn't interested."

"He's never been interested in his daughters, has he?"

"Never, and that's why Alexis and I fell in love with our cousins, and any other young man who would show us the least bit of attention." Again she paused. "I know you prefer Alexis to me."

"Jennie, that's simply not true."

"It's all right. Most men do."

Lewis stared into the fire once again. "Tell me what you think of me as a man."

"Why, Lewis," she said, looking him over from head to toe, "I think you're a handsome but thoroughly wet devil."

"Now you're being silly." But he couldn't help but smile. "You don't think much of me, do you? That infatuation was, as you said, when you were much younger. You're older now and expect more out of men, don't you?"

Jennie remained silent, only staring at him.

Lewis looked into the fire again. "This is what Franklin said I should prepare myself for."

"Have you received a letter?" she asked eagerly. "I've written several but received nothing in return. He must be, like you, going through a difficult time."

Lewis rolled his shoulders and let out a long sigh. "Perhaps it's time I found my fortune away from Charleston. Others in our family have. I might head to Kansas. The Bloodhounds, that unit out of Beaufort, wants me to accompany them into the territories."

"I'm sorry, Lewis, but you simply cannot go. Father is losing his mind, and *your* father is becoming a lech. Alexis and I need you here, whether you read for the law or not."

"I've told you before . . . ." Lewis faced her. "What . . . what did he do?"

"Nothing, Lewis. I just sit on his lap. From time to time."

"What time to time?"

"The times when he swears he'll kill himself. Thankfully, Father doesn't know about it. *He'd* kill him."

"Jennie, I didn't know . . ."

"Neither does anyone." She glanced at the doorway. "This is between you and me . . . and your father."

"Does he touch you?"

Jennie shook her head violently and her dark hair

flew around. "Absolutely not! He just cries on my shoulder." She colored again and looked into her lap. "I really shouldn't be talking to you about this. It's not proper, but it's why we need a man in this house."

"I—I'm sorry. I didn't mean to embarrass you."

"And I take his pistol away and unload it." Finally, she looked up. "I'm getting to be very good with dueling pistols. Unloading them, that is."

"He . . . cries . . . . on your shoulder?"

"Your father misses your mother. None of the women he's taken up with can make him content."

"You're sure he doesn't touch you?"

"Is there some reason you must dwell on our nasty little scene? Will you be telling tales out of school?" Jennie came out of her chair. "That's why I could never love you, Lewis. You, as with Alexis, were always in love with yourself." As she headed for the parlor door, she added, "Sometimes I look forward to being poor."

"And why's that?" asked Lewis, following her.

"Because there would be fewer choices. Only money gives you the freedom to choose." And pulling her nightgown tight, she hurried out of the room.

Lewis watched her go down the hall. One of the most beautiful girls in Charleston and no one wanted her. "Jennie . . . ."

But she did not hear him, and he had not raised his voice so that she could. He stood and watched her disappear into the darkness.

Walking back into the parlor, Lewis realized his cousin had persevered under the most difficult circumstances and had never once complained. All she asked was that he complete his tour of duty. It was the least he could do, and the hell with secret societies.

Lewis picked up his cloak and shook it out, spraying the floor with water. The fire was growing weaker and barely illuminated the room. Still, there were plenty of dark corners where he could hide, but only if he were a child.

Shrugging into his cloak, Lewis left the parlor and returned to the front door. There he listened to the storm. This one was going to last all night and well into the morning. At least that's what one of his classmates had said.

How did his classmate know? The cadet had spent time on the high seas with his father. And another classmate could stitch together anything and wore the best-looking uniforms. And there was another cadet who could cook as well as any servant. When Lewis had been invited to one of the Saturday night meals held on post, everything cooked by that cadet had been delicious.

How long had it been since he'd participated in one of those Saturday night gatherings, a gathering made up of ordinary cadets, not members of a secret group? Lewis didn't remember. All his free time had been spent on punishment tours and study. And worrying about a group who looked down on the common cadet, meaning the ones who could cook, sew, or knew how long the next storm would last.

Lewis stepped out on the porch and closed the door behind him. He'd return to the Citadel and graduate, and once out of school, he'd tend to as many women in Charleston as his uniform would allow. As good a way as any to test his cousin's theory regarding rich girls' attraction to military uniforms. Perhaps he'd even bed some of the women betrothed to those cadets who belonged to the secret society, but he would not quit. Turning up the collar of his cloak, Lewis went down the steps, leaned into the wind, and hurried down the street in the direction of his post.

Alexis felt Jennie rustle the covers as she climbed into bed. Contrary to what everyone thought, Alexis was not a heavy sleeper, but such a reputation did allow her to avoid many of the early morning chores around Cooper Hill.

Jennie was returning from a late-night rendezvous with her beau, and Alexis wondered who that might be. When Jennie's beau had carried their uncle to his room, the hallway had been in darkness and Alexis hadn't been able to see his face. At first she thought it was one of her cousins, but both Lewis and Franklin were away at school.

Who'd it been? Alexis was dying to know, and she lay in bed considering this young man and that young man, working herself into such a state that it was more than an hour before she fell asleep. What young man in his right mind would choose Jennie over her?

Alexis

Chapter Sixteen

The following morning Jennie was dressed and sitting at the dressing table, brushing her hair, when Alexis rolled over and looked at her. For a moment Alexis didn't know where she was. She looked around, trying to make sense of why she would be in Charleston at this time of year.

"You're in Charleston, dear," said her sister.

"Oh, stop showing off, Jennie. I know you can read minds."

Jennie gave her hair another couple of strokes, put down the brush, and left the dressing table. Heading for the door, she said, "Then I'm sure you remember that you don't have a personal attendant here as there was at Cooper Hill."

"Jennie, you can be so mean."

"Something else you should know. This is the city, and things move at a much quicker pace. If you don't want to miss anything, you'd best always be on time."

Alexis threw off the covers and sat up. "Jennie, I will

not allow you to lecture me."

But her sister was gone, closing the door behind her.

Alexis knew her sister was only teasing. Two women alone in Charleston would definitely need escorts. Plans had to be made and escorts provided for; all that would take time, and an escort who wouldn't wait for Alexis Belle, well, he wasn't much of a prospect.

And the balls began at the end of the week!

Hurrah! There she would meet plenty of young men who'd enjoy promenading along the Battery with Alexis Belle on their arm.

Alexis swung her feet over the side of the bed, and as she did, remembered the events of last night. She'd forgotten to ask Jennie what had happened. Not that her sister would tell her, but there had been all that shouting, what sounded like a shot fired, and a crash, and someone, perhaps Jennie's beau, carrying their uncle off to bed. Actually, with the storm raging, all Alexis could be sure she'd heard was the shouting.

What had Uncle Jean walked in on? Just wait until her parents heard. Jennie wouldn't be so cocky then.

But a more important question: Who was Jennie's beau. Who in the world could it be? All those letters Jennie had written before leaving Cooper Hill, and not once had she allowed her own sister to see to whom those letters were addressed.

Alexis prided herself on being a premier gossip—gossip was a girl's best friend—but she wouldn't learn anything about last night, or the identity of Jennie's beau, if she remained in her room all morning.

In record time Alexis was dressed, had joined her sister and uncle for breakfast, and, before she sat down, stuck out her tongue at Jennie's knowing smile. Oh, you just wait until our folks move in!

"Uncle Jean Louis," said Jennie as Ella Mae set a plate and a cup of coffee in front of Alexis, "I was thinking that Alexis and I might call on some families."

Her uncle said nothing but continued to stare at his plate. Alexis wondered what could be wrong. Their uncle's shirt was open and he wore no cravat. His shaving had been haphazard and he'd cut himself more than once.

Alexis shivered. How men could casually use a blade on their faces, she couldn't fathom. And she certainly didn't know what to make of her uncle's silence. Uncle Jean didn't appear to have suffered much last night, but still, he wasn't in his usual talkative mood.

Alexis looked across the table at Jennie in her calico dress and white apron. Her sister dressed like one of the servants.

Not her. She'd struggled into her hoop skirt, forced the crinoline under the table, and couldn't wait to see the latest fashions in the windows along King Street.

Alexis looked at her uncle again—still silent—and then glanced at Jennie. Uncle Jean had become more and more peculiar ever since his sons had left for their respective military academies. Of course, Uncle Jean had every right to be disappointed. Soldiering wasn't a gentlemanly occupation.

"That will be all, Ella Mae," said Jennie, dismissing the servant.

The Negro nodded and left the room.

"You wouldn't have any objection to Homer driving us around town to leave our cards, would you?"

Jean Louis nodded, and then picked up his knife and fork and sliced his sausage. Very deliberately he speared the sausage and placed it in his mouth. His bites were slow and deliberate, and all the time, he stared down the table, right between his two nieces.

"Good then," said Jennie, brightly. She looked across the table. "Alexis and I've grown out of touch with our friends since we left Madame Talvande's French School, and this will be an excellent opportunity for us to catch up."

To Alexis that meant catching up on all the gossip. The sooner she was dressed and ready to go, the sooner old Homer would prepare the carriage.

Alexis took a bite of eggs, then grits, and swallowed down some of her coffee. She pushed her plate away and got to her feet. A trip to leave cards demanded a closer examination of the gowns she'd brought to town.

Across the table Jennie looked up and made a face of disapproval, then returned her attention to their uncle. "May Alexis and I be excused, Uncle Jean?"

Their uncle nodded, continued to chew on his sausage, and stared down the middle of the table.

But when Alexis headed toward their bedroom to examine her gowns, Jennie told her to follow her to the kitchen, and, of course, there was nothing anyone could do when her sister was in one of her moods.

Alexis followed Jennie out of the house and into the kitchen where the servants were eating breakfast. The two elderly people hustled to their feet, but Jennie put a hand on their shoulders and told them to finish their meal. She also told them that if their uncle wanted anything, they were to come and fetch her.

Sighs of relief crossed both black faces. There should've been more servants at the city house, but Ella Mae and Homer were the only ones who could tolerate Jean Louis' idiosyncrasies. And since the Belles didn't believe in splitting up slave families, Jean Louis was stuck with them and they with him.

Fewer servants meant it was even more imperative that Jennie alert the Negroes to their plans for the day. You needed a small army of servants to keep up a house such as this, but more servants wouldn't be moving into town until the sale of Cooper Hill was finalized, and then, very few. And the Belle town house reflected the neglect. There was dust in the corners, and not a few cobwebs, and it didn't appear anyone had brushed off the furniture, and more furniture was on the way.

"Homer, Miss Alexis and I will be paying a call on several homes to leave our cards. Would you let us know when you have the carriage ready?"

"Yes, ma'am, I shore will."

She patted him on the shoulder. "Thank you."

The elderly Negro broke into a grin. "I'm sure all those white folks will be proud to see you." There wasn't a black person in the Low Country who didn't think Jennie Belle wasn't some sort of a witch, and it amused Homer to watch his fellow servants' eyes pop out when the Belle carriage pulled up in front of their house.

"We must remember we're doing this for Miss Alexis. It won't be long before she comes out, and the balls beginning at the end of the week will be a prelude."

The two servants looked at the identical twin, and

Alexis glowed. How could she quibble over any of this effort to reacquaint everyone in Charleston with her, the belle of the ball? And unlike her male cousins, she had no qualms over the spelling of their family name, and had often said she would miss being a Belle once she married.

"Alexis, dear, would you please see that Uncle Jean has some fresh coffee?"

"About time for him to start drinking," muttered Ella Mae.

"I saw him go into the church yesterday," Homer said.

"Then you've been drinking yourself," said his wife.

"Well," said Jennie, as she watched Alexis leave the kitchen with the coffeepot, "we're about at the end of that road, I would hope."

"Lordy, I hope so." The elderly woman touched her head where she had accidentally fallen, and "accidentally" was the term Ella Mae was sticking to.

Alexis left with the coffeepot, and as she did, remembered a promise she'd made to herself not to marry a man who mistreated his Negroes. A man who would mistreat his servants would mistreat his wife, and she'd seen a good bit of that at Cooper Hill.

Homer got to his feet. "I'll just be going to fix the carriage."

Jennie pushed him back down in his chair. "Your chores can wait until you've finished breakfast."

And where neither Jennie nor her sister were about to clear the table in the dining room, nor do any of the housework, Jennie knew very well that she had to husband the energy of these two Negroes. That didn't mean

Steve Brown

she'd go easy on them, or even become cross when they didn't complete their assigned tasks, but she'd treat them as she did Alexis: with great expectations.

"Homer, if Alexis and I are ready before the carriage is prepared, just holler up the stairs. We'll be in the south parlor completing our devotionals."

Alexis returned with the coffeepot. "Uncle Jean is gone."

"Gone?" asked Jennie and Mae. "Where?"

"He's not in the dining room, nor his room. I checked the parlors, too."

Homer followed the three women to the front of the house. The door was open, and they walked outside where Ella Mae and Jennie each looked up and down High Battery. Jean Louis was nowhere to be seen.

"I'll look upstairs," said Mae.

"I already told you he's not upstairs." Alexis was staring at the front door. It hadn't been left unlocked as she'd initially thought. "This door is broken." A shiver went through her. Runaway slaves could've broken in last night and slit her throat.

"Now don't you be worrying about that, Miss Alexis," Homer said. "I'm gonna fix that today."

Alexis looked at Jennie. "But who broke the door?"

"Honey," said Ella Mae, putting an arm around her and walking Alexis back into the house, "there's all kinds of things that break down around this place, and that door is just one of them."

"I hope this isn't going to hold up my sister and me from going out today."

"No, Miss Alexis," said Homer, closing the door as

137

they returned to the house, "you don'ts have to worry about a thing."

"Perhaps Uncle Jean went to his club?" asked Jennie.

"That's what he might've done," said Homer. "He don't do much work at his office."

Ella Mae glanced toward the door. "It's not safe for him to be walking the streets if he's been drinking."

"He's not drunk," said Alexis. They looked at her. "Well, he wasn't drunk at the breakfast table."

"Child," said Ella Mae, with a laugh, "it don't take long, and it don't take much."

Jennie was eyeing the broken lock on the front door. "Homer, when you drop Miss Alexis and me off, would you see a locksmith about this door?"

"I'll need a pass," said the old man.

"But everyone in Charleston knows you," offered Alexis.

"Yes, ma'am, but Charleston has changed since you were in school, Miss Alexis. All colored folks need a pass, and the freed ones most of all."

Their first invitation came from the Petigrus, saying the Belle sisters could call on them the following day. The note was brought to the house on High Battery by one of the Petigru servants. But a visit to the Petigrus' seemed to Alexis to be getting off on the wrong foot. The Petigrus were one of the last Unionist families left in Charleston, and if Alexis knew one thing, she knew who was on their way up and who was on their way down, and any son, or daughter, of a Unionist family was falling fast.

So, while Jennie made small talk with the mother in

the parlor, Alexis sat with the daughter in her bedroom and caught up on all the local gossip. This didn't
bother Jennie. She had work to do, the meeting with
cousin Lewis primarily on her mind.

Over afternoon tea with one mother after another,
Jennie's plea would rarely vary. "Alexis would dearly
love to see her cousin, but, as you know, Uncle Jean
Louis isn't fond of the decision Lewis made to attend
the Citadel. It's simply impossible for us to ask him to
escort us onto the grounds."

The mother would sniff and reply that she understood quite well a family's resistance to their young
gentleman becoming a soldier, but what's done is done.
"After all, not everyone can be an attorney."

"So, I thought you might be able to assist my sister."
And here Jennie would smile and add: "You know that
Lewis, he's such a rascal . . . ."

The mother would smile and nod at the follies of
young men. "How can I help you, my dear?"

"Well, we hoped when the cadets march to church
this Sunday we might join you in your pew." Citadel
cadets paraded through downtown on their way to
church each Sunday. It awed the general populace and,
hopefully, cowed the slaves.

"My dear, that is all well and good, but I'm afraid
you'd have to accompany us, or there might be those
who'd read some sort of commitment by my son into
such an appearance."

"Oh," said Jennie, leaning back and cooling herself
with a fan. "I hadn't thought of that." Then she would
smile and add, "Mother said we could depend on your
advice while we were in the city."

At that point the mother would generally lean over and tap Jennie on the knee with her own fan. "Your mother was right, my dear, and as long as she isn't in town, you should consider me your surrogate."

Jennie would flash another smile, thank the woman, and she and Alexis, who personally found all cadets unsuitable for such a remarkable young woman as herself, would accompany the family to church the following Sunday. And when the cadet was allowed to pay his respects to his family at the conclusion of the service, Jennie would take the cadet by the hand, look him in the eye, and thank him for socializing with that rascal of a cousin of hers and for including Lewis in any clubs, groups, or societies that might be a part of Citadel life. So, Lewis Belle was initiated into the cadets' secret society, and this acceptance encouraged Lewis to believe that bluster, boldness, and arrogance were good things when it came to charting one's path in life.

As for the impact this incident had on his cousins, quite a few sons were told by their mothers that the Belle sisters had been seen at church and these young men began calling on Alexis. Jennie, however, returned home, and during her sister's afternoon nap, she'd go into the empty servant quarters over the carriage house and bawl until she ran out of tears.

Chapter Seventeen

When the Belle family finally completed their move from Cooper Hill to Charleston in the spring of 1856, Alexis found her life rather restrictive and her parents dreadfully tiresome. She couldn't leave the house and wander around the property as she had at Cooper Hill. Not only that, but her mother would demand someone sit with her—for hours!—instead of doing what a mother should do: visiting with other mothers and taking Alexis along so she could dazzle their sons. The least her mother could do was to come down to the parlor and speak with her male visitors instead of having Jennie or Ella Mae or even Homer sit with them. After that, as far as she was concerned, her mother could take to her bed for the rest the day.

In Charleston there were plenty of beaus, but for some reason Alexis couldn't stop the rumor going round that she had a special place in her heart for the cadets of the Citadel. Alexis had no idea where this foolishness had started, though, during the fall balls, she and

Jennie had attended church with families who had sons at the Citadel. But it'd been Jennie who had gone out of her way to speak to those cadets, not her.

That had to be it! The Charlestonians thought she was Jennie and vice versa. Well, she would set them straight. Maybe . . .

Several fights had broken out between cadets and townies, though with different consequences: The young men of Charleston, coming from privileged backgrounds, had their high jinks winked at by the local authorities, but the cadets would walk punishment tours for showing disrespect to their uniforms and their school.

Alexis found she really liked to sally forth with the more combative boys, cadet or Charlestonian. Not because someone should defend her honor—that was a given—but because of how the whole scene so excited her, heat rushing from her throat all the way down to her privates.

Her sister made several attempts to end Alexis's promenades along the Battery with some of the rougher element, but, in this, Alexis had the full support of her father, a man desperate to marry off his daughter to the first young man to come along, as long as that young man's family had money. Claude wanted someone who could support Alexis, her mother, and himself, in the style to which they'd become accustomed.

So, at one of the spring balls, Alexis was on the arm of the most handsome and eligible young man in the city, while Jennie trailed along on the arm of a pimpled-faced boy who wore glasses and a suit that hung on his skinny frame. The boy was nervous, and for good reason. He was escorting one of the most beautiful women in the state, and he could not believe his good fortune.

This beauty had picked him from all possible suitors? Hoopskirt with a bodice cut low at the neck and hair in ringlets. He would definitely have to leave his card before he left Charleston.

So Alexis danced the night away and was fondled in one of the dark corners of the veranda. And though Jennie had the same bosom, same pale skin, and same legs, there were few dances for her, and all of those with the gangly young man whose family owned vast cotton holdings somewhere in the back country.

Jennie didn't know where. Jennie might've studied world history and could speak more than one language, but the girl was a Charlestonian through and through, and once you went beyond the "neck," or that area of Charleston above Boundary Street, you might as well be in Kentucky.

Her father had other thoughts. This young man might be the proper suitor for his daughter, and he opened negotiations with the family. As he told Jennie's mother: "No one knows of Jennie's eccentricity in Abbeville, and since that's where John C. Calhoun was raised, it must be a fine little town."

His wife simply reopened her Bible and prayed for her daughter's soul. It had to be the workings of the devil for her child to be so cursed.

So, that night when someone cut in on Alexis, her handsome escort joined his friends in the corner of the ballroom, and he was quite breathless. "I kissed them. I actually kissed them."

"What?" asked one of the young men.

"Her teats. We were out on the veranda and I kissed her down the neck and across the top of her bosoms. I did, I really did it!"

"Oh, no!" said one of the boys.

Another groaned in pain.

"So what?" said a red-headed fellow trying to minimize the damage to their egos. His face was covered with freckles.

"No," said Alexis's escort, "you don't understand. I think she liked it."

"Liar! Liar!" cried a couple of the boys in unison.

"Yeah," said another, "that's what you are unless you want to tell us what really happened."

"I am telling you. I kissed her teats and she liked it."

"Kissed her teats," said Sidney Craven with obvious disdain. "I'll bet I could have my way with her sister. Nobody cares what happens to Jeanne Anne, and the goods are just the same."

Heads turned and stared at the dance floor. It was well known that Sidney Craven had the itch for Alexis Belle, and now he was announcing that he would take her sister as a substitute. Or is that what he really meant?

"But if she's truly bewitched, you might lose an important part of your anatomy."

Sidney snorted. "Looks like any other girl to me."

"Yeah," said one of the boys, a dreamy look on his face as he watched Jennie with her partner on the dance floor. "Looks just like her sister."

"I heard Jennie Belle can turn water into wine," said another.

"Oh, Lord, what a trick. No more stealing from my old man's cache."

"That's blasphemy," said another boy.

"Yeah," agreed another. "Watch your mouth."

"Well, if you want to join me . . ." Sidney met the eye of everyone in the group. "But if you're afraid . . . ."

"I ain't afraid of nothing."

"I'm not afraid of any girl."

"Jeanne Anne can't resist all of us," Sidney said.

"What are you talking about?" asked the freckled-faced young man, interested in any scheme put forth by Sidney Craven.

"I'm talking about taking that girl and making her our very own whore."

Several gulped. Alexis's escort shook his head and walked away. The rest of the young men continued to stare at the Belle sisters on the dance floor.

"We do it to niggers, why not Jeanne Anne?"

One of them cleared his throat. "I think . . . I think . . . ."

Sidney took up a position between the five young men and the dance floor. "Hey, all I'm asking is whether you think it's right for Jeanne Anne to have that power over us."

"Nah," muttered the redhead, shaking his head.

"No. It's not right," agreed another.

"I don't know," said the young man with the dreamy look in his eyes. "I wish one of the Belle sisters would exercise their power over me."

"Appears one of them already has."

That was met with a gale of laughter.

"Hey," said Sidney, trying to return the conversation to the subject at hand. "Jeanne Anne wouldn't have a chance against the six of us."

"What are you saying exactly?"

"That she can't handle all of us. She's not powerful enough."

"I get it," said the redhead, snapping his fingers. "If we wait until she's older, she might be able to hex us all, but now—"

"Hell, Boykin, I didn't think you knew such big words."

"I know a lot more than you figure," said the redhead addressed as "Boykin."

"Yeah," asked Sidney, "but wouldn't you like to know what Alexis Belle looks like under all those petticoats? That's the question."

Several of the boys nodded, now understanding the complexity of the dare.

"So we get her alone," said the redhead.

The boy under the spell of the Belle sisters came to his senses long enough to say, "I don't know about that . . . ."

"Hey," said Boykin, gesturing at the Belle sisters on the dance floor, "if you're not interested in riding one of those, then stick to your father's sheep."

After the laughter subsided, Sidney added, "And who's to complain if we have our way with Jennie Belle?"

Burke Randolph

Chapter Eighteen

Burke Randolph shuffled down the gangway of the steamship *Atlantic Cloud*. Burke was in chains and he had a plum-colored frock coat draped over his arm. A tall hat had been jammed on his head, and his white waistcoat was soiled and filthy. His cravat had been stuffed into the collar of his ruffled shirt, and a pair of dirty plaid trousers clung to his legs and should have been strapped under the insteps of a pair of highly polished black leather boots. But those boots were missing, too, and for anyone who cared to look, Burke's stockings were soiled and torn and had holes where both big toes protruded. Burke had counted on making an impression upon landing in Charleston, and now he did, with the assistance of the chains that rattled as he came down the gangway, along with the bluish tinge under one eye.

At the end of the gangway Burke stopped and surveyed the harbor. The buildings of Charleston reflected sun off their copper roofs, glass windows, and a rainbow of colors off a row of houses near the water. There were over twenty wharves, a ferry across the Cooper River to Mt. Pleasant, and docks for the Wilmington Steam Packet and Railroad. St. Michael's spire towered over the city, a welcoming sight for any lookout after too many long days at sea.

Burke, himself, appeared to be about twenty, and his features were clean-cut but for a pair of sideburns that followed the angle of his jaw. His nose was almost Roman, high-bridged with thin nostrils, and the set of his jaw was determined; his lower lip cut. But his brown eyes laughed, and it was a good thing he found something amusing as the first mate gave him a good shove to complete his trip down the gangway. Burke stumbled forward, chains rattling and tall hat falling to the dock.

Another group of shackled men trailed Burke off the ship. These were the able-bodied sailors unlucky enough to have been born with black skin, and when mooring in Charleston, the Negro Seaman Act (passed by the state legislature) required all black sailors to be jailed while their ships were in port.

Burke turned around and faced the first mate, a man with enough muscle to exert his will upon any member of the crew. But evidently not Burke Randolph. Burke stood there, smiling and ignoring the pain in his foot from the stickpin stuck in the callus under his big toe. People glanced at Burke as they hurried by. Some actually gawked as the first mate instructed a sailor to remove the chains from his prisoner's wrists and the shackles from his legs. Burke simply stood there and grinned.

The first mate was tempted to flatten this arrogant

fellow who thought he could have the run of *his* ship and the ladies aboard it. Unfortunately, the captain had given strict orders, so the first mate watched as the chains were removed and the sailor dragged the shackles back up the gangway.

"Thanks for your hospitality," said Burke, pulling on his frockcoat and picking up his hat.

He brushed off the hat and gave a sweeping bow. Those along the rail waved or hooted. Several women blushed, hid behind their fans, or looked away.

"And my bags?" asked Burke.

"Sorry," said the first mate with a grin of his own, "but they were sorted through by the crew and tossed overboard."

"Why does that not surprise me?"

The first mate snorted and sauntered back up the gangway.

He stopped when Burke said, "You appear to be about as good a first mate as one might expect, but I wouldn't continue to ply your trade along this route."

"And why is that?" asked the mate, turning around and facing him from halfway up the gangway.

"Because I might sail on *Atlantic Cloud* again, and though this ship would certainly miss its captain, it will always be able to find another first mate."

Enraged, the sailor rushed back down the gangway. The man stopped only when a voice called out from the navigation bridge.

"That will be quite enough, Mister Cromwell."

Face red and panting, the first mate pulled up short. "Mister Randolph!"

Burke looked up, the sun making the captain no

more than a blur against the light. Then Burke saw it: a tumbling flash of light, twinkling as it arched out and fell toward him. He snatched the gold coin from the air, put it to his mouth, and bit it.

"Clean yourself up, Mister Randolph. Vagrancy is taken quite seriously in Charleston."

Burke nodded, and after throwing a salute in the captain's direction, strode off as if he'd come ashore clean and spiffy and ready for a night on the town.

The first mate watched this jackass go and made a promise to himself that when he was finished with his duties, he and several of his shipmates would go ashore and prowl the bars and taverns until they found a cleaner and a neater Mr. Burke Randolph and soil him once again.

Burke wove his way through the crowd along the dock, the unloading and loading, and the comings and goings of those in the merchant trade. Urchins and whores surrounded him, all touting their wares. The urchins bragged about their sisters, virgins all, and when Burke showed little interest, he was offered several narcotics, finally a young boy.

Burke pushed his way through the children and those that rubbed up against him. Their hands came away empty. There was no wallet, no money belt, nor was there any money, and no impression to be made upon the citizenry of Charleston, lest that be of a vagrant who'd be jailed and fined, or hit over the head for his boots. But there were no boots, and a few passersby wondered which whorehouse this gentleman might've patronized last night, so, in the future, they might avoid it at all costs.

Burke directed an inquiry to the remaining boy, as most of the whores and urchins had drifted away. "What about you, boy? I need a guide."

"I'm your man, sir. I know Charleston like no other." He eyed Burke speculatively. "But guides cost money. Sir."

Burke opened his hand and showed the boy the coin flipped to him by the captain of *Atlantic Cloud*.

A grin broke out across the youngster's face and he swept an arm in the direction of the customs house. "Sir, Charleston awaits your pleasure."

"First a Jew."

"Yes, sir. I know just the one."

A few blocks from the harbor, the boy led Burke off one of the cross streets and into an alley where the second-story galleries almost met overhead. Here, the sun was practically shut out, making the street quite dark and Burke very suspicious.

Glancing behind him, he asked, "Can I trust you, boy?"

The boy looked over his shoulder and smiled. "Most of the gentlemen I squire around Charleston walk down streets such as this, and not in as much daylight."

"Quite so," said Burke, and he followed the boy down the alley where a door with three golden balls hung over it. The windows flanking that door were criss-crossed with bars.

"You wait here."

"Yes, sir. I'm your man."

Burke shoved the wooden door back, and a bell rang as he stepped inside.

The showroom was dark, dank, and illuminated by oil lamps at opposite ends of a wooden counter, and under that counter, would be the good stuff: rings, pins, pendants, and snuffboxes galore, all laid out on trays covered in green felt. In the rear would be even better items, and on the wall behind the counter hung matching dueling pistols and several rapiers with silver hilts. The proprietor, a fat man, came from behind a curtain and took up a position behind the counter.

The pawnbroker was a sallow-skinned fellow who badly needed a shave. He wore a turban. "Welcome to my humble shop, sir."

His customer had bent over. *What?* The pawnbroker peered over the counter and found the man picking among his toes. "Sir?"

Burke stood up so quickly the pawnbroker stepped back. In his hand was the pearl stickpin and a drop of blood. "How much for this?" Burke wiped away the blood and presented the stickpin once again.

The pearl was dull in the semidarkness of the room, but when the pawnbroker passed the stone in front of one of his lamps, the milky ball caught the flickering light and shone brightly.

Still, the pawnbroker's face revealed little interest as he turned over the pearl in his fingers. "Perhaps a hundred dollars."

"I thought more along the line of two." Burke smiled. "Two thousand dollars."

The merchant turned the pearl over in his hand again. "I might offer as much as five hundred."

Burke reached for the pearl. "And I think I'll go down the street."

The pawnbroker evaluated Burke, taking him in from head and toe. "I'd be surprised if anyone took your offer seriously, sir. They might think this a fake." Still, he did not return the pearl.

"Then that would be their loss." Burke gestured at his soiled clothing. "But you, sir, appear to be clever enough to see that I have little to lose, and with the proper backing, even more to gain. Standing before you is a sporting man who has fallen on hard times." Burke smiled. "Or had those hard times fall on him."

"A thousand dollars," countered the merchant, "that is my best offer."

Burke reached for the pearl again. "Fifteen hundred."

"Twelve-fifty."

Burke withdrew his hand. "Make it a thousand in gold, and agree to hold the pearl for thirty days and you have a deal."

A few minutes later he reappeared on the street. The boy leaped to his feet as Burke slipped a purse inside his pants, then righted the soiled hat on his head.

"And your next destination, sir?"

"The bank of Charleston, a clothier, and finally a hotel and a hot bath." And a game of poker. A very expensive game of poker.

But instead of poker, the game he became involved in was one of rescuing damsels in distress, and it paid quite poorly compared to poker.

Chapter Nineteen

Burke was hurrying down the alley and toward the light of the cross street when a horse and carriage turned in, practically on top of him. In the coach's box, or driver's seat, an elderly Negro was fighting off a well-dressed young man attempting to seize the reins from him.

A rather bold maneuver, thought Burke, and he wondered how a gray-headed Negro could've lived this long if he tangled with young white men in Charleston.

His guide threw out a hand. "Step back, sir!" And the boy forced Burke off the cobblestones.

This was nothing new to Burke. He'd been stepping aside for runaway carriages since he'd been a child, and he knew how to use a stoop and doorway. He and the boy pressed themselves against the door as the carriage raced by. Seconds later, the elderly Negro lost control of the reins and the carriage pulled to a stop a short distance away.

Before Burke and his companion could step down from the darkness of the doorway, three more young men followed the carriage and its horse into the alleyway, racing past Burke and his young companion. They split up as they went at the carriage and the Negro. Down the alley, doors shut and locks were thrown.

Stepping from the stoop in his stocking feet, Burke felt the boy grip his arm. "No reason for you to become involved in the business of some Negro, sir." The boy tugged on Burke's arm as the elderly man was shoved away and fell to the cobblestones. "It's obvious that he's offended those gentlemen in some way."

The doors on both sides of the carriage were jerked open, and a woman screamed from inside.

"Still say it's none of our business?" asked Burke.

"It might be yours, sir," said his guide, releasing Burke's arm, "but it's none of mine." And he raced off down the alley.

"How about calling a cop?" shouted Burke, using a word that was slowly working its way into the American lexicon.

The boy only ran faster.

Oh, well, thought Burke, I'm sure he's had other experiences that would make calling for a policeman a bit risky.

Burke returned his attention to the carriage where young men were attempting to climb inside. Again the woman screamed, and one of the young men came flying out of the carriage and landed on his rump in a pile of horse droppings. The force with which the young man been shoved out could only mean the woman had used her foot.

Now that would be a woman to meet, thought Burke, but only if she wasn't angry with you.

The young man got to his feet, shook his fist at the carriage, and cursed. After brushing off his pants, he charged the carriage door once again, along with the two young gentlemen who had finished thrashing the elderly Negro.

The woman screamed again, but this time the threat came from a young man climbing in the carriage from the other side. The woman's scream appeared to inspire the others. As Burke approached the carriage, the three on this side fought to be the first inside, and of course, found it impossible for all three to go through the carriage door at the same time.

"Get off me!" screamed the woman.

The young man on the opposite side fell back and practically in Burke's face as Burke had foregone the pleasure of taking on the three fools on the far side.

The young man grabbed the sides of the carriage door, snarled, and went at the woman again. Burke followed this lone attacker inside, and as he did, saw the animal-like rage on the faces of the other three.

My God, but they want this woman in the worst way, and from their looks, it has nothing to do with romance.

Burke locked his hands together and clubbed the young man over the back of the neck. Without a sound, the young man collapsed in the lap of the girl. When Burke went to pull him off, the lapel of his jacket was grabbed by a red-headed young man jammed in the door on the far side of the carriage.

A carriage that was moving once again!

All Burke could figure was that the fight had spooked the horse, and the young men, in their eagerness to put their hands on the woman, hadn't delegated one of their number to hold the reins.

Burke tried to shake off the hand reaching across the carriage, but another of the three grabbed his arm when he did. Burke and the three teetered in the door-way until a helpful shove from the woman sent all four of them sailing out the door to land on the cobblestones below. Luckily for Burke, he was the last one out and landed on this pile of humanity.

Outnumbered four to one, Burke quickly pulled himself into a tight ball and rolled away from the carriage. Only at the corner of the alley and the cross street did the last of the four assailants vacate the carriage, kicked out by a pair of feminine stockings and shoes. Then the elderly Negro raised his whip, laid it across the rump of the horse, and the carriage wheeled out of the alley and was gone.

My God! What a woman!

Stumbling to his feet Burke backed away, almost tripping over another stoop.

Uh-huh. Too bad she's not still around to pull your bacon out of the fire.

The young men were on their feet now, moving in his direction. Actually, there were only two of them as the third was screaming and reaching for his ankle.

The other two ignored their companion and advanced on Burke, faces red from exertion and embarrassed at being bested by a girl. They brought up their fists, and both young men looked like they knew their way around a ring. Down the alley lay the fourth member of their party, drawing the attention of passers-by, who called a policeman. The officer began blowing his whistle.

"Boys," said Burke, touching his pants and finding

the purse still there. "I'm ready to tangle with you, but one of your number appears to need a bit of help."

"You scoundrel, we'll show you." The young man's hair was flaming red and he had a multitude of freckles across his face.

The man next to him wasn't so sure. He glanced at their friend lying on the ground and begging for help. At the far end of the alley, the fourth member of their party lay unconscious.

"Say," called out another policeman, walking toward them from where the carriage had turned the corner, "what's going on in here?" As he moved up the alley, he appraised the young man lying on the ground and holding his ankle.

The redhead pointed at Burke. "It was him, Riley. He attacked Sidney and dragged him into the alley. We were across the street and saw the whole thing."

"That's simply not true," protested Burke as he backed away from the policeman.

Another policeman joined him, and then another from behind Burke, entering the alleyway from the opposite direction. Very quickly Burke found himself boxed in.

Well, thought Burke, the police in any city would more likely than not club a nasty looking fellow like himself over the head, and then inquire to his side of the story.

And that's just what they did. Burke found himself lying on the cobblestones and not thinking of the purse being lifted from his pants, but remembering the pale face, rich black hair, and angry blue eyes.

What a fighter that girl had been!

Chapter Twenty

Two days later, a redhead, and this time a woman, came 'round to see Burke, and she had quite a way with the guards. Her dress lacked a hoop, and Burke took this to mean that the woman was no lady. Still, Burke got up from where he sat on the stone floor and came over to stand at the bars when hailed by the guard.

First, he noticed how attractive the redhead was; then he noticed her smell. She smelled like newly baked bread. The girl's eyes were green; her face round and freckled, and her curls fell to her shoulders, as if daring anyone to make an issue of the fact that her hair wasn't netted in a chignon. The girl appeared to be his age, give or take a year.

Beside her stood a guard, munching on a cinnamon roll. "This must be the one you mean, Susannah." The guard looked from the woman to Burke and back again. "Though I don't see any family resemblance."

"Oh, that's my cousin for sure. Been brawling again,

have you, cousin?" The redhead looked Burke up and down. "You're not in Charleston an hour and look at yourself. My father will expect an explanation."

Burke started, "There is an explanation—"

"I'm sure there is, but the judge won't be interested. What he'll want to hear, if he allows Susannah Chase to take you home, is that you won't be dragging any more of the fine young men of Charleston into dark alleys and giving them a proper thrashing."

"Then tell His Honor that he has my word of honor."

The guard had been listening closely to what was being said. Now he returned to his cinnamon roll with enthusiasm. As far as Burke could tell, the cinnamon had clearly gone to the guard's head. Anyone brighter would've seen through their charade.

"I'm sorry, cousin," said Burke, hanging his head. "Your family gives me an opportunity to start anew in Charleston after I disgraced my family in Richmond, and I've already disgraced you."

"You've certainly done that, and my father will decide whether you're shipped back to Richmond or not."

Burke gripped the bars of his cell. "I promise, cousin. I'll do the best I can."

The guard snorted in disbelief. When he did, he took some of the roll down the wrong way. The guard hacked and coughed until the redhead slapped him across the back several times, then cleared his throat by spitting on the floor.

The redhead eyed the damp spot. "That's no way to treat my rolls, Johnny."

"Sorry, Susannah. You know I have the utmost respect for your baking."

The redhead smiled and patted the guard on the shoulder.

Pounding the guard's back hadn't startled Burke as much as when the redhead patted his shoulder. Was she this familiar with all men? Oh, what did it matter if she could free him from this wretched cell?

"And, cousin, your wenching, drinking, and gambling, are you prepared to give that up while in Charleston?"

Burke paused long enough to cause the guard to smile. The guard must be wondering, if those were the terms of his release, whether he would prefer to remain in the lockup.

"Well," demanded Susannah.

"Yes, cousin," said Burke, looking properly chaste.

Minutes later, Burke was swearing to a magistrate that he would conduct himself with such decorum that all Charleston would be honored to have Burke Randolph in their city.

The magistrate, an elderly man, cautioned him. "Son, you should listen to your cousin in these matters." He gestured at the redhead who stood off to one side. "Not only does she make the best cinnamon rolls in the Low Country, but you couldn't do any better for a wife."

Burke almost choked on the suggestion as much as the guard had choked on the redhead's roll.

Susannah stepped over and took his arm as Burke cleared his own throat. "Believe me, cousin, that's not one of the terms of your release. I'm already betrothed."

"To whom," asked the magistrate, "and when's he going to make an honest woman of you?"

"Your honor, I am an honest woman."

"Well, of course you are. I didn't mean any offense."

"None taken, your honor."

The magistrate shuffled through his papers. "I have no idea why no charges were brought by the young gentlemen you attacked. One of them was seriously injured. You'd do well to remain in your lodging or at the bakery for the next week."

He shook a pen at Burke. "What I'm saying is, I don't want to see you on the street, Mister Randolph, and I'd better not hear of you fighting any duels." He looked Burke up and down. "And purchase some new clothes. You do have other clothing, don't you?"

"I had his chest taken from the ship to the bakery," said the redhead.

"Very well." He waved the two of them out. "Then be off with you, and, Susannah, give some consideration to marrying someone other than that sailor. You never know what sailors do once they've disappeared over the horizon."

"Oh, I think I do," said the redhead with a smile, "and it's probably quite a bit like what they do when here in Charleston."

Outside the courthouse, Burke asked, "May I ask what happened in there? Not that I don't appreciate your services, Miss . . ."

"And, I, sir, don't appreciate your language. You make me sound like a common streetwalker."

"I didn't mean—"

"I know what you meant, but you're in Charleston now and you'd best be on your best behavior. And that includes your language."

The redhead glanced around and then took Burke's arm and led him away. Across the street several people watched them go. One of them was the street urchin who'd accompanied Burke to the pawnbroker, another a young Negro who trailed them down the street.

"Would you know the condition of the young lady in the carriage?" asked Burke.

"Taken to her bed, if I don't miss my guess. But I'm sure she'll recover, thanks to you."

"And the four young men?"

"They really did that? Four of them attacked Miss Belle's carriage?"

"Absolutely, and I'm willing to testify to their actions."

The redhead looked him over as they strolled along. "Not until you do something about your clothing."

"Fine, but what happened to them?"

"Two are out and about, and probably looking for you. Don't look behind us, but that's one of the Cravens' colored boys. Another of the scoundrels is recovering at home. I'm not sure if Sidney will ever walk again, and by maiming him, you've made enemies of one of the most prominent families in the Low Country. The other boy, the one in the coma, was a hanger-on, so I doubt you'll hear much from that quarter."

A pang of remorse shot through Burke. His father always said he'd come to no good, and now this woman, whom he didn't know from Adam, or rather Eve, was practically saying the same thing.

Been in Charleston less than an hour before running afoul of the law? Even his father would consider that some kind of record.

"We may have a problem with the terms of my release,

Susannah, if that's your name."

"It is. Susannah Chase."

"Well, for your information, I'm a sporting man."

She pulled him to a stop. "Then I might as well take you back to the docks and see you off. The tide goes out this evening."

"No, no, I'll do my best to keep my word."

"For at least a week, you hear me." Tightening her grip on his arm, they started out again. "That and the fact someone wants to thank you."

"Who?"

"Well," said Susannah with a smile, "you don't think I bail every young gentleman out of jail, do you?"

"Actually, I'm not sure exactly what you do."

"I'm a baker by trade, and that's what you're about to become, at least for the next week or two." She eyed him. "Unless you'd prefer sailing on the evening tide?"

"No, no. I can tolerate anything for a few days."

"It might be more than a few days. The lady who sent me wants to thank you properly, and for a lady, the timing might be difficult to arrange."

Burke remembered those blue eyes, that pale face, and rich black hair . . . . *That* woman wanted to see him?

Burke wondered what this redhead would think if he told her the woman had already visited him . . . whenever he'd fallen asleep on the stone floor of his jail cell.

Chapter Twenty-One

Amos Craven looked down at his son, who lay in bed, one leg propped up to alleviate the pain. Amos stood there and frowned until his son opened his eyes. First, fright filled those eyes, then anger, and finally defiance.

"Well, my boy, you're in a pretty pickle." Amos glanced at his son's lower extremities. "You'll be using a cane for the rest of your short days."

"Cane? Short days?"

"Yes, you fool. Here you're not yet twenty and, as an invalid, you'll always be a drain on your physical resources and my financial ones." Amos sighed. "Though I always thought you'd break an ankle leaping from some woman's bedroom window, not be run down by a carriage in some alleyway. The police are still looking for the carriage."

Sidney lifted up on his elbows. As he did, pain raced up his leg and tears formed in the corners of his eyes. "I was set up by a band of ruffians, I'll have you know."

"Yes, yes," said his father, nodding, "I'm sure that's

the way you'll always tell the tale."

"Father—"

"What humbug! You were up to no good, of that I'm sure. You're not the only youngest son who believes he must become the premier game-cocker, horse-racer, card-player, and most mischievous fellow who ever lived in the city of Charleston."

Sidney's eyes still contained tears, but he would not wipe them away. Not in the presence of his father. His older brother stood to inherit the plantations, the slaves, and the arrogance that went along with them. He would be left with nothing. Nothing but a burning anger to crush anyone who rose up against him. Of course, that was going to be a bit difficult without sufficient assets, and with a broken ankle.

"Look, Sid," said his father, his voice softening, "it's time you put these childish games behind you, time you find a wife and start a family. You have a sister and brother who've married well, and it's time for something to be arranged. If you want to put your best efforts into that, then I'll do anything I can to assist you."

Now the dam broke and the tears ran. Wiping the tears away, Sidney gestured at his ankle. "And who would have me, now that I have this . . . deformity?"

Amos saw those tears and pitied the boy. Would the boy have turned out any differently if he'd been first-born? Or was a person's character set at conception? Or was character learned from a mother? Difficult to blame the mother in this case.

Sometimes Amos wished he had someone to discuss children with, but each of his children, the married son and daughter, and Sidney, all had been borne by different mothers, and all of the women had died from some malady or disease. If his own luck ran so sourly, what chance did this reckless son of his have?

But he'd try. After all, you should do as much as you could for a . . . cripple.

There! He'd said it, rather thought it, as many others would. If Sid had learned something from his latest bout of foolishness, perhaps some good might come of this yet.

"Father?"

"Yes?"

"I've always fancied Alexis Belle. If I'm to marry, could you put in a word for me with her father? I understand the twins have returned to Charleston."

Amos considered this. That might work. It was common knowledge that, because of their factor, that Jew, the Belles had lost Cooper Hill, and what was left of their assets Jean Louis Belle quietly drank away at their club.

If the twins had returned to Charleston, what would Claude be doing with his free time? Scheming to make sure his daughters married well so that he and his invalid wife could spend the autumn of their lives in relative comfort. The Craven fortune could provide such an autumn.

"Alexis Belle. You shall have her." Amos reached down and patted his son's shoulder. "Consider it a deal already done."

So, several weeks later, when the Belle brothers returned from their annual visit to Savannah, Amos picked up a drink at the bar and joined Claude and Jean Louis in the comfortable chairs in front of the stone fireplace. Only moments earlier Claude Belle had stood at that same bar and had listened to reasons why South Carolina should secede from the Union.

If the abolitionists thought they could violate the Constitution, and their damnable majority was gaining the upper hand in Congress, they had another think coming. Change "the law of the land" to favor a bunch of Northern shopkeepers and South Carolina had every right to change its status within the Union.

"Jean Louis," said Claude, taking a seat before the fire, "there's something I want to speak to you about."

His brother continued to stare into the fire. "More bad news, I would imagine."

"Not at all. Margaret has some concerns."

"You handle them. After all, you're her husband."

"Margaret is concerned about your drinking."

Jean Louis pulled his attention away from the flames. "What of it? She remains in the south parlor all the time."

"And the fact you now have two young women living with you, that also worries Margaret."

Jean Louis looked hard at his brother. Had Jennie said something? He'd deny everything.

"Jean Louis, you knew this day was coming."

His brother returned to staring into the fire.

"What shall I tell Margaret?" asked Claude.

"Tell her whatever you wish."

"And then there's your obvious dissatisfaction with our annual visit to Savannah."

"I don't like that man." The comment was followed by a quick swig from his glass. "As I've told you in the past, the world of trade is full of liars."

"Percival is our brother-in-law."

"And a damn annoying one to boot."

"Why? Because he's done well?"

"He's a damn merchant, Claude."

"The better to care for our sister and her children, wouldn't you agree? I counted six last time we were there. At least he didn't move away like Pierre."

Pierre was Pierre, Junior, who had taken his portion of the Belle inheritance and purchased land in Louisiana. It'd been a long time since they'd seen their older brother, and through the grapevine, they'd learned Pierre's estate now straddled the border of Louisiana and Texas. A small mercy that he hadn't returned to Charleston to lord it over them.

Amos Craven walked over, drink in his hand and a servant in tow. "May I buy you two gentlemen a round?"

Jean Louis looked at his brother from under hooded eyes and smiled.

"Thank you, Amos," said Claude, raising his glass, "but I just refilled my glass. Talking at the bar can make one dry."

Amos glanced at those arguing at the bar. "Did they ever settle anything?"

Jean Louis snorted. "That'll be the day."

"Jean Louis," asked Amos, "Claude's glass may be full but what about you?"

"Thank you, Amos," said Jean Louis, looking at his brother once again, "but I've been told that I've had more than my share." He gestured at the chair between them. "But do join us. Claude and his family have moved to town, and I might need some advice about handling in-laws."

Amos dismissed the servant and took a seat between

the two brothers and shifted around, getting comfortable. "I don't know what to say. Most of my in-laws want nothing to do with me. They think their wives will drop dead if I'm brought around."

To that the brothers said nothing. It was well known that many an eligible widow's family shunned Amos Craven because of the untimely death of his three wives. So, the three men sat there, sipped from their glasses, and stared into the fire.

Well, thought Amos, this is a lively bunch, and certainly not receptive to seeing the merits of their niece or daughter marrying his son. So, he proposed a toast to Claude's return to Charleston. The brothers toasted that and other negative remarks about life in the country.

"That, of course," said Jean Louis, "is why I've left the running of Cooper Hill to my brother. Now he's finally learned the error of his ways and will live out the remainder of his life in Charleston."

Amos Craven agreed it was much simpler to live in Charleston than struggle with the daily demands of a plantation. The brothers nodded and sipped from their glasses. After that, there was a short discussion of Jean Louis' sons and their experiences at their respective military academies.

"Louis prefers to be called "Lewis" these days." When Jean Louis saw Amos's puzzled look, he added, "It's a malady that strikes a young man soon after entering the service of his country. François is now 'Franklin.'"

Amos didn't understand, but he wasn't surprised. The Belles had always been a rather clannish group, who, at the drop of a hat, would remind you of their family's origins. And they had a tendency, after six generations in this country, to speak French at social gatherings, and then there were those tales about one of their daughters.

What was her name? The name wouldn't come. Oh, well, it mattered little. Alexis was the Belle his son had his heart set on, and asking around, Amos had been pleased to learn his son had set his sights on one of the most beautiful girls in Charleston.

Claude was attempting to explain the changing of Jean Louis' sons' names. ". . . something to do with our surname and the harassment that comes from being—"

"Highborn," finished Jean Louis. He, too, remembered the jests made at their expense while growing up and certainly didn't want to relive those days.

"Oh," said Amos Craven, still lost.

"Jean Louis' boys should've studied in Columbia. By now they'd be reading for the law. I don't know what they think they'll do as soldiers."

"Fight the impending war," said Jean Louis with some degree of gloom and staring into the fire again.

"Won't the abolitionists let us go?" asked Amos.

Claude gestured at those discussing politics at the bar. "Some say the Yankees will fight."

"But if we give them no cause . . ."

Amos looked from one man to the other. As most men running large plantations, Amos Craven was up at the crack of dawn and worked late into the night. He had no time to dally in politics, and in truth, the master of any plantation had no equal with which to discuss politics, even if he cared to. The only time available were the months Amos's family spent in Newport Beach

each summer, and there, abolitionists were thick as fleas.

"Why would they want to hold us?"

"Believe me, Amos," said Jean Louis, "I share your sentiments. Our mother always taught us that you shouldn't remain where you weren't wanted, and I'd think that would also apply to the Union." He took another swallow from his drink.

"Certainly, François—I mean, Franklin, would not fight on the side of the abolitionists."

"I'm no longer sure. Franklin has tumbled for a girl in Lowell, and you as well as I know their thinking on those matters."

Amos nodded. Falling in love was something his heart well knew, and he had the tombstones to prove it.

"I hope it doesn't come to war," said Claude. "I have daughters who wish to marry and start families."

And that was the opening Amos needed to propose the marriage of his son Sidney to Alexis Belle.

At the bakery, Burke Randolph was covered with flour and sweating like any slave as he shoveled rolls in and out of the oven. Susannah was out front, giggling like a schoolgirl and talking with her friends about her "white slave." Returning to the city of his birth was looking better and better. Well, certainly not Richmond. There he'd be at the mercy of his family.

The bell rang again and Susannah called out to him from the front of the store. "Burke, there's someone here I'd like you to meet."

Burke closed his eyes and said a prayer for patience. To have to sweat in this kitchen was bad enough, but to be on display for all of Susannah's friends to see . . .

He slammed the oven door shut, and from the backroom, Susannah's father stuck his head around the corner and frowned. Almost fell out of his chair, the old man did, craning his head around from where he kept the books, and a bottle, in a beat-up desk.

Poor man had lost his wife to smallpox, and his only son had gone to sea. Both Susannah's brother and her fiancé had sailed around Cape Horn to make their fortune in the goldfields of California. Been gone over four years now and might never return. To Burke Randolph, Susannah's father had the look of a man wishing to find a fallback position. And that fallback position was looking more and more like Burke Randolph.

That'd be the day! Not only were he and the redhead not from the same class, but this baker's daughter was the bossiest woman alive.

"Burke?" asked Susannah from the door. "Did you hear me?"

"Yes," he said, staring at the hot oven door, the paddle still in his hand, "but I have rolls to tend to."

"They've all fallen. I heard the oven door slam shut."

"Well, you can't expect me to get my work done if I stop every few minutes."

Susannah stepped into the kitchen. "Stopping every few minutes? I doubt I've interrupted you more than twice today."

"And twice more than necessary."

"Nonsense. Women enjoy meeting their baker."

"Then offer my apologies or your customers won't have any baked goods."

"Burke," asked Susannah, walking over to the oven,

"have I given you cause to be angry with me?"

"*No!*"

Again the father's face appeared at the rear door while Susannah glanced toward the front of the store.

"Sorry, Mister Chase," said Burke, "but I'm not the sort to bake bread the rest of his life, and if you can't see that, then you're as dense as any tradesman."

Susannah's father said nothing, only returned to his paperwork, and probably his bottle. Susannah took Burke's arm and walked him toward the front of the store. This redhead didn't take "no" for an answer.

"I don't care to meet any more of your friends!"

"Burke, it's not my friend that's come to see you, but yours."

"What do you mean? I know no one in Charleston."

"But she's here," said Susannah with a smile. "The lady who sent me 'round to see that you were freed from jail."

It took a moment for the thought to connect with his overheated brain, and then Burke walked over and peered through a small opening in the wall.

On the other side of the counter stood the girl Burke had seen for the briefest of moments in the rear of the carriage. But a woman he'd never forgotten. Skin like porcelain, pale blue eyes, black hair under a bonnet, and a figure barely restrained by her bodice.

Chapter Twenty-Two

On the day her carriage had been attacked, Jennie returned to the town house where Homer and Ella Mae practically had to carry her inside. Thankfully, no one was there but Homer, Ella Mae, and Alexis.

Jennie was hysterical. She had no idea why those young men had attacked her, but she recognized them: the ones she'd discouraged in coming around to see Alexis.

Her sister didn't believe a word. "Jennie, why would those boys be interested in you?"

"I . . . I don't think they were interested . . . ." Jennie pulled the covers up to her neck and looked around. She trembled. Alexis sat on the side of their bed, Homer stood at the foot, and on the other side, Ella Mae.

"Then why would they play a trick on you, instead of me?" Alexis shifted closer to her sister. "And tell me about this young man, the one you say came to your rescue."

"He . . . he threw them out . . . of the carriage."

Homer looked away, embarrassed.

Jennie saw this. "Homer—Homer . . . what is it?"

"I was just worried about you, Miss Jennie. Now, if you don't mind, I'll just be putting the carriage and the horse away."

Jennie nodded rapidly as he left.

"Tell me what he looked like," said Alexis, smiling, "your knight in shining armor. Was he tall, dark, and handsome?"

"I don't think he was a Negro," said Ella Mae from where she stood on the other side of the bed.

Alexis looked at the woman as if she were crazy.

"Now shush with your questions, Miss Alexis. Can't you see your sister's upset?"

"Well," said Alexis, tossing her head as she slid off the bed. "I just wanted to know."

"I'm sure you'll find out all about it in the morning."

Once Alexis left, Ella Mae held out the mug.

After a sip, Jennie made a face. "This is brandy."

"And I'm going to sit right here until you finish the whole mug."

The following day Alexis commandeered the carriage to take her shopping. Her trip, Alexis said, was to find a gift for poor Jennie, who remained in bed and needed to be perked up. Her sister was showing tendencies of becoming like their mother, and they certainly didn't need another invalid in the house.

Neither Homer nor Ella Mae believed a word, but this was not unusual. Very few people believed anything Alexis Belle said, and for good cause. Alexis's reasoning could be rather complex and convoluted.

On the plus side, Alexis was free of her daily prayers and studies, all of which her sister supervised. Just because her sister was a few minutes older, she thought she was the boss—a rather coarse word, she'd admit—but Jennie acted like she was the boss of the whole world! Alexis couldn't wait until her parents returned from Savannah and set her sister straight.

Still, it was nice to have this holiday. With her parents away and her sister bedridden, she'd investigate this young gentleman herself. Alexis immediately sent word to two of the biggest gossipmongers in the city that they should call on her sister, and when the girls arrived, Alexis only permitted them to stick their heads in the door of Jennie's bedroom, and then they were shooed out "because Jennie needs her rest." In the drawing room Alexis was able to catch up with the latest goings-on, and slyly inquire about any new men in town.

The girls *had* heard. Burke Randolph was working in a bakery!

Then how could this man be of any consequence, say, as a member of the Randolph family of Virginia?

Alexis was also motivated by the lowering of her own family's status upon their return to the city. Anyone who was anybody owned a plantation, maybe more than one, and Alexis knew she'd remain at the mercy of Virginia Hampton unless she reestablished her own rightful position in Charleston society.

Virginia Hampton, a member of a family that had more money than God, reigned supreme over the world of Charleston debutants. Not to mention it intrigued Alexis that the young man who'd saved her sister had taken on four others, and for his trouble, had been clapped in jail. The whole idea of a knight-errant was just too much to pass up.

Still, there was a more important reason to inquire about young Randolph. The only thing more valuable than gold or silver in Charleston was secrets. Alexis knew her own family secrets were being used to keep her from her rightful position in Charleston society, and she would not stand for it! It was imperative that she know everything about everyone, and the sooner, the better.

Because there was something wrong with one of Homer's arms—Alexis wasn't sure what, and she certainly wasn't going to ask; servants were always coming up with one reason after another for not doing their chores—it was some time before the Belle family carriage made its way up King Street. Whenever it passed an alleyway, Alexis peered left and right to see if any young men were about to accost her, and, of course, if a knight-errant was waiting in the wings. Alexis became so nervous that by the time Homer stopped in front of the bakery and opened the carriage door she jumped in fright.

"You all right, Miss Alexis?"

"Er—yes. Fine. Just fine." She took Homer's hand— his good one—and stepped down into the street, looking left and right.

Immediately the aroma overwhelmed her. It smelled like Christmas, and since Christmas was celebrated for five days at Cooper Hill, no one could forget those mouth-watering treats. Inside, the smells so overwhelmed her that Alexis didn't noticed Homer had followed her inside. Not completely unusual, but most servants usually waited outside until asked to perform some task.

A bell rang over Alexis's head as she came through the door, and a redhead smiled from the far side of the counter. Behind her, on shelves mounted into the wall, were all sorts of breads, rolls, and confectionary treats.

"Ah, Miss Belle. I'll be right with you."

Two young women, certainly not of her class, glanced at Alexis as she tapped her foot impatiently. With a laugh from the redhead, the two women left, and the baker's daughter continued to smile as she said, "I imagine you're here to meet your young gentleman."

"I don't think he's my young gentleman," said Alexis rather stiffly.

"I'm sorry, Miss Belle. I didn't mean to infer any sort of intimacy." The redhead turned toward the rear of the shop and called out, "Burke, would you please come out here?"

From the rear came the sound of an oven door being slammed.

The redhead flashed a nervous smile, excused herself, and disappeared into the rear of the shop.

That's when Alexis noticed Homer near the door. "I'll call if I need you."

"Well, Miss Alexis, since your sister isn't here—"

"I said I'd call."

The elderly man nodded and left the store with the bell ringing over his head.

The baker's daughter escorted a flour-covered man out of the kitchen. The man even wore an apron. "Miss Belle, this is Burke Randolph, the man you asked me to have released from jail."

My Lord! Not only was the man nasty but a jailbird. None of this was making sense. First Jennie had lied about the attack. It was simply impossible to believe those boys would've had an interest in her, and now this man, wearing an apron, no less, was supposed to be her sister's knight in shining armor? No way this man could be a Randolph from Virginia.

"Miss Belle," said Burke, giving her a short bow, "proud to make your acquaintance."

What did her sister see in this man? Oh well, if you cleaned him up, perhaps he'd be fine enough for this baker's daughter. "Mister Randolph, I do believe you have me at a disadvantage."

"Oh, yes. Sorry, Miss Belle. I'm Burke Randolph of Virginia. Perhaps you've heard of my family."

Oh, yes. One Randolph had signed the Declaration of Independence; another had attended the Constitutional Convention; several had died in wars. Many were lawyers, some even doctors, though being a doctor wasn't something to brag about.

"Of course I've heard of the Randolphs, though if this is true, why you're working in a bakery is beyond me."

Susannah and Burke glanced at each other, and although Susannah wanted to hear more, she tactfully disappeared into the rear of the building.

"Don't go far, Miss Chase." Alexis had no intention of being left alone in a room with any man, even with a counter between them.

"I'll be right here watching the oven."

"Miss Belle," said the so-called Randolph, "I doubt you're familiar with the terms of my release."

"Why should I be?"

"Still," he said with a smile, "I want to thank you for what you did."

"It was only right. You did prevent my sister, I mean me from being . . . ." Violated was much too strong a term. ". . . being approached by those young men." Alexis's nose rose. "Rather disgusting creatures, I would imagine."

"Not exactly," said Randolph. "They appeared to be more of your crowd."

"My crowd. I certainly don't think so."

Randolph looked through the window. "Still, your Negro acquitted himself quite well. Is he all right?"

Alexis saw Homer peering through the window. "Well, that is his responsibility." Growing bored with this whole affair, she asked, "And how long will you be in Charleston, Mister Randolph?"

"I don't know," said Burke with another easy smile. "I assume that has to do with the congeniality of the young ladies of Charleston."

Alexis drew herself up. "Sir, you are being much too familiar."

"I'm sorry. I didn't mean to offend. What I'd like to make clear is that I don't think any two women could've been more gracious than you and Miss Chase have—"

"I don't think it's appropriate for you to include Miss Chase and myself together."

"Er—well then," said Randolph, his brow furroughing, "be that as it may, I'd like to thank you for the effort you made on my part. You were certainly much more gracious to a newcomer, under the circumstances, than one would expect, especially one who has fallen on hard times—"

"Mister Randolph, are you saying you are without resources?"

"I guess you could say that." Randolph flashed that ingratiating smile again. "I've been forbidden to gamble while in Charleston."

Alexis had heard quite enough. A gambler! What a perfect choice for her sister, a woman without resources herself!

"If there's anything else I can do for you, Miss Belle, don't hesitate to ask."

"I doubt that will be necessary, and now, Mister Randolph, I have other appointments."

"Er—yes, and thank you again for stopping by."

The bell rang as Homer opened the door, and the Negro flashed a knowing smile at the man behind the counter.

"Well," asked Susannah, reappearing at the counter again, "did the girl of your dreams turn out to be everything you expected?"

"You know," said Burke as he watched Homer assist Alexis into the carriage, "I'm not sure I like that woman."

Susannah watched the old Negro climb into the driver's box. "What's there not to like? She's one of the most beautiful ladies in Charleston, and her family has money."

Burke smiled as he took the hand of the baker's daughter. "Then I'll have to meet more young ladies before making up my mind."

Susannah pulled her hand away. "I don't see how you can do better. Everyone's a step down after that woman and her twin."

Burke glanced at the window as the carriage pulled

away. "You mean there's another just like her?"

"Like I said, her twin."

"And that was Jennie Belle?"

"Yes," said Susannah. "Rather nice for a lady, if I have to say so myself."

Burke shook his head. "Sorry to contradict you, but the woman who just left here wasn't all that nice."

"Well," said Susannah, smiling and taking his arm as she escorted him back into the kitchen, "you know how stiff these society people can be, Mister Burke Randolph of Richmond, Virginia."

Rachel

Chapter Twenty-Three

When Franklin Belle left West Point after graduation, he had no idea where he should go or what he should do. No one from his family had attended his graduation; no one believed he should become a civil engineer; actually, they couldn't understand what he'd been up to the last five years. When he'd returned home after his second year, the normal leave for any cadet, every discussion with his brother, his uncle, and especially his father, had ended in a shouting match over whether he would side with the abolitionists against his own people, if it came to that. So Franklin sat in a bar in New York with orders stationing him at a fort in the mouth of the Savannah River. Staring back at him in the mirror behind the bar was an adult version of himself, alone again.

Hell, he thought, tossing down another drink, he could always head south. What he needed to do was make up his mind about this woman who, for the life of him, he couldn't get out of his head.

But how to do that?

With several drinks to fortify him, and the encouragement of his fellow patrons, a group of them stumbled down the street to the train station. On their way a policeman stopped them but allowed them to proceed when he realized they were just a bunch of harmless drunks supporting a reluctant suitor. The policeman could never have been so wrong.

Going to see a woman without an invitation was a rather bold move, whether you lived north or south of the Mason-Dixon Line. But after being locked away in one of those worlds so often noted for unrequited love, such as military academies, Franklin drew false courage from the men complimenting him on his shiny, new gold bars and boarded a train for Boston.

It didn't stop there. The first gentleman who engaged Franklin in conversation was a salesman for a Lowell textile mill, and the salesman wanted to know, if push came to shove, if the Southern states would leave the Union. The salesman had good reason to be concerned. Textile mills employing men such as this drove the economy of Massachusetts, not to mention the city of New York owed much of its success to the cotton fields of the South. Lloyds of London actually came into existence and prospered because of the slave trade. This salesman, a minor cog in a system producing enough cloth to circle the world more than twice, became Franklin's boon companion, and in the warmth of this friendship, Franklin continued north.

It was up to reasonable men, said this salesman, to do what they could to preserve the Union, and, of course, their way of life. Others traveling in the same compartment seconded what the salesman from Lowell said. The abolitionists were the problem, and it was the responsibility of clear-thinking men on both sides of the Mason-Dixon Line to preserve the Union, and their own livelihoods.

Unfortunately for these men, and their livelihoods, Massachusetts senator Charles Sumner had taken to the floor of the Senate again to denounce "The Crime Against Kansas." In this speech Sumner attacked the slave owners for proposing that the territories of Kansas and Nebraska decide on their own whether to enter the Union as a slave state or not. Sumner held the packed Senate gallery in rapt attention as he heaped scorn on one particular lawmaker, Andrew Pickens Butler of South Carolina. He accused Butler of choosing a mistress who, "though ugly to others, is lovely to him . . . I mean the harlot slavery."

The following day Preston Brooks, a congressional representative from South Carolina, and a cousin of Andrew Butler, snuck up on Sumner in the empty Senate chamber and began to club Sumner over the head with a walking stick. When Sumner tried to escape, Brooks followed him into the aisle, and when Sumner went to his knees, Brooks continued to beat him until his cane broke. The congressman was fined three hundred dollars, and Brooks justified the beating by claiming he was repaying an insult to his cousin.

Overnight the fragments became "sacred relics" and were bid on by Brooks's constituents. A group of South Carolinians even sent Brooks a new cane inscribed: "Hit him again!" and newspapers in the South editorialized in favor of someone finally standing up to the abolitionists. The traveling salesmen and his fellow companions, who had toasted Franklin as a brother in arms on his trip north, suddenly underwent a sea change in attitude, and when Franklin passed through New York on his way to Charleston with his new bride, both bride and groom were subject to that change.

Joshua and James returned home with Franklin in tow. They'd found Nicholas Eaton, and quickly learned that the father supported the son. As for whether Joshua Mullins would continue in the employment of the Eaton family, that would be decided sometime in the future.

Joshua returned home to prepare the family for the worst, only to find his wife had filled their house with delicious foods, a dining room adorned with flowers, and had the minister and his wife sipping tea in the parlor. This time it was Franklin who almost fainted. Staggering into the parlor and finding a seat among the chairs dragged in for the occasion, he wished he could take back the whole day.

He'd been a fool to come to Boston. Not only had he ruined Rachel's life but his own. He had no way to properly support a wife, and as for Rachel living in Charleston, that was too crazy an idea to consider; except the servant girl was upstairs packing Rachel's trousseau. Wasn't there anything he could do to stop this madness?

The preacher broke into his thoughts to ask whether Franklin was a Protestant or not. Franklin blinked, looked at the man in the severe black clothing, and said that he was. That said, the minister escorted the groom into the dining room where the marriage license was signed, witnessed by James, and where Franklin remained seated until his bride-to-be came downstairs.

Scrambling to his feet, Franklin felt the room move. But his new brother-in-law was there with a glass of wine. Two glasses later, Franklin told James he was ready. Evidently Rachel was not. She stood in the hallway, crying, and wearing a plain white dress with no hoop or embellishments. Once she finally calmed down, the preacher's wife, a lover of great opera, began playing a lively piece called *The Bridal Chorus,* which would later come to be known as *The Wedding March,* or "Here Comes the Bride."

The minister smiled. He'd seen all this before: A girl in the family way, and her family trying to make things right before sending their daughter away; but instead of the newlyweds heading to Ohio, these newlyweds would be traveling south. So the ceremony was performed, the meal picked over by the unhappy guests, and the couple driven to the station, while the minister and his wife were sent home with several plates for their new icebox.

Rachel never stopped crying, even on the train.

Oh God, thought Franklin. I've been lonely all my life, never able to fit in, and I gave up a life of solitude for this? Finally, he'd had enough and bolted from the compartment.

"Franklin, don't desert me!" shouted Rachel.

Gripping the sides of the corridor as the train sped down the track, he threw over his shoulder. "I'll be right back. I just need a drink."

Oh, God, thought Rachel. Of course the man would drink. No matter what Southerners said, the evil that was slavery ate at their very souls; hence the drinking.

In a car where beverages were served, Franklin quickly downed his first drink. Around him the car buzzed with conversation and it took some time for Franklin to understand what people were saying. The conversation was about the sea change that'd occurred while he was in Boston.

"Senator Sumner clubbed down in the sanctity of the American Senate!"

"Rotten scoundrel, Brooks. Should be hung from the nearest lamppost!"

"That won't happen," offered another man. "Our nation's capital is in the South, and Washington's filled with secessionists."

It wasn't long before his fellow travelers gathered around Franklin. They clapped him on the back and bought one round after another for the lieutenant. Now, if he could just keep his mouth shut. Franklin soon learned that was the least of his worries.

"It won't be long before you'll teach those secession-ists some manners," said one of the passengers, bending down and breathing in Franklin's face.

"Yes," said another. "Southerners believe they have the market cornered on manners, but this assault on Senator Sumner reveals their black hearts."

"Wish I was going with you, son," said another man, slapping Franklin on the back.

Franklin wasn't sure what the man meant and blurted out: "You want to go to Charleston?"

"You've been posted to the heart of the rebellion?" asked the man, regarding the young officer with even more awe.

"Hear, hear," said those gathered around.

"Yes, yes," shouted others. "On to Charleston."

A drunk stood in his seat and shouted that they should commandeer the train and head south, right into the heart of secessionist territory.

"Right on!"

"Hear, hear!" shouted another.

"On to Charleston!" was the cry filling the club car, and that's when the Negro porter put away the liquor.

Then came cries to liberate, not only Charleston, but also the wine and beer. Very quickly, the porter was shoved from the car, and once the porter was gone, a celebration broke out and the liberated liquor passed around. Franklin was pushed forward as the drunks seized control of one passenger car after another.

To seize control of the engine took someone agile enough to climb over the coal car even when inebriated. Several tried and fell off, and in the passenger car behind them, Franklin Belle lay, knocked to the floor between seats as the mob had surged forward. Telegrams flew down the line when the train passed through its regular stops and left passengers to stand and curse as the train raced through each station.

Thinking they had a runaway on their hands, when the train slowed taking a curve, the railroad had two engineers hoisted aboard and into the hands of the mob. One engineer fought free and leaped from the train, breaking his arm. He returned to the previous stop and told authorities that secessionists had seized control and were determined to take the train to Charleston.

More telegrams called for policemen on horseback, and if they weren't available, what about a troop of cavalry. As the train passed through the countryside approaching New York, a troop of cavalry rode alongside, swarmed onboard, and laid out every man who raised a hand against them, and some who did not.

Finding one of their own lying unconscious between the seats, the soldiers carried Franklin off the train, placed him on a wagon, and had him taken to the army hospital with other members of their troop who'd gone down at the hands of the mob. Upon arriving in New York City, Rachel Belle, née Mullins, found herself all alone and totally bewildered as to what had happened to her new husband.

Chapter Twenty-Four

The management of the railroad learned they had not only a bunch of unruly drunks on their hands, but a wife who'd lost her husband. Rachel was of little help. She'd been reduced to tears again, and any moment just might just swoon.

Alone in a train station in New York? Alone in New York City without an escort? It was too impossible to conceive.

A nurse was summoned to get the full story from her, and the nurse did, but only after being sequestered with the distraught bride for several hours in the office of the terminal manager. Leaving Rachel with her handkerchief and her tears, the nurse made her report to several members of the terminal staff and railroad management, all huddled around a male secretary's desk.

"Her husband must've been trying to stop the mob," offered one, after hearing from the nurse.

"Yes," said another. "There was only him against all the others."

"He shouldn't have left his wife alone."

"What would you've done?" asked another. "He's a soldier. It was his duty."

"Yes," said another man, "the train was out of control and he made a valiant effort to stop it before being struck down."

"Yes, yes," said the other man. "That must be it."

"He should be given a reward for his efforts."

"Let's not get ahead of ourselves," said the manager of the railroad, speaking for the first time. He looked at those huddled around the secretary's desk, especially the terminal manger. "But where in the world could the husband be?"

When the men looked at the nurse, she said, "You're asking me?"

"The wife did not know?" asked the manager of the terminal.

"Not in her condition," said the nurse, glancing at the office of the terminal manager. From inside came more sobs.

"Yes, yes, we understand," said the manager of the rail line. "Have the train searched for the husband," he ordered.

"It's already been searched," reported one of his subordinates. "Twice, and then sent along its way."

"Several hours late," offered another.

"The wife said her husband was in uniform," said the nurse. "Is there anyone in uniform being held by the authorities?"

The subordinate glanced at a hastily composed list and shook his head. "All civilians."

"Then where can he be?"

"He could've been thrown off like our employees," suggested the local manager of the rail line.

"It's possible," said another.

The nurse had a suggestion. "He's in uniform, right?"

"We know how he's dressed," said the terminal manager, impatiently.

"That's not what I meant," said the nurse, but no one was listening to her.

"We should put out an alert," said the man with the list.

"That's a lot of track to cover," said another, scratching his chin. He looked out the window and saw the sun going down. "We're certainly not going to find him tonight."

"Gentlemen," asked the nurse, "were any soldiers injured in the fracas?"

The men around the desk did not know.

"If so, perhaps we should check with the military hospitals."

As Franklin Belle came to his senses, his wife of less than one day was being escorted to the most upstanding hotel in the city. The railroad company spared no expense, and to make sure there was no question as to the bride's honor, they had the nurse accompany her. Sometimes traveling salesmen frequented the most upstanding hotels, and as everyone knew, the morals of traveling salesmen were not much better than any sailor home from the sea.

Rachel ended up sprawled across another bed, and once again, burst into tears as she remembered conversations she'd had with her mother while lying across her own bed. Except she wasn't in her own bed, and if memory served, Mary, her younger sister, had already claimed her room upon learning her older sister was being turned out.

Exhausted and distraught, Rachel cried herself to sleep.

Franklin woke to find himself in a military hospital, and he had no idea why he was there. His uniform hung on a wall rack next to his bed, and it took three days for his memory to return. During that time no one at the army post was in the mood to give out any information to civilians, and certainly not information about officers. Look how they ran the railroad.

On the first day of her husband's amnesia, Rachel was barely able to feed herself, and she could hardly put two words together. The hysterics really began in earnest when the nurse asked if there was someone the railroad should contact.

Perhaps her family?

The second day, asked if she'd like to return home, Rachel burst into tears and started on another crying jag. The nurse took a couple of minutes of this and summoned the hotel doctor.

The doctor had seen hysterical women before, wives abandoned in this very same hotel. It took only a tea-spoon of laudanum to knock out the woman. That's what the hotel wanted: either the woman asleep or gone, but she would be silent. There were other guests to consider.

The third day the nurse got some breakfast down

her, then commented: "I doubt your husband will know where to find you if you don't return home."

Rachel put down her coffee and looked the nurse in the eye. "My home is in Charleston now."

"Very well," said the nurse, and by noon the same day, the railroad had Rachel and her bags on the next packet sailing south.

Franklin arrived the following day, after sneaking off base. He'd been told to remain in the hospital until the army could check out his story. As to the whereabouts of his wife, that would take considerably more time to sort out.

Outside the hospital and off the grounds, Franklin found a civilian population eager to help. All he had to do was make sure no one heard his accent, and people would move heaven and earth for him. After all, the nation could be split asunder any day and the Republic would need all its young officers.

In New York City he immediately went to the station and demanded to know what had happened to his wife.

"Sir," asked the manager of the terminal, rising up behind his desk, "where have you been?"

Franklin explained.

The manager looked to his secretary, a thin man watching from the doorway. "Arthur, would you bring the scheduled sailings into my office?"

The secretary did, and they learned a ship sailed for Charleston that very afternoon, one of the old clipper ships trying to remain in business by offering speed in this day of steamships that could sail in any weather.

Onboard the ship bearing Rachel south stood an Irish dandy watching the coast of Carolina appear off the starboard side.

"I must say, Mrs. Belle, but you have quite the nerve to enter Charleston harbor alone."

Rachel finally had to have some air, and she'd acquired this Irishman as she strolled around deck. Rachel hated the drab little cabin she was assigned to, though it was actually first-class, the railroad and the shipping company sometimes exchanging favors. But this man, Murphy, wouldn't stop pursuing her as she strolled around deck, her parasol protecting her from the noonday sun. It was going to be warm in Charleston.

"My family lives in Charleston now."

"Well," said the dandy with a wide smile, "with that accent of yours, you certainly don't sound like it."

"My husband graduated from West Point. We will await his assignment in Charleston."

"And why's he not traveling with you, if I might be so bold to ask?"

Rachel was prepared for that. "He went ahead of me."

"Of course he did," said Murphy with a laugh. "To prepare his family for that accent."

Rachel looked at him coldly. "You make it sound as if I won't be welcomed in South Carolina."

"Oh, I don't think there'll be any problem, as long as you keep your mouth shut." When Rachel didn't laugh or even smile, Murphy bowed and said, "If your husband isn't at the dock to escort you home, I'll offer my services."

"Thank you, sir, but that won't be necessary."

She put her dilemma before the captain at dinner

that night. Unfortunately, the Irishman sat across the table from her.

"If my family isn't ashore when we dock, might I stay aboard until they contact me?"

The captain had little interest in remaining in Charleston harbor any longer than necessary. He had more than one black able-bodied seaman aboard. Still, he said, "Of course, Madam. You're a guest of the railroad and shall be offered every courtesy. I, myself, will send someone ashore to find your family."

"And," said the dandy, smiling at Rachel from across the table, "if your husband isn't there, I shall be your escort." A glance at the captain and the smile disappeared from Murphy's face. "To make sure the lady's properly taken care of." The Irishman leaned forward on the table. "Didn't you say the Belle family owned a plantation, Cooper Hill?"

"That is correct."

"Well, that should be easy enough to find. As long as we don't have to take this boat up the Cooper River."

"Ship," corrected the captain.

"This . . . ship can go inland?" Rachel had heard of boats that could do so, even seen them on the Charles River the few times she'd been in Boston.

"No, Mrs. Belle. What Mister Murphy means is that once he's located a boat to take *you* up river, then and only then will we make the transfer."

At breakfast the following morning, Rachel was told the dandy had gone ashore at first light. A little over an hour later, Murphy returned with news that he'd reserved passage for Rachel on a boat going up the Cooper River.

"Its pilot says the trip should be no more than a couple of hours. He's to move some furniture from the plantation to the town house."

"Well," said the captain, "it appears this is where you leave us, Mrs. Belle."

Rachel, who was becoming emboldened because of the amount of time she'd had to consider her plight, asked, "Why not take the train inland? Or a stage-coach?"

Having never visited South Carolina, the Irishman said, "There are few railroads in South Carolina, and the ones available are not suitable for a lady."

"And the stagecoach?"

"The boat is the preferred method of travel in this part of the state," explained the captain. "There's a canal farther upstream."

"Yes," said Murphy with a nod. "I was told the road to Cooper Hill is quite roundabout. In South Carolina everyone travels by boat, either up the Ashley or the Cooper."

So Rachel and her luggage were transferred to the boat, and once he saw her off, the captain issued instructions for his first mate to go ashore and send a telegram to the rail line, assuring the manager of the New York terminal that Mrs. Belle had, indeed, arrived in Charleston and been reunited with her husband.

A telegram had also arrived the previous day and had been delivered to the town house on High Battery. Lewis Belle, home from his first tour of duty, read the telegram more than once, could make no sense of it, and threw it in the trash.

There was no Mrs. Belle in this house, and if he had his way, there'd be none for a long time to come. That evening Lewis went on the prowl for someone who'd be impressed by his exploits with the South Carolina Bloodhounds in "Bleeding" Kansas.

Chapter Twenty-Five

"That's Cooper Hill," said the pilot from amidships where he steered his boat. Their new captain was a nasty-looking man with a broken nose and he wore a straw hat and dirty white clothes. His engine huffed and puffed as it made its way upriver.

Rachel sat forward with the dandy and under her parasol. It was good to finally be home! If this could ever be called home.

A large white mansion sat on a slight hill overlooking the river, and working in water up to their knees behind dikes were Negroes sloshing around and swinging tools Rachel didn't recognize. Actually Rachel hadn't recognized anything since leaving Charleston, the similarity between Boston and Charleston ending at the harbor. Certainly New Englanders had waterways to take you inland, but no river in New England was draped with moss that hung from low-lying trees spreading their branches hither and yon. She was told it was called Spanish moss.

Rachel couldn't help but smile as she considered what she'd been told about these Southern waterways. Supposedly, the Cooper and the Ashley, both named for the same English nobleman, formed the Atlantic Ocean where they emptied into Charleston harbor.

What conceit possessed Charlestonians! Everyone knew New England was home to the best schools in the Republic, or why did so many Southerners attend Harvard and Yale?

"Magnificent," said the dandy, referring to the six columns across the porch of the plantation house. There were matching magnolias at each side of the house, two piazzas, an upper and lower one, and a carriage in the crushed shell turnaround.

The pilot navigated the boat toward the wharf where two Negroes made ready to receive the lines. Behind them, a small black boy raced away, running up the road sheltered by cedars. Then the boat was tying up, and the dandy was on the dock and offering his hand.

Finally! Solid land!

Lucky for her she'd not become seasick. From what Rachel had seen of seasickness, it wasn't anything a lady should have to endure.

"Miss Rachel Belle of Lowell, Massachusetts," announced the Irishman to the two Negroes.

The two slaves looked at each other as, down the path, raced the carriage with the little boy at the reins. He pulled the single-horse vehicle to a stop and leaped down to open the carriage door. The other two Negroes simply stared as Rachel climbed inside.

Before joining her, Murphy said to the Negroes, "Have Mrs. Belle's belongings brought up to the house."

Then he climbed in behind her, and the little black boy closed the door, scrambled into the driver's seat, and put a whip to the horse. The carriage jerked forward and raced up the driveway to the Big House.

On the porch stood a girl who appeared to be a few years younger than she, hoop dress, and hair netted into a chignon. The closer they came, Rachel realized the girl was quite a beauty: rich black hair, the whitest skin, and pale blue eyes.

As the dandy gave Rachel a hand down, the young woman walked to the edge of the stairs. "We've been expecting you for hours," she said rather impatiently and led them through the double doors and into the entrance hall of the plantation house.

*   *   *

While their daughter sailed for Charleston, Rachel's family attended church and tried to hold their heads up, an especially difficult task as their church was the same church where the Eatons owned a pew. The Mullins didn't own a pew, and might never, if it became common knowledge that their daughter had been forced to marry some Southerner who'd gotten her in the family way. Few people spoke to them, and as for the Mullins, they spent most of their time on their knees praying, and that included James, who was considered rather stiff-necked after completing his education at the military academy.

After the service the minister took each of the Mullins' hands and reassured them that God did work in mysterious ways. When Joshua turned away, Simon

Eaton's driver was at the church door to take his arm and gestured at the carriage in the street. Joshua felt his legs weaken, and for a moment, he throught he might have to put a hand on James's shoulder to stand.

"Mister Eaton would like for you to call this afternoon at four."

"On the Sabbath?"

"That is correct. I'll arrive at your residence fifteen minutes before four."

"Should I . . ." Joshua cleared his throat. "Should I bring my ledgers?"

The driver drew himself up. "Mister Eaton is as devout a Christian as any man, so I doubt this meeting is to discuss business. Leave the ledgers at home."

At the Sunday meal Emma tried to keep up everyone's spirits, but only the younger children could be fooled and were finally sent off to their rooms to prepare for the evening service. James looked around the table and saw the devastation he and his sister had wrought. Rachel was gone and he was to fight a duel that would end his military career before it even began, and that's if he survived the duel!

His mother chatted on about this and chatted on about that, but nothing she said could cheer up his brother and his wife. Peter was as able a fixer as any on the factory floor, but his wife was pregnant and they wanted a home of their own, not to continue living with her parents. Rachel and he had dashed all hopes for that. And since this was the Sabbath, there could be no card playing, no reading of novels, or working around the house, so everyone ended up in the parlor, passing the time by reading their personal Bibles and glancing at the grandfather clock. Quite a few pages had been turned in those Bibles when the knock finally came at the door.

Peter's wife broke down and began to sob, and at the door Emma kissed her husband while Peter shook his father's hand and James insisted on coming along.

The driver, however, was firm. "I'm sorry, but I wasn't told to bring anyone but your father." And he returned to the carriage in the street.

James put up a fuss, but his father clapped him on the shoulder and told him everything would work out, that God did work in mysterious ways.

The driver watched Joshua walked to the street and climb up with him to sit in the driver's box. "Sir," protested the driver, "you're to sit inside."

"Sorry, son," said Joshua with a smile, "but I wasn't raised to be all that grand and I'm not going to start now."

The driver shrugged and cracked his whip, and the carriage moved down a street where more than one neighbor stared as the carriage passed by.

Joshua simply looked straight ahead and held onto the one constant in his life: his books were all in order and he had excellent penmanship. The absolutely best set of books kept by any bookkeeper in New England, and Mr. Eaton had said as much on more than one occasion.

The thought did not comfort him.

At the Eatons' the carriage passed through an iron gate swung open by the driver, and then up a gravel driveway to a brick home flanked by deep lawns. When the carriage came to a stop, Joshua climbed down and stepped up on the porch as the front door swung open. A servant escorted him down an ornate hallway, through a parlor, and into a room with glass walls that held the sun most of the day. It would appear Simon Eaton knew not only how to stretch pennies but how to make the sunshine last all day.

The room was warm and cozy but chilled instantly when Joshua noticed Eatons' attorney sitting beside his boss. From this room, and through its glass walls, these two had watched his arrival.

Dressed in plain black, very much like the plain black suit Joshua wore, Simon Eaton was a plump man with tufts of white hair near his ears. The rest of his head was bald and pink, and though he looked like a fat angel, Eaton didn't smile when Joshua walked into the room.

Eaton introduced his lawyer, whose name was "Wingate," and both men gestured to a chair in the middle of the room. Joshua nodded and took a seat in what appeared to be the inquisition chair.

"I see you rode over in the driver's box," said his employer. "Are you trying to embarrass my family even further?"

"No, sir. That was not the intent."

Before they could get farther afield, the attorney said, "Mullins, I'm not sure if you're aware of the law, but it's illegal to fight duels in the state of Massachusetts."

"Yes, sir, I know that."

"And," said the attorney, referring to notes in a bound book in his lap, "cadets of the United States Military

Academy must forfeit their commission and can be brought up on charges if they participate in duels."

Joshua shifted around in his chair. "I did not know that, but it seems reasonable."

"What seems reasonable," injected his employer, "is that those dilettantes running West Point know the taxpayers aren't going to coddle the sons of rich men."

Joshua only nodded. His son, James, was no son of a rich man, but he wasn't here to dispute this minor point.

"We all can agree that a crime has been committed, can't we?" demanded Eaton, leaning forward.

"Sir?"

"You don't believe a crime was committed against my son?"

"I believe," said the attorney, jumping in again, "that Mullins is asking for clarity on that point."

Instead of clarity, Joshua got passion. Eaton almost came out of his chair. "Your son struck mine! And after what's happened to our great senator, Charles Sumner, I won't tolerate this sort of assault on anyone in my family."

The attorney put a hand on his client's arm. "Simon, all of us are in agreement that there should be some sort of restitution."

"Still," Joshua said, "I'm not sure I would call it a crime." Nor had Simon Eaton ever called Charles Sumner a great senator, but often referred to him in the most derogatory terms.

Eaton leaned forward, his pink face turning red. "A crime was committed against my son and there should be satisfaction." Eaton felt his attorney's hand on his arm again and sat back in his chair. "Still, we're not barbarians, such as those living in South Carolina."

"Yes, sir. What do you suggest?"

The attorney held up a telegram. "This is from the War Department, your son's first assignment. As I explained to Mister Eaton, with the assault on Senator Sumner, this is not the time to be running officers out of the army."

Joshua's face was impassive, when, in fact, he was shocked. There'd been a great deal of speculation by James and his mother as to where the boy would be stationed, but his employer already knew of James's posting. Being the Sabbath, it was blasphemous but quite efficient.

Wingate read from the telegram. Brevet Lieutenant James M. Mullins was to report to a military base in New England.

Well, thought Joshua, that would relieve his mother.

"Mullins," asked Eaton, "do you see our problem?"

Joshua did not and said so.

"If your son and my son want to settle this matter, they could very easily do so since they will be in close proximity. Nicholas has another year at Harvard. Do you understand now?"

Joshua did. Emma had sent their daughter away, but it was their son Eaton wanted sent away, and probably not anywhere above the Mason-Dixon Line.

"So," said the attorney, "what we're proposing is that Mister Eaton use his influence in Washington to have your son posted as far away from Boston as possible."

"And where would that be?"

"Our country desperately needs troops out west."

"How far west?"

"California."

Oh, God, thought Joshua. California was the other side of the world, not to mention the state was full of Indians and gold diggers, both of whom would cut your throat as soon as look at you.

Joshua cleared his throat to be able to ask, "And the resolution of the broken engagement?" No reason to wait for the other shoe to fall.

"Brevet Lieutenant Franklin M. Belle will be assigned to the territorial area of Kansas and Nebraska."

Joshua felt his shoulders slump. It was one thing to send his daughter south. In Charleston Rachel had a chance for some sort of a life. But Bleeding Kansas. Rachel's new husband might soon be dead.

And finally Joshua understood. His employer wanted, not only his pound of flesh, but his son to have a chance to court Rachel once again, when she returned from Charleston, wearing widow's weaves.

"Would you have any objections to these suggestions being made to the Secretary of War?" asked Wingate.

Joshua swallowed his fear. His wife had said they'd pay penance, but this was too much. Still, he agreed to the terms, and once he'd left the room, Simon Eaton turned to his attorney.

"I told you there'd be no objections. Mullins has been rock solid for my company the last twenty years."

The attorney nodded.

Still, there was one concern. "You saw to it that Nicholas sailed for Liverpool?"

"Yes, sir. I was there when the ship set sail."

"And the earliest my son can return to Boston?"

"Would be two weeks from today."

"The captain carries my letter?"

"Yes, sir, and your factor will distract him until it's time for Nicholas to return for his final term at Harvard."

Eaton let out a sigh and finally relaxed in his chair. "You're lucky you don't have children, Wingate. When you try to reason with them, or try to teach them something you've learned . . . . Nicholas has always been a difficult child. His mother and I raised him like we did the others, but he's flighty. Nicholas has been influenced by that liberal element at Harvard. Despite arguments by both his mother and me to the contrary, Nicholas was preparing to indulge Miss Mullins in her suffragist ways."

"You mean allowing women to vote?"

Eaton nodded.

"My goodness, sir. What's the country coming to?"

But Nicholas wasn't sailing for Liverpool. He was on a ship bound for Charleston.

When his father's attorney left him aboard the packet, Nicholas had wandered out on deck and back down the gangway. Nicholas had grown up in the textile business so it didn't take long for him to learn which ship was sailing for Charleston. Ships that carried his father's cloth left Boston every day, and chests filled with goods were occasionally moved from one ship to another for the quickest passage.

So it wasn't all that difficult for Nicholas to book passage to Charleston. As for his belongings, it was as simple as paying a couple of stevedores to move his chest from one ship to another. Onboard the southbound packet, he shared a cabin with a fellow Bostonian traveling to Charleston for the very last time.

"There's not enough money to tempt me to go south of the Mason-Dixon Line."

"And why's that?" For the first time Nicholas was having second thoughts about following the woman he loved into enemy territory. Still, someone must rescue her from a fate worse than death.

"The damn secessionists are up in arms," said his traveling companion, "and the faster I can liquidate my holdings, the better."

Nicholas chuckled. "Southerners are always upset over something."

"Sir, you are right on that account, and the beating of Senator Sumter was the last straw for me."

Nicholas knew of the beating and heaped more scorn on the Southerners and their cowardly ways.

His companion stared at him from his bunk on the other side of the cabin. "And feeling as you do, you still venture south."

"It's a personal matter," explained Nicholas.

"Well, sir, I'd think twice before I offered any of your opinions once you're in Charleston."

Again Nicholas chuckled. "Certainly there are men of good will still living in the South."

"Yes, sir, and you just might see one from your lofty perch as they ride you out of town on a rail."

Chapter Twenty-Six

By the late 1700s rice had proved to be such a reliable crop that planters in the Low Country began importing labor to remove the cypress and gum trees and to ditch and dike the land. Most Indians were already dead or dying from diseases contracted from the Europeans or they'd escaped into the upcountry and been absorbed into other tribes. For this reason the slaves who came to labor in the rice fields of South Carolina had to be captured by their fellow Africans and shipped overseas. Slave brokers, ever quick to improve the quality of their "product," trained future "recruits" in rice production similar to the conditions they'd find in the Carolinas, and these "recruits" brought along other skills, such as the ability to clean and husk rice.

With the development of tidal flooding, rice became so profitable that even merchants, physicians, and attorneys were leaving their professions, purchasing land and slaves, and becoming planters. The invention of the rice mill had the same impact on production as the cotton gin had on cotton, and over the years, the rice planters found common cause with the cotton planters, so that in 1832 both groups supported John C. Calhoun against the rising tariff. Still, no one threatened to secede when a tariff bill was later passed by Congress to protect American rice.

After the Nullification Crisis, the planters formed their own social and political organizations, and by 1840, had their slaves so well disciplined that they'd created an aristocracy confident enough to carve out a nation of its own, much like the Founding Fathers had done almost a hundred years before. Up north, profits from cotton and rice did not go unnoticed, and more than one rich Yankee purchased plantations in the Low Country, plantations very much like Cooper Hill.

Rachel and the dandy were led through the entrance hall with its descending and curving staircase, then to one side of the house where a dining room ran the length of the building.

"This is where we shall be served our midday meal," said the dark-haired beauty.

This place is huge, thought Rachel, looking in both directions. Nothing at all like where she'd grown up. At the far end of a long mahogany table, linen and silverware had been laid; overhead were a series of chandeliers; and many silver bowls with roses floating in water served as centerpieces. Rachel quickly lost count of the number of chairs. How many people did this room seat?

Across from the dining room was a study, and when they stuck their heads inside, they saw that the smaller room was connected to a drawing room, and on the other end, a parlor where a piano and her brother James might've held court.

But James and the rest of her family were in New England, so Rachel followed the attractive young woman throughout the house and tried to understand why the girl's voice wasn't the voice of welcome and homecoming but sounded more like something repeated for guests who just happened to drop by. Why, she didn't even know the young woman's name. So Murphy was left to say all the correct things, and Rachel simply smiled and kept her counsel. Truly, she was a stranger in a strange land.

Rachel had seen few Negroes in her lifetime, and now they surrounded her, outnumbered her, and she found their presence slightly intimidating, as when they entered the kitchen, an outbuilding where all the cooking was done. There, scores of servants dutifully stood by, heads bowed, except that these weren't servants as she'd come to know, but honest-to-God indentured servants who could never work off their obligation.

True, she'd seen slaves in Charleston when their small boat had come ashore, but all that had happened in the wink of an eye. Here Rachel found herself slowing to a stop and gawking. Some of the slaves had lighter skin, one or two had the pale blue eyes of the girl who led them through the house, but they were all slaves.

Murphy took Rachel by the arm and escorted her back into the house where the impatient girl continued their tour. Then it was upstairs to see the sleeping quarters, parlors, and where Rachel supposed the women of the house could escape the responsibilities of downstairs. Except there had to be little work for any white person with all these servants. Actually, several slaves followed them as they passed through the house, hurrying to open this door, closing that one behind them. You'd never have to lift a finger if you lived in this place.

And there was something else peculiar about this house. Lord, there were plenty of things she wasn't used to, and for this reason it took Rachel several minutes to realize each room was missing pieces of furniture that upset the room's balance. But it wasn't just the furniture but paintings that had been taken down, and nothing covered the rectangular or circular spots on walls on either the upper or lower levels.

Their guide dismissed the third floor with a wave of the hand and said "they could see the stores later." Then the three of them, and their entourage of slaves, returned downstairs to the smell of a midday meal being brought into the house by a long line of slaves.

And she was to spend the rest of her life here!

Rachel felt the walls closing in, the number of Negroes surrounding her, an elderly black man who had followed them everywhere . . .

She left everyone and hurried outside. Following her came the dandy and the plaintive call of the young woman.

"Where are you going? Dinner is about to be served."

Rachel continued to the end of the veranda, and as she did, the little boy slipped down from the driver's seat, flashed a big smile, and opened a door to the carriage. A row of rocking chairs dotted the veranda, and Rachel held onto one of them just to remain on her feet. Her legs felt weak, her stomach was doing flip-flops, and she tried to control her breathing as she looked over rice fields that seemed to go on forever.

"You all right, Mrs. Belle?" asked Murphy.

"Mrs. Belle?" asked the pale-eyed young woman, who had followed them to the end of the porch.

"This is Mrs. Rachel Belle of Lowell, Massachusetts."

Their host didn't appear to understand. "But my mother isn't here. She's in Savannah."

"No. I'm Mrs. Belle," said Rachel, turning around. Still, her new title didn't roll off her tongue that easily.

"I'm sorry, but I don't understand."

Rachel smiled. "Franklin's wife."

"My cousin's expected any day now," said the girl, brightly. "He's just graduated from West Point."

"Yes," said Rachel, continuing to smile. "That's where we met."

This appeared to be too much for the delicate girl. Her hands fluttered and her mouth worked but no words came out.

"You's Mister François wife?" asked the elderly man, the one referred to as Homer.

François? Who was that?

"What are you saying?" asked the blue-eyed beauty. "Are you saying you married my cousin François?"

"No," said Rachel, patiently. "I married Franklin Belle once he graduated from West Point."

"But that's impossible."

"Oh," said Rachel, a growing edge to her voice, "but I assure you that it's so. He and I were married less than a week ago. You must've received telegrams telling of my arrival."

The girl looked around, then beyond the boy at the foot of the carriage and toward the Negroes loading furniture on the boat. The girl didn't appear to find what she was searching for. "Then where is he? Where's my François?"

"Madam—" started the dandy.

Rachel cut the Irishman off. "I don't know who you're talking about. I married Franklin Belle Saturday night and we were to await his first posting in Charleston." Rachel cleared her throat. "Franklin was held up in New York and will be here shortly. I was sent ahead."

"No!" shouted the girl as she backed away and bumped into one of the rocking chairs. "You can't be married. François and I were to marry." She glanced at the dandy. "Who is this man and what has he put you up to? I was expecting the Colemans, but you're not them. Who are you?"

The dandy introduced himself, and Rachel repeated she was the wife of Franklin Belle.

"No, no, no," shouted the girl and she stamped her foot.

"Miss Alexis . . ." tried the old black man.

The girl turned on him and began to hit him with her fists. As she pounded away, the old black man simply stood there and took it. "No, no! You can't have married François." Eyes full of tears, she shook her head violently. "No, no, I won't have it!"

"Well, I did," said Rachel, who had closed with the girl.

"Is it possible there's been some error?"

Both women turned on Murphy, but Rachel was the first to speak. "Are you saying you doubt the validity of my claim?"

"No, no," said the dandy, "I was only saying—"

"I doubt everything you say," said Alexis, her nose rising. "Why, by the sound of you, you're a Yankee. Why would François have anything to do with you?"

"François or Franklin?" asked the dandy, trying to establish some common ground.

"We married because Franklin loves me," said Rachel. She would not suffer this fool any longer. Why, the little twit was insinuating that her marriage was not legally binding!

"François does not love you," taunted Alexis. "He does not. Does not. Does not."

"Does," said Rachel, being drawn into the childish game she had occasionally been baited into by her younger sister.

"Doesn't, doesn't, doesn't . . . ."

Alexis stopped short when Rachel slapped her. Her pale blue eyes widened and her mouth fell open.

Murphy stared at Rachel.

But it was the old black man who spoke. "Now there's no reason for that."

"You stay out of this, nigger," said the dandy.

Alexis turned on him. "Don't be calling my nigger a nigger." She drew herself up and pointed toward the wharf. "Get off my property, and it's still my property until the Colemans arrive."

"You little twit . . ." started Rachel.

"Mrs. Belle," said Murphy, taking her arm, "perhaps it would be more prudent to take our leave?"

"Yes," said Alexis. "Go now and never return."

And Rachel allowed herself to be led across the veranda, and then down its steps to the waiting carriage.

The girl followed them. "And don't be saying you're married to François when you reach Charleston. I won't have it."

From her seat inside the carriage, Rachel stared at the blue eyes flashing at her from the porch. For the first time in her life she was without words.

But the blue-eyed beauty had plenty. "Remember what I said. I will not have you spoiling the occasion when François returns from West Point."

"Driver!" shouted the dandy as he slammed the door shut.

The carriage jerked forward and started around the turnaround. As it raced between the cedars and down toward the wharf, Alexis's sister came out of the house and watched it go.

"Who was that?" asked Jennie, wiping her hands on an apron. "I was in the yard giving one of the children some castor oil. I hope the Colemans know a thing or two—"

"Yankees!" spit out her sister.

"Alexis, we don't own Cooper Hill any longer. You can't speak to the new owners anyway you like." Jennie watched the carriage race toward the river.

"They weren't the new owners."

Alexis knew in her heart of hearts that François hadn't married. True, she hadn't heard from him since he'd last been home, but everyone knew that men didn't take their correspondence as seriously as they should.

"Did you offer the lady the use of the facilities?" asked her sister. "It's more than an hour to Charleston by boat."

"Jennie, they were just some riffraff who got off to

stretch their legs. You can't expect me to squire everyone around Cooper Hill now that we no longer own the place."

Jennie watched a well-dressed man help a blond woman, equally well dressed, down from the carriage. As she watched, the man glanced in their direction, and then escorted the woman to the boat. When Jennie turned around to question her sister, she noticed Homer trying to get her attention.

To her sister, she said, "Don't you need to lie down, my dear? You shouldn't be out on the veranda. You know what the sun does to your skin."

Alexis put the back of her hand to her forehead and arched her back. "Now that you've mention it, I am feeling a bit faint." She'd simply die if François were married! Married? Impossible! No one had told her, so it could not be so.

"Tammy," called Jennie into the interior of the house.

Moments later a little black girl appeared at the double doors. "Yes, Miss Jennie."

"Could you see Miss Alexis upstairs? She's been out in the sun again."

"Yes, ma'am," said the little black girl, smiling. She *knew* what it was like to spend time out in the sun.

"Jennie, can I really lie down? I thought the bedcovers had been packed away."

"Not on your bed, dear. We saved your bed on the off chance you might need a nap. It was quite a long drive out here." Jennie patted her sister on the arm and led Alexis into the house. "Now, I want you to rest. The Colemans will be here soon, and I'm sure they'll want to meet you."

"I don't know . . . I might not be up to it."

"We'll see how you feel after your nap. I understand the Colemans have two sons, and I'll need your help entertaining them while I show the parents around Cooper Hill."

"Sons? Well, if you insist."

Jennie returned to the porch and looked toward the wharf. "Homer, please have the carriage brought up to the house."

"Yes, ma'am, and you might want to have a picnic basket fixed for them white folks. It's a long way back to Charleston and I don't think they've ate." The Negro stepped down into the turnaround, put fingers to his mouth, and whistled.

At the wharf the black boy looked toward the house. An instant later the carriage was racing up the path between the cedars, and by the time it had been turned around, Jennie had her bonnet on and carried a picnic basket in her hand.

Homer held open the carriage door, and once Jennie was inside, he climbed into the driver's seat with the boy. Moments later the carriage had returned to the wharf where the last of the Belle furniture was being loaded.

Homer got down from the driver's seat and opened the carriage door. He took the picnic basket from Jennie as she leaned out of the carriage and waved to the people on the boat. The blond woman didn't return her gesture, only stared.

Undaunted, Jennie said, "Please ask the husband if his wife needs to return to the house before making the trip downriver."

"Yes, ma'am."

Homer took the basket to the boat and gave it to the dandy. Without smiling, Murphy accepted the food and listened to the inquiry. He nodded and took the basket to the bow.

"You have an invitation to return to the house," said Murphy holding out the basket. "If you care to."

"No, thank you, and please return the food."

"Mrs. Belle, I don't understand what's happening here, and it's certainly none of my business." He glanced at the carriage. "I can only assume the young lady has been reprimanded by her mother and she's trying to make amends."

"I still don't want the food."

"Yes, ma'am, but I'm new to Charleston, and I wouldn't like people to think that I made a habit of being rude to families as prominent as the Belles of Charleston."

"Very well," said Rachel, "then you keep the basket."

The dandy gave a short bow and returned to where the boat was tied to the wharf. To the elderly Negro, he said, "Thank your mistress for the basket, but I'm assured the lady doesn't need to return to the house."

Homer allowed that he understood and returned to the carriage where he climbed back in the driver's seat. Seconds later the carriage was headed up the shaded lane to the Big House, while Rachel Belle was left to sit in the bow wondering what she'd do for lodging once the boat returned to Charleston.

Onboard the clipper ship headed for South Carolina, Franklin paced back and forth while the captain smiled. Taking the pipe from his mouth, the captain walked over to where the young officer paced.

"Nothing to worry about, laddie. We'll drop anchor before nightfall."

"Yes" muttered Franklin. "I only hope that's soon enough." He glanced at the sails as if he could will the clipper more speed.

"You have family meeting your wife, don't you?"

"Yes, sir, I do." A telegram had been sent ahead by the manager of the rail terminal; of that, Franklin had been assured.

"Well," said the captain, pulling on his pipe as the clipper ship flew across the water. "Then that's that."

Not exactly, thought Franklin. When his new wife arrived at the house on High Battery she'd be greeted by his drunken father or his lecherous brother. Franklin didn't know which one was worse.

Chapter Twenty-Seven

All the way downriver Rachel was in a quiet panic. In contrast, the dandy and the boat's captain didn't appear to be overly concerned. Murphy, finished with his picnic lunch, trailed his hands in the water, dried them with his handkerchief, and came forward. Sitting across from Rachel, he joked about the strange girl and how her mother had sent her down to the wharf with a peace offering.

Oh, God, thought Rachel, he's seen through my charade and he's taunting me because I have nowhere to turn. My husband's missing, possibly dead, and I'm adrift in a part of the country I know nothing about. And it probably wouldn't help to let these people, including this Irishman, know what I really think about them.

Rachel took out a handkerchief and dabbed away the perspiration over her upper lip. She really needed a fan. The sun was going down and still the air was hot as blazes. The air seemed to be filled with moisture, and if the weather were like this back in Massachusetts, you'd expect snow, except that it was much too warm. Rachel watched the approaching skyline of Charleston and tried to ignore the anecdotes told by Murphy about Yankees who found themselves at sixes and sevens in the South.

Where was Franklin? And where was his family? Would she literally have go out on the street and ask where the Belles of Charleston lived? People would know, wouldn't they? Belles had been living in Charleston for generations, hadn't they? Oh, my, how could she have married a man she knew so little about?

She'd go to church. Her father always said whenever she had doubts, doubts about anything, she should pray. Well, she had plenty of doubts! But she wouldn't be going there to pray.

She'd go to the Episcopal Church. People who belonged to the Episcopal Church knew everyone in town. At least they knew the movers and shakers.

Turned out Rachel had nothing to worry about. Their nasty-looking captain and the dandy took the strange girl all in stride—Southerners can be rather peculiar, to say the least—and when the boat motored into Charleston harbor in the moonlight, two Negroes were there to haul Rachel's luggage and the three pieces of Belle family furniture onto the dock.

Holding out his hand to help her ashore, the dandy explained, "These men will take both of us to the Belle town house." He smiled for the umpteenth time. "And I'll stay with you until you're safely with your family."

"Oh, thank you, Mister Murphy." A sense of relief

washed over her so complete that Rachel wanted to give him a hug, but she knew she dared not.

The furniture was lifted to the back of a wagon, along with Rachel's chest and bags. Actually, only three were hers, one was Franklin's.

Franklin, why aren't you here? You're causing me to meet your family alone.

Rachel smiled as she was helped into the driver's seat and the reins of the wagon turned over to the Irishman. Still, it would make a splendid story to tell the grandchildren. She blushed at the thought of children and what it might entail to produce them.

A few minutes later the wagon stopped in front of a stately mansion, and the house appeared to glow because it fronted the harbor. Across the street people strolled along a wide wall, and from her seat on the wagon, Rachel could see the moonlight shimmering across the water.

"Here we are, Mrs. Belle," said the dandy from the cobblestone street below.

Gripping her around the waist, he lowered Rachel to the curb in front of a three-story building at the end of a short walkway. For longer than necessary, Murphy held Rachel around the waist, looked deeply into her eyes, and said he hoped he'd see her again and also meet her husband in the future.

"If he's not inside," added Murphy with another one of his ingratiating smiles, "then we can wait for him while we stroll along the Battery."

"I really don't think that will be necessary." Rachel forced her way out of his grip and headed for the house.

The Negroes appeared to have done all this before. They unloaded the furniture, one piece at a time, and carried them down a grassy alleyway alongside the house. At a wrought iron gate beside the house, one of them produced a key and let them inside. Each Negro wore a piece of paper fixed to a string that hung around his neck: a pass to be out after dark.

"We have to consider the possibility of a first-class hotel," said Murphy, trailing Rachel up the sidewalk. "If your husband isn't here, I mean. I have a reservation at the Charleston Hotel, and you can accompany me there."

"Really, Mister Murphy," said Rachel over her shoulder, "and I thought you were a gentleman." She started up the stairs.

He came up after her. "Mrs. Belle, I certainly meant no offense."

"You can apologize to my husband."

Rachel beat Murphy to the door and knocked on it.

"I could've done that, Mrs. Belle."

"Then be quick about it. I haven't seen my husband in several days." Not since we were married and placed on a train heading south. And I'm still a virgin. Oh, my, but she'd heard that was going to hurt.

No answer to her knock.

Murphy reached past her and knocked again. He smiled, and she returned the smile, and they waited as the Negroes came down the grassy alleyway and returned to the wagon for another piece of furniture.

No answer to the second knock.

Oh, God, thought Rachel, please let there be someone here. Please let this be my new home, and she closed her eyes and said a silent prayer. She opened her eyes when Murphy touched her at the waist. Startled, she stepped back.

"You stay right here, Mrs. Belle. I'll go around back and see if the owners are supervising those colored boys."

Murphy left her at the front door, went down the steps, and followed the two Negroes around to the rear of the house. Rachel was left alone and nervously looked across the stone promenade.

No one there. And no one in this house. Wasn't there anyone who wanted her, besides this Irishman?

Upstairs, Lewis heard the knock, and he stopped unlacing the bodice of the woman sitting beside him on the bed.

The woman noticed, too, but her words slurred as she asked, "Lewis, is there something—?"

"Shhh!"

They sat still for a moment, Lewis holding the woman tightly, leaning against her, and taking in the smell of her perfume. Women needed a bit of lubrication to ease them out of their clothing, and the half-empty bottle of wine on the table near the bed stood as testament to his effort.

The woman was quite drunk, and if he didn't hurry, she'd pass out on him. Not that Lewis hadn't had his way with women who'd passed out before, but he did like to hear them respond when he worked his magic on them. Lewis relished his reputation as "a naughty boy," and that reputation had lured many a woman to his bed.

Lewis parted the tresses trailing down the back of the woman's neck and kissed her as he returned to unlacing her corset.

"Ahhh . . . ," she said.

Then another knock.

What?

It distinctly sounded like someone at the front door, but then came a sound from the back porch, and that sound carried up the back of the house to the open window.

Were there slaves loose tonight? Too many fires had been set lately, and everyone knew who was doing that.

"Lewis . . . ?"

Oh, God, why wouldn't people leave him alone. Only minutes after he'd brought her upstairs, a telegram had been delivered and now lay on the table near the front door. The telegram was from the War Department and probably contained his brother's first posting, though why Franklin hadn't received orders at gradu-ation Lewis had no idea.

If this woman hadn't been waiting, Lewis might've opened the damn envelope. As it was, his family was making their annual trip to Savannah, his cousins were squiring the new owners around Cooper Hill, and the servants had been ordererd to remain in their quarters if they knew what was good for them. He thought he had the whole house to himself, and now someone was hammering on the front and back doors.

Damn!

"What's happening, Lewis?" The woman pulled away, and as she did, gathered her bodice around her.

Lewis glanced at those breasts before standing up

and tucking in his shirt. "I'll make them go away."

"Perhaps your family has—"

"My family's in Savannah. I've already told you that."

The look on the woman's face caused Lewis to realize such a tone wasn't the sort of lubricant to keep a woman in the mood. He bent over, nuzzled her neck, and kissed her with passion. Her arms came up around his neck, and Lewis had to pry himself away and lay the woman back on the pillows stacked against the headboard.

"Hold that feeling, my dear." He smiled down at her. "I shall return."

The woman smiled back up at him. "Do hurry," she said in a hoarse whisper.

"Not even wild horses . . ."

Murphy returned to the front porch as the Negroes fetched the third and final piece of furniture.

"Nobody back there, Mrs. Belle. Just a porch to protect the furniture from the weather." He tried looking through the beveled glass but could see nothing. The only light he saw was off in the distance, or was that the effect of the glass?

The Negroes glanced at the white people as they returned from their third trip around the side of the house. At the same time, the latch was thrown, the front door suddenly opened, and standing there was her husband!

"Franklin!"

And with unladylike glee Rachel leaped into his arms. The startled man put his arms around her and glanced at the man tipping his hat.

"Mister Belle, name's Colin Murphy, and I'd like you to know Mrs. Belle was never out of my sight, whether going upriver or coming back down."

"Going upriver . . . ?"

Clearly the man had no knowledge of their trip up the Cooper, and why should he? He'd been patiently waiting for his wife at the town house, not the plantation home.

Rachel kissed Lewis again, lowered her feet to the porch, but held onto him tightly. Her face was flushed and she was quite antsy. Thankfully, no one noticed.

Murphy gestured at the Negroes unloading the luggage from the wagon. "There were three pieces of furniture your family wanted moved from the country to the city, and I supposed it was suitable that these darkies placed them on the back porch."

Lewis nodded numbly. He couldn't make sense of this. All he knew was he hadn't been with a woman for a very long time, and there was an eager one hanging on him, her breath hot in his ear. Forgotten was the woman upstairs but that wasn't all that surprising. Most women in Charleston knew they had to work hard at keeping Lewis Belle's attention.

"Thank you," he said, finally able to extricate himself from the clutches of the woman. He held her back and looked at her. "Where'd you come from?"

And Rachel quickly ran through her adventures since her husband had gone forward to the club car to have a drink. Even though puzzled, her husband was gracious enough to thank the dandy. He did not, thankfully, invite the man into the house. Instead, he produced a card from his breeches, and that's when she noticed Franklin's shirt was unbuttoned. Red-faced, Rachel let go of his arm and rushed inside.

As she did, she heard Franklin say, "Perhaps you could join me for a drink at my club and I could thank you properly."

"Absolutely," said the Irishman as he watched the young woman with the delicious figure disappear inside. Murphy returned the favor by giving Lewis a card. "I'll be at the Charleston Hotel. I'm in town to examine some horses."

The husband glanced at the card, said "thank you," and then followed his wife into the house.

"Er—Mister Belle, this is the lady's luggage." Murphy pointed to where the two Negroes, both hands full, were climbing the stairs. "And the key to the gate to the rear of the house."

"Thank you," said the husband, taking the key and one set of bags, then watching as the chest was placed inside the door. "Well," said the husband with a wink and a smile, "I guess my wife and I have some catching up to do."

The boat Franklin Belle disembarked from was an old clipper ship brought out of retirement by soldiers of fortune on their way to support William Walker, an American adventurer who had seized control of Nicaragua. This wasn't Walker's first foray into Latin America. A few years earlier he'd seized Baja California but had to forfeit his claims when he ran out of supplies. Now, with the Liberal Party of Nicaragua in danger of losing power to the Conservatives, the Nicaraguan Liberals had called on Walker's military expertise to win back their country. Walker had double-crossed the Liberals and seized control of the country with the intention of uniting all of Central America under his rule. This time he would not run out, and Franklin's clipper ship was full of supplies headed for Managua.

The adventurers invited Franklin along. After all, if Walker were successful, he'd bring his new country into the Union as a slave state. Franklin said if he were interested, he'd turn up the following morning before the ship sailed, but right now, he had to tend to some personal business.

A woman! It's a woman, shouted the men as they watched Franklin go down the gangway.

One specific woman, thought Franklin, and he ignored the calls of the carriage drivers and beggars as he stalked toward the house on High Battery. He'd been cooped up too long on the ship, in a hospital, and before that, on a train, and try as hard as he could, he couldn't come up with a better excuse for what had happened to him: getting drunk and being knocked out and dragged off to an army hospital. It was beyond belief.

He needed time to think, and he needed a better story. If Rachel's brother learned of this, he'd demand Franklin meet *him* at dawn on some field of honor. And James would be right! How did anyone lose his bride of only a few hours?

Rachel sat at a table in the kitchen eating cold meat, bread, and asparagus, and being watched by her husband. Rachel could tell her husband was excited to see her because of how he lavished attention on her, asking about her adventures and never once mentioning his. Those small courtesies and his nervous excitement also meant that, after five monastic years at West Point, Franklin Belle was ready to consummate their marriage. Her mother had counseled Rachel to get on with this wifely chore, for only when a woman had children could she leave her mark on the world.

Rachel put down her fork and thanked him again for the food. Across the table her husband beamed, leaned over, and poured more wine.

"Franklin, I don't drink spirits."

"My dear," said Lewis Belle, pouring an even larger glass for himself, "after what *you* went through, I need a drink."

Rachel laughed. Franklin could always make her smile.

Lewis Belle was doing a great deal of smiling. After graduating from the Citadel, he'd immediately gone west to Kansas as a member of the South Carolina Bloodhounds. In Kansas, Lewis had participated in the pro-slavery raid on Lawrence, and watched as the palmetto flag was raised over the headquarters of the free-soilers, or out-of-state militia who didn't want Kansas entering the Union as a slave state.

Lewis returned to Charleston a legitimate war hero and he greatly elaborated on the number of free-soilers who had fallen at his hand. Lewis told everyone that he welcomed the coming struggle with the abolitionists and the establishment of a new country, but first he wanted a woman, and the first one, rather the second one he came across was his brother's wife. Oh, well, it wouldn't be the first time he'd lain with someone who thought she was bedding Franklin Belle.

Rachel burped, smiled, and covered her mouth with her napkin. "Oh, I'm so sorry."

"Well," said Lewis with another smile, "spirits seem to agree with you." Lewis got to his feet and came around the table to take her hand. "And now, it's time to show you our boudoir."

Rachel's face reddened as she came out of her chair, and she could not bring herself to look her husband in the eye. Truth be known, she was rather pleased that she'd consumed so much Madeira. Maybe it would soften the pain.

Lewis took her by the arm and escorted her back into the house. Rachel noticed that her bags were missing from the first-floor landing and figured when Franklin had left her, he'd taken them upstairs. Actually, while upstairs Lewis had checked on the woman in his bedroom. Passed out from all the wine, the woman snored away. Lewis covered her with a blanket and returned to the kitchen where Rachel was wolfing down her food but puzzled at the inclusion of the asparagus. Lewis said it was a favorite in Charleston and she should get used to it.

As they passed through the downstairs hallway, Rachel saw the telegram on the table. She clutched his arm. "From my parents?" she asked.

Lewis saw the envelope and shook his head. "My orders."

"Oh, Franklin," said Rachel, still gripping his arm, "where are we to be sent?"

Lewis smiled down at her. "You think I'd open my orders without you being here?"

Rachel looked up into his face and loved him even more. Franklin Belle was the dear she'd always imagined him to be.

At the top of the stairs, and down the hall, was the spare bedroom. Now that his uncle, aunt, and cousins lived here, there was hardly a bed to spare, but Lewis found one, and nibbling on Rachel's neck, he escorted his brother's wife into the spare bedroom and closed the door behind them.

Chapter Twenty-Eight

Much had changed since Franklin had last been in Charleston. The economy was going ahead full throttle, and you could see the results along the harbor. He counted one or two new wharves; less water stood in the streets, the open sewers had been closed, and crews worked late into the evening removing horse droppings. There were more fire companies, even one manned by slaves, and more mounted police, but those mounted police gave no relief to the Union man being thrashed by several Nullifiers. Other Charlestonians surrounded the group, egging the fighters on, and Franklin was horrified to realize he recognized the man.

Nicholas Eaton! What the devil was he doing here?

Franklin waded into the crowd, demanding that they unhand the New Englander. It only took a moment for the crowd to turn on him. The blue uniform did it.

Coming out of a restaurant across the street, Burke Randolph and Susannah Chase saw the melee, as did the dandy who had accompanied Franklin's wife upriver.

Leaving his cane in the hands of Susannah, Burke waded into the fight beside the dandy, and they knocked down or pushed away several men as they fought their way to the man in uniform. Franklin almost took a swing at them before he realized Randolph and Murphy meant him no harm. With Burke fielding the blows, Franklin and Murphy each seized an arm and hauled Nicholas to his feet. As they did, more locals garnered the courage to take on the abolitionists. When they closed in, Susannah came up from behind and laid out one man, then another with Burke's cane.

"Susannah, return to the restaurant!" ordered Burke.

The red-headed girl laughed and gestured with her free hand for another thug to come ahead. "And you, sir, like this fool here, have mistaken me for a lady."

When the ruffian stepped inside the cane, brushing it aside, Susannah brought her fingers up into the man's throat. The bully gasped for breath and backed away, holding his throat.

Burke flattened another man, then put his hand around the waist of the redhead and gathered her in. "Where the devil did you learn that?"

"My father taught me to always strike a man where he least expects it, and if you don't slap him, he always expects to be struck in one place."

The brawl had drawn the attention of a mounted patrol, and several horsemen moved in to protect a fellow man in uniform. The mob dispersed as the policemen used their horses to break it up.

Franklin wiped the blood from a busted lip as he backed into a horse's flank. "Thank you, sir," he said to the policeman.

"You're welcome, mister, but this won't be the last time this happens if you insist on wearing that uniform in Charleston." The horseman leaned down to Franklin. In his hand was a torch that illuminated Nicholas Eaton's face. "And the sooner that Union man learns to keep his mouth shut, the less trouble we'll have. I warned him earlier tonight."

Franklin glanced at Nicholas, who hung between him and Burke Randolph, the two taking the weight of Eaton between them. Nicholas's head slumped forward, his eyes were closed, and he couldn't stand without assistance. Franklin looked at his own clothing, ripped and torn again. He'd be run out of the service if anyone saw him in such a state.

Burke introduced himself and Susannah as the horses whinnied and neighed around them. Franklin returned the introduction, and that drew the attention of the dandy, who was brushing his hands on his pants.

"I must say, sir, that you do get around." Murphy surveyed the men lying on the cobblestones or crawling off into the darkness. "And your choice of pleasures is beyond my comprehension."

"Pardon?" asked Franklin, puzzled.

"Why I mean your wife, sir. I left her with you only moments ago at your town house, but you, sir, prefer street brawling to spending time with such a beauty."

It only took seconds for what the Irishman said to fall together like tumblers in a lock. Rachel was at the town house and his brother with her, and Franklin knew what happened to a woman left at the mercy of Lewis Belle.

Franklin looked around. No carriages or hacks to be

seen. Responsible owners had shut their windows at the first sound of the fight or driven their carriages into other parts of town.

Franklin turned to the policeman who carried the torch. "I need your horse."

"Get your own, sir, and change out of that uniform before you do it."

Franklin pulled several coins from his pocket and pressed them into the man's hand.

The policeman counted the money in the light of his torch. "Climb aboard, sir. You've just hired yourself a ride."

When Franklin swung up behind the policeman, his companion protested, saying they had their rounds to complete.

"Sorry, Charlie," said the policeman, once Franklin had settled in behind him, "but this fellow says he knows where a nigger might be setting a fire."

And with that, the other members of the troop formed up and followed their companion and the Northern officer down the street to High Battery.

In the spare bedroom Lewis had stripped off his shirt and loosened his belt. Rachel could see his rippling muscles in the light from the bedside lamp. She shuddered with a combination of fear and desire. Her dreams had come true. She was married, and the night she'd dreamed of was finally here. Tonight they'd put the circumstances of their union behind them and begin their lives anew. They'd build a life together, and wherever the telegram on the downstairs table sent them, they'd go as a couple. This house and this bedroom were only the first stop along their way.

Lewis sat on the edge of the bed, one boot removed and his hands on the other. He looked up to see Rachel staring at him. He smiled and patted the bed beside him, but Rachel blushed and ducked behind the dressing screen. Lewis chuckled, took off the second boot, and let it clunk to the floor, then reclined on a pile of pillows. Undressing behind that privacy screen was one of the most beautiful women he'd ever seen, and growing up in Charleston, he'd seen quite a few. Forgotten were the nights with his fellow Bloodhounds and the stark terror of his first skirmish, the surprised look on the man's face as Lewis skewered him.

He was back home in Charleston. Soon his hands would no longer tremble, and he'd hold someone who'd be able to keep that dead man from waking him in the middle of the night. Or hearing the screams of the women and children as the Bloodhounds rode through Lawrence, Kansas.

Lewis was drawn back to the here and now when the hoopskirt was tossed over the dressing screen and came to rest on the edge. After that would be the woman's corset, and then Lewis figured the woman would be sitting in the chair practically naked as she removed her shoes. Lewis rose up off the pillows, swung his feet off the bed, and sat there, fidgeting. He wanted to cross the room, throw back the screen, and seize the woman. Instead, he bit his lip and tasted blood.

From the other side of the screen came the girl's voice, and if Lewis hadn't been so high-strung, he would've heard the nervousness in that voice.

"Franklin, can you do something about the light?"

Lewis swung around to blow out the lamp. In his haste he almost knocked the lamp off the night table.

"That better?" he asked, but only after catching the glass chimney and resetting the lamp on the table. "Ouch! Ouch!" The glass burned to the touch.

"You all right, Franklin?"

"Just . . ." Lewis cleared his throat. "Just can't wait to be with you."

"And me . . . with you. Yes, that's much better. Thank you."

Lewis jerked his fingers from his mouth when Rachel came from behind the screen wearing her nightgown. When she passed in front of the window moonlight revealed her figure . . . the softness of her throat . . . the long tangles of blond hair . . . the swell of her breasts, the curve of her hips.

"Beautiful," he was able to get out after clearing his throat.

Lewis came off the bed and took Rachel in his arms, and it was only the blood roaring through his head that made it impossible for him to hear the front door crash open.

Chapter Twenty-Nine

When it came to babies, Jennie considered her sister one of the worst. Not only had Alexis been rude to whoever had stopped by earlier in the day, she was of absolutely no help once the new owners arrived. The Colemans' boys were both under the age of twelve, and instead of entertaining them, Alexis took a seat in a rocker on the veranda, called for a glass of lemonade, and demanded that one of the servants hover over her with a fan.

"The heat," she said in explanation to the inquiries by the new owners.

This made Mrs. Coleman ask what the remainder of the spring would be like.

"Hot," muttered Alexis and she rolled the glass of lemonade across her forehead.

It was left to Jennie to show the couple around the house, and while Mrs. Coleman inspected the kitchen, her husband and Jennie set off with Homer to survey Cooper Hill.

This entailed riding across quite a few acres where Jennie explained this or that and apologized for places where the carriage could not go. But that would've entailed Jennie riding on horseback and been totally unsuitable. The overseer rode along and just listened. He'd contradicted this girl before and paid the price. If Jennie Belle said the rice business was slumping because of competition from some place called Borneo, who was he to argue.

"Miss Belle," said the new owner, with a bright smile, "if all the Southern girls are like you, then our Northern gals had better polish their manners and study their sums. May I ask where you learned what you know about rice production?"

"You're being very kind, Mister Coleman, but I've lived at Cooper Hill all my life, and a plantation isn't run like a factory. There, I'd assume, you went off to work each day and left the running of the household to your wife."

"Yes. It's only proper."

"Well, this is plantation living, and even if I don't actually work with the help, I know everything that goes on. And what I don't see, I hear about, as I'm sure your wife will quickly learn."

Beside them, the overseer nodded, wearily.

"But the numbers you've quoted, the yields I can expect, just about everything to watch out for . . . ." He flipped the pages of a small journal resting on his knee. "I didn't start taking notes right away, but look at this."

All those pages caused Jennie to blush and look away. She'd gotten carried away again, just like the times when her father had had to rein her in.

"I'm sorry," said Coleman, glancing at the white man on horseback. "I don't know all the conventions of Southern living. Have I committed a faux pas?"

No, no, thought Jennie. Just reminded me of why I shall never wed. "I have a head for numbers, Mister Coleman, and my father occasionally asks me what I remember."

Instead of looking up the information in one of his journals or calling in the overseer. Of course, that didn't begin in earnest until her father had become more comfortable speaking to her as an equal, and a future spinster.

"Well, you're easily the most clever girl I've ever met." Seeing that none of this put Jennie any more at ease, he asked, "Er—what else do I need to see?"

They returned to the house well before sundown and found Alexis ready to head back to town. If they were going to live in Charleston, let's get on with it.

Jennie found she, too, was ready to leave. The more of Cooper Hill she'd ridden over, the more morose she'd become. So, once she'd excused herself and gone upstairs to the third floor storeroom, always a good place for a decent cry, she repaired the damage to her face and returned to the veranda.

The Colemans were there to see them off and watching Alexis with fascination as she fanned herself inside the carriage. "Your sister seems eager to return to the city, Miss Belle," said Mr. Coleman with another smile.

"Yes, sir," said Jennie. "It breaks her heart to leave home, but she'll soon find many a beau in Charleston."

"As I'm sure you will."

Alexis never liked traveling by carriage. She preferred the boat, but the boat had left earlier, and stretching out before them was a long, rutted-out road. In places it was hard to actually make out the road, and where logs had been placed in corduroy fashion, no carriage, no matter how well built, could keep its passengers from being jostled around. Alexis complained, but all Homer could offer was his apology.

As darkness fell, they reached the home of a neighbor and dismounted for supper. The wife asked the girls if they wouldn't care to spend the night, but Alexis said she must return to Charleston, that she expected a gentleman caller the following day and it was important to have a good night's sleep.

The neighbor's wife smiled across the table and agreed if that were the case, it'd be best for them to soldier on. After supper, one of the family's cousins, who'd heard the Belle twins were dining at his aunt and uncle's, arrived to escort the carriage the rest of the way to Charleston. There was little Jennie could do to discourage him, so she had to sit there and listen to the young man try to impress her sister as he rode beside the carriage, and of course, it was like Jennie wasn't even there. North of the Neck, one of the slave patrols picked up their security, and they entered Charleston and headed for High Battery.

Franklin slid off the policeman's horse and raced up the steps. When he found the door locked, he threw himself at it, and after a couple of licks, the frame cracked and the door flew open.

The two policemen looked at each other, slid down from their mounts, but remained in the street. A few moments later a carriage rolled to a stop behind them. Sitting between Burke and Susannah was Nicholas Eaton, and the New Englander was complaining that he couldn't feel his legs.

"We need to get this man inside where he can be properly attended to," said Burke.

"Well, fellow," said the member of the patrol who'd given Franklin a ride, "if you know what's going on, we'd appreciate a clue."

"Yeah," said his companion, glancing at the door standing open, "it appears we've just participated in a breaking and entering."

Assisted by one of the policeman, Burke carried Nicholas into the house. Along the way the injured man moaned several times, and loudly, but the noise he made was nothing compared to the shouts and screams coming from upstairs.

Rachel heard a door slam as her husband slid the gown below her shoulders.

"Rachel, are you up there?" came a male voice from off in the distance.

Who was that? Who was calling her name? Could there be someone downstairs? Or someone at their door? Breaking out of the glow surrounding her, Rachel asked herself where she knew that voice?

Someone was coming upstairs and in a hurry.

Lewis's hands were on the woman's breasts, but she was pulling her nightgown over her shoulders.

No, no! She couldn't stop him now!

Lewis forced the nightgown down and the woman back on the bed. With his free hand, he pushed at his breeches.

To her husband who was kissing her shoulders, Rachel asked, "What's happening?" And what would they do if someone actually opened the door?

Using one leg, her husband forced her legs apart, and then she felt him hard against her, but at the same time there were those footsteps down the hall.

A door was flung and a woman screamed.

Rachel turned and looked at the bedroom door.

"You're not Rachel," came a voice from down the hall.

She heard her name called again, but there was little she could do. Her gown was around her waist, her mouth covered by Franklin's, and he was almost lying across her. Rachel tried to break though the haze created by the wine and the warmth of being with the man she loved. In this she had some assistance. Down the hall came the sound of doors being thrown open and then bouncing off walls as they flew back and tried to close.

"Rachel! Are you up here?"

Who was it? James? What was happening?

While one of her husband's hands held her down, the other found the hem of her gown and pushed it up. The nightgown was around her waist now, her breasts and lower extremities exposed. She wore no undergarments.

"Franklin . . . ?" she asked, moving her head away so he couldn't kiss her.

Suddenly the door swung open and a man stood in the doorway. Rachel turned her head and gaped at the figure standing there.

Franklin?

She looked up at the man hovering over her.

Franklin saw Lewis lying between the legs of his wife. "You bastard!" He hurled himself across the room.

Lewis stood up in time to catch his brother, but there wasn't enough time to do that and pull up his breeches. The two fell back and crashed into the wall. The lamp fell to the floor, the glass chimney shattered, and whale oil spewed everywhere.

Franklin was the first to his feet as Lewis tried to figure out whether to defend himself or pull up his breeches. While he made up his mind, his brother's fist rocked him. Lewis fell back and bounced off the wall. Lights flashed, the room darkened, and it didn't have anything to do with the whale oil burning on the floor just inches away from his arm.

"You dog!" shouted his brother. "I'm your brother."

Franklin hit Lewis again before he could stand, and Lewis collapsed to the floor, holding up his hands in surrender.

"Enough . . . ."

As Franklin staggered over to the bed, trying to keep his balance, he glanced at his wife in the light from the burning oil. Though fire was the single most feared calamity in all Charleston, Franklin couldn't help but notice his wife's torn nightgown, one breast revealed and both long, white legs.

Franklin grabbed the bedcovers, and instead of covering his wife, he threw them over the fire, stamping out the flames. The room went dark until another woman stuck her head in the bedroom door. In her hand was a lamp.

"Lewis," asked the woman, "what's going on here?"

This woman's bodice was twisted to one side and she was barefoot. She saw Lewis sitting on the far side of the bed, and another man who looked like Lewis standing over him.

"Annabelle?" asked Franklin. "What are you doing here?"

The woman held up the lamp so she could see. "Franklin?" Then she saw the other woman on the bed. "Who's that?"

Rachel was still trying to cover herself with her torn nightgown and wondering if she could cross the room to the privacy screen without even more exposure.

"I guess you could call her my wife," said Franklin with a sneer.

Rachel looked from one brother to the other, trying to understand. As she did, another face appeared at the door.

This was a redhead, and after taking in everyone, she said, "I hope all the beds in this house aren't full because I have a seriously injured man on my hands."

From downstairs came the voices of their cousins, and especially Alexis Belle, who demanded to know who these people were and what were they doing in her house.

Jennie

Chapter Thirty

A Charleston house is a huge house, especially for the wealthy, with plenty of rooms to go around. And all family members know their room assignment as they've been using those same rooms their whole life, while waiting for the first killing frost so they can return to their plantation home.

On the ground floor of the Belle home were the stairs to the upper floors, and to the left and right of those huge stairs, two large rooms on both sides of the first floor. One side held the plantation office, and this room contained all the records from Cooper Hill and other plantations, or portions of plantations, owned by the Belles. Generations of data passed down, and the new owners had a right to this information, even the right to copy it.

The new owners would also need a town house to shield them from Cooper Hill's deadly summers. The poisonous air off the swamps (mosquitoes) could kill you, though the Colemans let it be known they'd spend their summers at Newport Beach or at their residence up north. Spending summers in northern climes was *de rigueur* for wealthy planters until the assault on Senator Charles Sumner made any Southerner's reception rather chilly. As a result, more and more Charlestonians felt trapped in their own city, and became rather quarrelsome, even though they had the Yankees to blame for their predicament.

The room across the hall from where the records were kept was filled with meats on hooks, fruits of slave labor from Cooper Hill. It had been the Belle's factor, Abraham Marcus, who made sure a steady stream of foodstuffs would continue to flow into the town house, and he steadfastly argued against the sale of portions of any plantations still owned by the brothers. Still, Marcus knew the Belles would soon have to surrender those holdings, too, if they continued to live such a lavish lifestyle. Where the family's food would come from after that, Abraham Marcus had no idea.

But for now the sale of Cooper Hill had wiped away all indebtedness and the Belle family could begin anew, and Claude and Jean Louis Belle truly believed one of their descendants would eventually repurchase their ancestral home, perhaps someone more suited to being a gentleman farmer. Of course, being up before the crack of dawn and spending your day in the saddle never felt like the life of a gentleman to either brother, and that's why Jean Louis had chosen to practice law.

Upstairs was where the family lived. It was also where, under lock and key, were kept the sugar and other staples, along with the wine, all stored on the third floor. There were few gatherings in the kitchen, as city code prevented a kitchen from being part of the main house, but this did not bother the planter or his family. They had more than enough slaves to carry food from the outbuildings to the second floor and to a room where the family dined.

Along with this upstairs dining room, and a room to keep the food warm, were drawing rooms, parlors, dressing rooms, and more than enough bedrooms, but no baths. The chamber pot was still in use and emptied each morning by the household staff. Indeed, each servant had an area of the house they were responsible for, and more Negroes would soon be brought into town from Cooper Hill. There were too many favorites to be left behind, another extravagance that would become a millstone around the Belle family's collective neck.

So Rachel moved into Franklin's room but never really settled in. How could she? Her husband had caught her in bed with another man. His twin brother. Would this nightmare ever end?

There was a knock at the bedroom door.

Rachel stared at the door in terror.

Oh, who could this be? Franklin coming to collect his husbandly due? Or had he come to beat her? Or would he be drinking again?

Gripping her dressing gown tightly, Rachel took a seat on the far side of the bed. "Yes?"

Her cousin-in-law opened the door, leaned into the room, and gave her a cheery smile. "May I come in?"

"Yes, yes, of course." A bit of tension went out of Rachel. "After all, this is your home."

The beauty with the pale blue eyes and dark black hair closed the door, came over, and took a seat on the bed. The girl smiled, which Rachel found tremendously off-putting. This was the same person who'd treated her so shabbily at Cooper Hill, and she couldn't quite understand why her attitude had changed.

No, no. That wasn't correct. This was Jennie Belle, and the dreadful creature from the plantation house had been her twin sister, Alexandra.

She said, "I just came up to make sure you were comfortable."

Rachel was having a hard time controlling her breathing. She gripped the bedcovers and held on tight. The room had a tendency to move. "I missed you at Cooper Hill."

"You've been to Cooper Hill?" The blue-eyed beauty appeared to be puzzled.

"Yes," said Rachel, nodding rapidly. "I went upriver on the boat that brought the last of your furniture downriver. It's on the back porch, or that's what I was told."

Concern crossed the girl's face. "And with whom did you travel upriver?"

"Oh, just the two men and me." With her breathing under control, Rachel attempted a small smile. She released her hold on the bedcovers.

"Which two men?" Jennie could not believe someone as sensible as Franklin could've married a woman who would travel into the backcountry with total strangers.

"You've already met one downstairs. Mister Murphy."

"And he was with you at all times?"

"Oh, yes," said Rachel. "I wouldn't have accompanied him if he hadn't been a perfect gentleman on the ship."

"I don't remember seeing you . . ." Jennie was trying

to make sense of this, and none of it made sense, nor looked good.

"Oh, that's because it was Alexandra who showed us around."

Jennie remembered the riffraff run off by her sister earlier in the day. Now things were beginning to make sense. "Well, I hope Alexandra wasn't rude to you."

"Really, it was nothing." Rachel's hands fluttered and she found it more comforting to grip the bedcovers. "I'm sure Alexis has a good many things on her mind."

"Yes. It appears the sale of Cooper Hill has upset her more than we expected."

"I can understand," said Rachel, looking around the bedroom. "Changing domiciles isn't easy."

"Well," said Jennie, taking Rachel's hands, "you're Franklin's wife and this is your home now."

"Thank . . . thank you."

Rachel was having a hard time meeting this girl's eyes. She'd traveled openly with a man other than her husband, had sailed to South Carolina alone, and had been found in another man's bed. What must these people think, that Northern women lived fast and loose?

"No, no," said her new cousin-in-law, smiling again, "it's us who should be thanking you. Franklin's always been much too busy for girls."

"I—I didn't know Franklin had a twin." She gripped Jennie's hands. "You must believe me on that account."

"What are you saying, that Franklin didn't tell you about Lewis, or Alexis and I?"

"He told me nothing." Rachel stared at the bedcovers. "Only that he loved me." Tears began to roll down her cheeks. "And I'm not sure he does. Love me, that is."

Jennie scooted over and put her arm around the older girl's waist. "Now, now, there's nothing to be upset about."

Rachel's head came up, almost colliding with Jennie's chin. "Nothing to be upset about! My husband found me in his brother's arms."

"Er—yes, well, why don't you tell me what happened."

As Rachel explained her confusion over the twin brothers, Jennie's face stiffened. Releasing her, Jennie turned to the door and called out, "Ella Mae."

An old Negro woman opened the door and entered the room. In her hand was a mug, on her face a smile.

Jennie took the mug and handed it to Rachel. "Take a sip. You may not like the taste, but I want you drink the whole thing."

After a sip, Rachel made a face. "Really, I've had quite enough spirits for one night."

"Please drink it. Drink it all." Jennie got to her feet. "Rachel, this is Ella Mae, and she's the mistress of this house. When she tells you to do something, you must comply, understand?"

Rachel almost dropped her drink. She could not believe any Southerner would kowtow to any Negro. What power did this woman hold over these white people? She'd read about voodoo but never expected to meet one of its practitioners.

The old black woman put a hand on her shoulder, and Rachel flinched. "Don't you be worrying about anything, Miss Rachel. Soon we'll have all this straightened out."

Rachel looked at the white girl who was at the door. "You're going to leave me?"

"Believe me, you're in good hands. If you haven't noticed, a lot has happened and I need to make as many things right as possible." Jennie released the doorknob. "Rachel, would you happen to know the man down the hall? He was calling for you."

"Calling for me?"

"And there was a letter in his coat pocket in which he speaks of you in the most intimate terms."

Rachel looked from the white woman to the black one and back to the white one again. "But I know no one in Charleston."

"The letter is signed 'Your beloved Nicholas.'"

"No, no," said Rachel, spilling some of the whiskey. "That's impossible. Nicholas is in Lowell."

"Then you know this man?"

"I only know one Nicholas. Nicholas Eaton." Rachel stared at the bed as the mug was taken from her hands and the spill quickly brushed away. "He was my fiancé in Boston."

"You were engaged to this man?" asked Jennie.

Rachel looked up. "Yes . . ."

"But married my cousin?"

"Er—yes."

"Then what's Mister Eaton doing in Charleston?"

"I have no idea." Rachel straightened up on her bed. Actually her and Franklin's bed. Oh, my Lord, she was supposed to have relations with her husband tonight.

Shadows on the wall jumped and jiggled. Her breathing became uneven and her chest felt tight. The girl and the old black woman appeared to be moving.

Rachel blinked, and the room stopped moving.

Could Nicholas really be here? He'd written on many

occasions of his devotion to her, usually when he went to sea for his father's textile firm. But Nicholas was in Boston . . . where his father owned not only several textile mills but had access to more than one shipping line.

Oh, my Lord, no, no, no! Her breathing came faster and faster, and it was all she could do to remain upright. When she did, the room really did move.

Jennie was describing the young man who lay in a bed down the hall. "Who does that sound like to you?"

But Rachel didn't hear her. She'd passed out and fallen facedown across the bed.

Chapter Thirty-One

"François, I need to speak with you."

Jennie said it from the door of the plantation room, as she intended for her cousin to join her in the hall. Instead Franklin remained behind Pierre Belle's massive desk, holding a piece of yellow paper in his hand, shoulders slumped. When he looked up at her, he let the telegram slip from his fingers.

"François?"

Slowly his eyes focused on her. "Oh, hello, Jennie."

"I need to talk to you."

Jennie had been forbidden to enter this room, for this was where men handled their business, and now she entered reluctantly. It wasn't the same as being summoned to her father's study at Cooper Hill for some obscure figure or calculation.

For the first time she noticed Franklin's uniform was torn and dirty. "What has happened to you, François?" Jennie spoke in French, not English.

He stared at her from the chair, then replied in the

same tongue, telling her that he had graduated from the United States Military Academy—not that anyone in this family cared—gone north to ask for the hand of Rachel Mullins in marriage, and then become separated from her in a train accident. His wife had preceded him to Charleston; on his way home, he'd run across Rachel's former fiancé, Nicholas, whom it would appear would not take "no" for answer. This would require that he fight a duel, and that would cause him to be dismissed from the army.

Franklin smiled sardonically. "Then I come home and find my wife in the arms of my brother."

"Well, we know how despicable Louis can be and he's never disappointed us yet." As Jennie entered the room, she glanced at its shelves of hundred-year-old journals and books on how to plant everything from rice to indigo. "Where is Louis?"

"I threw him out and told him not to return until I . . . ." Franklin glanced toward the hallway. "Until she and I are out of the house."

"Well, I'm sure Louis will land on his feet."

"He always does, but for me, it only gets worse." Franklin picked up the telegram at his feet and held it out. "This countermands my original orders to report to Savannah, a place I thought might ease Rachel into Southern life." He shook the telegram at her. "These are new orders: to report to Kansas, and no dependents are allowed within the territories."

Jennie gasped and her hand came up to her throat. "Surely that can't be true. Louis has just returned from Kansas. He said there's to be more fighting."

"Yes," said Franklin, with a sick little laugh, "brother

against brother, it would appear."

"François?" asked Jennie, coming around the desk and standing nearby, "why did you not tell us of your engagement? Despite what you believe, there are people in Charleston who care about you, but you have written few letters over the last few years, and certainly nothing that would have prepared us for such happy tidings."

Franklin's face broke into a smile. He laughed. "That's what I'd expect from a girl who's spent most of her life in the country: a sunny outlook."

"I know Charleston, too."

"No, you don't. Charleston has changed, and this is the last time I'll return." He sat up and straightened his tunic. "I knew this uniform wouldn't fit in, but all my other clothes were in my chest and my chest had been sent on ahead."

"It arrived yesterday and I had Homer put it in your room."

"Anyway, I was a fool to walk to the house."

"Or you were looking for a fight." Jennie ran her hand through Franklin's short, black hair.

Franklin took her hand and looked up. "So young and perceptive. Jeanne Anne, how old are you? You can't yet be sixteen."

Jennie drew herself up. "I'll be fifteen next year."

"And already bearing the weight of the world on your shoulders. It's not fair. You should have time to be a girl before the world requires you to become a woman."

Jennie pulled away. "It's been obvious for quite a while that you don't want anything to do with Charleston. You were the one always touting its shortcomings."

"Only for its failure to embrace the modern age. Christ, Jennie, only in Charleston is it unlawful for a carpenter to use a steam-powered machine."

"François, I know you've spent the last five years in the company of soldiers but please do watch your language."

He apologized for taking the Lord's name in vain.

"Sometimes I worry about the company you keep," Jennie said. "Those ideas, they came from Abraham Marcus, didn't they?"

Franklin stood up and pushed back his chair. "One of the best friends this family ever had. Don't underestimate that Jew."

"Actually, this conversation has gone too far afield. At a later time we can discuss familial economics or why you didn't let your family know of your engagement, but your wife needs you now."

Franklin fell into English as he looked into the hallway. "I don't think I'm the one she needs."

"François," said Jennie, still speaking in French, "she has no one else to turn to."

"Nicholas has money. She should've married him instead of me."

Jennie took Franklin by the arm and walked him into the hall. "I'm sure everything will work out for the best. Now go upstairs. You have a wife to attend to."

When they came out of the plantation room, Alexis stood there, crying. "François, can it be true? You are married?"

Franklin took his cousin in his arms and tried to comfort her. "There, there. As your sister says, everything will work out."

Sobbing, Alexis was barely able to get out: "But—but I always thought . . . ."

Franklin held the girl away from him. "You always thought what?"

"Oh, nothing," said Alexis as she pressed close again.

"Alexis," said Jennie from behind them, "Franklin needs to be with his wife."

This caused Alexis to cry much harder. Franklin unfastened Alexis's hold on him and released her into the arms of her sister. Before going upstairs he gave the two of them a rather forlorn look. For Alexis, this only encouraged more tears.

Jennie held her sister, the two of them rocking back and forth as they watched their cousin climb the stairs.

"Alexis, dear, you must stop carrying on like this."

"But—but I thought he loved me."

"Alexis, not every man in the Low Country will become infatuated with you."

"You don't know that." Her sister wiped away the tears with a small embroidered handkerchief. "How would you know? Did you have a vision?"

"Alexis, how many times do I have to tell you that I don't have visions."

"But everyone thinks . . . my friends believe . . . ."

Jennie let out a long sigh. "And that's why the talk will never end. Alexis, please allow Franklin to get on with his life. Don't burden your cousin with your childish infatuation."

"Oh, you are so horrid. Sometimes I can't stand the sight of you."

"I only mirror the image I see."

"Now what does that mean? You're always speaking

in riddles. No wonder all my friend think you're strange." Alexis crossed her arms and the handkerchief dangled from one hand. "You and I are the same age so my friends are supposed to be your friends, but they won't have anything to do with you."

"Alexis, you must learn to watch what you say. Words can be hurtful."

Alexis uncrossed her arms, and as she did, snapped the handkerchief. "You're only a few minutes older than me. That doesn't mean you know everything, or what's best for me." She cast a glance upstairs and shook her head. "My life's over. The only man I ever loved has married another."

"Alexis, you're being irrational."

"Oh, yes, you're the rational one. The loveless one. You have no friends. No one in this family trusts you. You're all alone in this world. See what your cleverness has gotten you?"

Bewildered and saddened, and not for the first time, Jennie reached out for her sister, only to have her flee upstairs.

When Alexis reached the second floor, she turned around and shouted, "You did this to François! You drove him away!"

Jennie's shoulders slumped, and a tear appeared in the corner of each eye. Quickly, she wiped the tears away. This was not the time, nor the place, for a good cry.

Homer appeared out of the darkness of the hallway stairs. "Need anything, Miss Jennie?" He reassured her with a smile.

"Oh, probably several things, but I don't know where to begin."

"I was told to tell you that Mister Randolph and Miss Chase had to be getting on home."

A pain sliced through Jennie, and it surprised her. She hadn't known how much she wanted to get to know the man who had come to her rescue, or at least thank him. "I'm sorry to hear that. I was going to get around to them sooner or later."

"I helped Mister Burke with that Eaton boy."

"Help? How's that?"

"Well, he wanted some strange things, but I done got them anyway."

"What do you mean?"

"He had me bring a bucket of hot water upstairs from the kitchen."

"Why?"

"To clean Mister Nicholas's head where he got cut in the fight."

A knock came at the front door.

Homer crossed the hallway to answer it.

"Is that all he asked for?"

"Oh, no, Miss Jennie. He wanted a needle and thread to sew the boy up." Homer smiled as he turned the handle and pulled open the door. "He stitched up that young man's head right smartly, but not before he dunked the needle and his hands in the bucket of hot water. That must've burned."

It was Dr. Rose at the door.

"Evening, Doctor Rose," said Homer with a large smile. To Jennie, he concluded by saying, "Then made us give him a clean piece of sheet for Mister Nicholas's head."

Dr. Rose looked from Homer to Jennie as he came in

the door. "Clean sheets for dressings? What's this all about?"

Homer nodded to the doctor. "Said he learned it in Europe."

"Europe?" asked Rose. "I thought the injured party was from New England."

Jennie asked Rose to follow Homer upstairs.

"That's not necessary, my dear. I've been in this house plenty of times. I know my way around." Rose crossed the hallway for the stairs. "Had to leave in the middle of Beethoven, but they told me a young man had been trampled by a mob."

"I don't know anything about a mob," said Jennie, following Rose to the foot of the stairs, "but the friend Franklin brought home is in the spare bedroom."

"Conscious?" asked the doctor, going upstairs.

"Not when I last saw him. Homer, if you don't mind . . . ." And she gestured with her head for the elderly man to follow the doctor.

As Homer followed him, Rose said, "I said I know the way."

"Then Homer will show you to the proper room. We have more than one guest in this house tonight."

"Well, I hope none of them is ailing. I'd like to get back to the recital in time for the encore."

In the kitchen Jennie found the empty mugs left behind when Susannah Chase and Burke Randolph had been offered coffee. Ella Mae, not understanding these two people's standing in the Charleston pecking order, had escorted the visitors out here, blaming their accommodations on the number of injured parties occupying the rooms upstairs.

Jennie looked around the empty room. Only a small fire and a lamp gave the room any light, or character. This time of day, at Cooper Hill, the kitchen would be filled with smells, activities, and the songs of servants. Jennie gripped the edge of the table where Rachel had been fed by Lewis and burst into tears.

Ella Mae had followed her into the room and now she put a hand on the girl's shoulder. "There, there, Miss Jennie. Your folks will be home in a few days."

Jennie nodded, stifled her tears, and wiped them away. "And Franklin's . . . wife, how is she?"

"Well," said Ella Mae, smiling, "I don't think some colored person is the best one to be comforting Miss Rachel right now."

Jennie faced her, a woman who'd always been such a presence in her life. "I—I don't understand."

"That's because you're not a Yankee meeting your first Negro."

It took a moment for this to sink in.

"And if I say so, I don't think Mister Franklin is the one to be with his wife tonight."

Jennie wiped her tears away. "I'll—I'll go right up." She started away.

"Miss Jennie, what's happening in this house?"

From the kitchen doorway Jennie faced her and smiled. "Nothing more than Franklin bringing home more guests than we'd expected."

"Well," said Ella Mae, with a hearty laugh, "that's one way of putting it."

Upstairs Jennie found the doctor and her cousin

wrestling with Rachel in the hallway, and very close to the stairs. For this reason Homer stood at the head of the stairs in case someone stumbled in that direction.

"No, no!" said the distraught woman. "I must see him."

Rachel still wore her dressing gown, but her blond hair had come out of its netting and now fell across her shoulders.

When Franklin pulled his wife away, the physician said, "You must keep this woman away from me or I can't work."

Held by Franklin from behind, Rachel pleaded with Jennie. "I must see him. I really must."

Jennie took her hand and gripped it. "Please calm yourself, Rachel, and tell me who you wish to see?"

The woman stopped struggling. "Why, James, of course. You said he was here."

Jennie looked at her cousin.

"James is her brother," said Franklin over his wife's shoulder. "Back in Massachusetts."

His wife canted around, still in the grip of her husband. "But you said James was in the next room." She looked at Jennie. "That's what Franklin said."

"I thought it was Nicholas Eaton in the next room."

Franklin nodded to Jennie over his wife's shoulder.

"Nicholas?" asked Rachel. "What would Nicholas be doing here?"

Jennie looked at the doctor, who was brushing down his jacket. "Don't look at me. I don't know the young man's name."

"No, no. I wondered if it'd be all right for Rachel to see her brother."

"The unconscious man is her brother?" asked Dr. Rose.

"No, no, no," repeated Franklin. "It's not her brother."

"Franklin," Jennie said, "Rachel's concerned about this young man, whoever he might be, and it might relax her if we let her see him." Jennie looked at Rose who simply shrugged.

"Yes, yes," said Rachel, nodding. "I must see James."

Franklin shook his head, not in defiance but from general weariness.

Another knock at the front door, and Homer turned to go downstairs. Before he did, the elderly Negro said, "Oh, I forgots to tell you what the other doctor said about the ice."

"What doctor?" asked Rose. "Another doctor has been here?"

"Ice?" asked Jennie.

"Well, that white man who put Mister . . . well, whatever-his-name-is in the spare bedroom. Said to keep ice on that young man's head."

"Who was this man?" asked Rose.

Jennie shook her head. It was getting so that you needed a dance card just to keep up with the guests.

"Well," asked Rachel, crossing her arms, "are you going to let me see my brother or not?"

"Any chance we might get some whiskey into her?" asked the doctor.

"I don't drink spirits," said Rachel. She twisted her head around to look over her shoulder at Franklin. "You know that, dear."

"It's for the best . . . ."

"No," said Rachel, shaking her head. "Father simply

wouldn't allow it." She looked down the steps and her eyes widened in surprise.

"You're with me now," said Franklin, gripping her from behind.

"Rachel," asked Jennie, "if we let you see James, would you drink some more whiskey?"

But Rachel wasn't listening. She'd burst out of Franklin's hold, brushed past Jennie, and started downstairs.

"James!" she shouted. "Oh, James, I thought you were upstairs."

Jennie turned and looked. Standing in the entrance hall with Homer was a blond young man in a uniform similar to the one her cousin wore.

"Who's that?" asked Jennie as the doctor and her cousin joined her at the head of the stairs.

"James," Franklin said. When Jennie looked at him for further explanation, he added, "My brother-in-law."

Chapter Thirty-Two

Dorothy Laurens, who went by "Dottie," and Millicent Pinckney, who preferred her childhood name "Pink," belonged to two of the Charleston families that had arrived in the Low Country somewhat earlier than the Belles had arrived from France. Of course, there was no "somewhat earlier" if you were discussing the arrival with Mrs. Laurens or Mrs. Pinckney, as the two women had agreed on a mutual date years ago to keep the peace between their two families.

"Dottie" Laurens and "Pink" Pinckney would also be at the head of any invitation list if you were giving an important party, and the Belles of Charleston were giving such a party as Jean Louis presented his new daughter-in-law, Rachel, to the city. The two women arrived "fashionably late," but, because of their age, were allowed to go ahead of others in the receiving line.

Jennie Belle, who knew everyone, along with the blond young man standing beside her, James Mullins, a lieutenant in the United States Army, introduced everyone to each other. Jennie would say to make this Yankee and his uniform welcome in Charleston, at least for the evening. Then Jennie would smile and pass the guest along to the brother of the bride, and since the ice was broken, James would introduce Nicholas Eaton, who sat in a chair beside him in the receiving line. And everyone agreed that no matter how long the line was, or how tedious some of the guests became, or the fact that both men were Yankees, Nicholas Eaton was always in good humor even though he was confined to a wheelchair.

Sitting in a Queen Anne chair beside Mr. Eaton was Margaret Belle, looking pale and exhausted, but who perked up whenever someone bent down to speak to her or gave her a peck on the cheek. Next in line was her husband, Claude Belle, who had recently moved his family into the city from Cooper Hill, and then daughter Alexis, standing in for the mistress of the house since Marie Belle, wife of Jean Louis, had passed away many years ago.

And then the bride and groom, looking radiant and ill at ease at the same time: Lt. and Mrs. Franklin Belle, whose maiden name was "Mullins," and whose family everyone should remember because the Mullins were associated with Eaton Textiles, a firm that bought boatloads of cotton from some of the very planters attending the reception tonight. The Mullins family sent their regrets that they could not travel south during this busy time in the textile business, and this was why Simon Eaton had sent a representative of his family, son Nicholas. Lewis Belle, the other son of Marie and Jean Louis, was nowhere to be seen.

Anyone who was anybody was there, and "Dottie" Laurens and "Pink" Pinckney were soon holding court in a corner of the drawing room on the second floor. Working both together and separately, these two women soon had the truth, or what they perceived to be the truth, about everyone in the receiving line, and many who were not.

"Well," said "Pink" Pinckney, fanning herself with a small paper fan. These drawing rooms could really heat up, especially when the young people began dancing. "I can't say that this marriage brings any shame to the family."

"The bride is beautiful," responded Dottie Laurens with a wave of her own fan. "Even if she's not wealthy, her family is well connected. I doubt anyone will ever have to look for work."

"Fortunate for Franklin and Lewis, as I understand Cooper Hill has been sold."

Dottie tsk-tsked. "Hasn't been a true planter in the family since their father ran off to Florida and got himself killed, leaving a wife and all those children."

Lowering her voice, Pink stopped fanning herself long enough to ask, "There's not been anymore talk of Anne taking up with the family factor, that Jew, has there?"

That stopped Dottie's fan, too. "Not for years, but I do believe Lewis Belle inherited his mother's interest in romance. Where is Lewis anyway?"

"I was told he returned to Kansas with the South Carolina Bloodhounds."

"That so? Joseph Rutledge, you know him, Frances Rutledge's boy, said Lewis shipped out with William Walker's people when they called at Charleston a few weeks ago. Joseph wanted to go along, but his mother put her foot down."

"Good thing she did. My grandson says Joseph's going to get himself killed with all his pranks. Anyway," said Pink, cranking up her fan again, "either one's a proper fight. Kansas, Nicaragua, or Cuba, we need another state to make sure our voice is heard on the floor of the Senate."

Dottie looked at her friend. "Pink, I had no idea you kept up with politics."

"Everyone best keep up with politics. The Yankees are hellbent on taking away our property rights."

"Been learning how to talk like a man, have you?"

Mrs. Pinckney gave a mild snort. "The future of this city will depend on its women as it has in the past. Why back in my grandmother's day—"

"Pink, remember who you're talking to. I know what our grandmothers did during the Revolution."

"Well," said Mrs. Pinckney, "I would hope so."

"But why would Franklin go north for his education? Now he has an abolitionist for a wife, and where does that get him? It's one thing to have a Yankee living in your house, quite another to have an abolitionist."

"Are we sure Rachel is an abolitionist, or should we simply condemn her for being from that part of the country?"

Mrs. Laurens leaned over to whisper behind her fan. "I've heard both the new bride and the Eaton boy have traded words with Claude and Jean Louis, and that Margaret had to make a rule that politics would not be discussed in the house."

"Politics should never be discussed when ladies are

present, but are you telling me that when the men get together for their cigars and brandy, no politics are discussed?"

"That's what I was told."

"Amazing." Pink looked across the room at the woman in the Queen Anne chair. "Never would've thought Margaret had it in her. I heard she never leaves her room."

"She'd best. Her girls are much too young to enforce any rules, and there's the fact that Jean Louis likes his Madeira. Someone has to keep an eye on him."

"Hmm," said Pink, "but if that's the case, why haven't we seen Jean Louis with a glass? He's only taken a drink when participating in a toast, and that's with punch."

Dottie stared at the man who stood next to the bride. "Don't know. Perhaps he found Jesus. It's happened before."

"Maybe the 'no politics' rule is one all households should enforce. Never seen so many people upset, well, not since the tariff of '28."

"No politics discussed in Charleston? People would rather give up breathing."

"Quite right, and I understand that's why the Eaton boy's in a wheelchair."

"Do say. I heard it was a riding accident."

"Not what I've been told. Young Eaton left the house one evening in the company of Franklin, and they ended up in a tavern where Nicholas couldn't hold his tongue when some of our more articulate debaters engaged him over the issue of slavery. I understand the argument spilled into the street, and it was such a quarrel that Franklin was lucky he wasn't injured when he came to young Eaton's aid."

"An injured groom. Don't think that would sit well with any bride."

"Perhaps it would," said Pink, eyeing the far end of the receiving line. "Possibly cool the groom's ardor."

Dottie smiled in agreement. Both women had their wedding night horror stories.

"Still," said Pink, continuing to stare at Rachel Belle, who stood across the room, meeting one guest after another, "I ask you, Pink, dealing with husbands as we must, does that girl look like she's become a woman?"

"Pink," said Dottie, "what an outrageous thing to imply."

"I find it hard to believe myself. Northern girls are known for their unrestrained ardor."

Dottie was staring at the bride. "Still, you might have something there, my dear. Of course, I would never speculate on the state of another's marriage."

"Wouldn't be ladylike. Have you heard if there are any plans for Nicholas Eaton to return home?"

"I was told by Helen Grimké that the poor boy has vertigo and that sea travel is out of the question at this time."

"So Mister Eaton will remain in Charleston when the husband departs for Kansas?"

"That's what I understand."

"Hmmm," said both women in unison and their fans began to work in earnest.

"I suppose Franklin's agreeable to that as long as Mister Eaton is confined to a wheelchair."

"Well, as long as Mister Eaton *is* confined to a wheelchair. Remember my cousin Percy who everyone thought couldn't move a muscle and everyone waited on hand and foot?"

"Oh, yes, your family spent their lives providing for him, didn't they?"

"And come to learn Percy could get around quite well, and that he'd been visiting beds other than the one everyone thought he was confined to."

"Hmm," said the women in unison as they looked from the bride to the man in the wheelchair and back to the bride again.

Jennie Belle caught their eyes and smiled at them until the two elderly women returned her smile. Jennie quickly broke off her smile when a tall man with good shoulders entered the receiving line. Most everyone had passed through, and perhaps that's why this young man had waited to introduce himself; he was spending considerable time talking with Jennie Belle. Neither Pink nor Dottie knew the young man, and they knew everyone who was anyone in Charleston.

"Who is that young man?"

Virginia Hampton passed by as the question was asked and glanced at the receiving line. "Burke Randolph of the Randolphs of Virginia."

"Oh, my, but he's quite attractive," said Dottie. "Would you happen to have Mister Randolph on your dance card, Virginia?"

"Yes," said Pink, "I hear the musicians tuning up."

Across the room a string quartet began to harmonize their instruments.

"I don't think my father would permit me to dance with Mister Randolph. He's much older than I."

"That doesn't appear to be keeping Jennie Belle from engaging him in conversation," observed Dottie, "and she's younger than you."

"Yes," Pink said, "she literally seems to have stars in her eyes."

"Some gambler might be the only beau Jennie Belle can find."

"Virginia, please don't be that way. As a member of the sorority of women, we should support all women in their quest for the proper marriage."

"Yes, my dear," agreed Pink, fanning herself once again, "I know you see other girls as competitors, but as a young lady who comes from a prominent family, you should encourage everyone to become engaged and marry."

"Indeed," Dottie said. "Charleston society doesn't need a pack of unmarried women prowling about."

"It's not healthy, Virginia."

"Oh, I'm sure Virginia is having too much fun for such serious conversation. Are you still seeing Sidney Craven?"

"Can't say that I am," said Virginia, rather airily. "He appears to have found someone else to call on."

"And your father allowed this snub, my dear? That is very hard to believe."

Virginia gestured toward a young man using a cane to cross the floor. "Besides, I don't think my father would want me to be courted by a cripple."

"'A 'cripple' is such a harsh word. Isn't there a more polite word you could use?"

"Yes, my dear. I know I'm not your mother, but do take this in the spirit that it's offered."

Virginia thought for a moment and said, "Engaged to someone who might have to use a cane for the rest of his life."

"Marvelous, my dear. Simply marvelous."

"Bravo," said Dottie, almost applauding. "Well done."

And they watched the receiving line break up as Sidney Craven crossed the room and spoke to Alexis Belle. Claude took the hand extended by Sidney and shook it. Alexis's father smiled and said something. His comment didn't appear to be enthusiastically received by his daughter.

"Poor Alexis, always wearing her heart on her sleeve."

"She doesn't look all that happy with your former beau, Virginia."

"She can have him, for all I care. You know, I might just have a word with that Lieutenant Mullins."

"The brother to the bride?" asked Pink.

"You mean, just walk up to him?" And Dottie's fan went to work again. "Oh, my, but the younger generation is much bolder than back in our day."

"What I meant to say is that I'm sure I can find someone to introduce me. I didn't learn that much about him when I was in the receiving line."

"Well, my dear, you'd better hurry. I hear Lieutenant Mullins leaves for California soon. He's just passing through."

That brought Dottie's fan to a stop. "How do you make that trip these days? I understand they have rail service across the isthmus now."

Pink shook her head. "I've never thought that was any way for a lady to travel."

"Why would a lady travel to California in the first

place?" Dottie's fan started up again. "It's all rough-necks out there. Imagine, a state coming into the Union with rabble running it."

"Couldn't be any worse than the ones governing those states north of the Mason-Dixon Line."

"Well, if you'll excuse me," said Virginia, clearly bored.

"Yes, yes, my dear," said both women.

As Virginia left, she heard Mrs. Pinckney say, "If you think about it, California has to be much safer than Kansas."

"Any place would be safer than Kansas," said Dottie, leaning in behind her fan, "unless you were speaking on the floor of the Senate."

The ladies laughed behind their fans, the musicians began to play, and soon Virginia Hampton was moving with James Mullins within their quadrillion area.

"My, my, but that girl doesn't waste any time."

As the women looked on, other couples joined them in performing the quadrille, a square dance for four couples, and across the room, Sidney Craven leaned on his cane as Alexis stood nearby. By the way the girl's skirt moved, both women could tell Alexis was tapping her foot to the music.

"I don't think that match will work out."

"Of course it will, Pink. Just give it time."

"Only if Claude includes a good number of lectures about the merits of young women marrying well."

Then Jennie Belle came promenading by on the arm of Burke Randolph. Both young people were speaking in French.

Jennie said, "I didn't know they still spoke French in Virginia, Mister Randolph."

"Please call me 'Burke.'"

"I don't think so. Perhaps later."

"Oh," asked Burke, with a coy smile, "will there be a 'later?'"

"Well," said Jennie, "there will certainly be a later dance."

"Miss Belle, I can't believe your dance card isn't filled."

Jennie looked away. "It never is."

Burke glanced at the young men standing in clusters, some standing alone. Wallflowers all, that is, until some girl finagled a way to get them on the dance floor. "Their loss, my gain."

"I don't mean every dance will be available, and I hope you wouldn't ask me to dance too many times."

"Oh, that would make you angry?"

"No. It would cause me severe embarrassment, as you very well know."

"To have one man monopolize your time?"

"Mister Randolph, you're from Virginia. You certainly know what proper decorum is between people our age." She regarded him as they continued to dance in place. "How old are you anyway?"

He grinned down at her. "Is that a polite question for a young lady to ask?"

"For a woman to ask a man, yes."

Burke chuckled. The girl was truly bold. "Twenty-three."

"Twenty-three?" asked Jennie, losing a step. "My goodness, you're almost ten years older than I."

"That's funny," he said, smiling down at her once again. "I couldn't tell there was much of a difference, could you?"

Jennie flushed and looked away. The music ended, and he bowed and she curtsied.

"May I fetch you a cup of punch, Miss Belle?"

Jennie glanced around. When she did, she saw James Mullins asking her sister to dance, and her sister forgetting to ask Sidney Craven for permission to take her leave. She'd have to speak to Alexis about that, the rudeness, that is. On the engagement front, Jennie was as opposed to Alexis marrying Sidney as her sister was. Jennie remembered the horrid-looking faces sticking their heads inside her carriage and the sickening crunch as the carriage ran over one of those boys' ankles.

She shivered.

"Miss Belle, do you need a wrap?"

"No, no. It's nothing."

"Well, you don't look like you'd care to have a cup of punch with me. You know, a woman as striking as you might attract another partner while I'm gone. There's always that to look forward to."

"Oh, I'm sorry. I was just thinking . . . ." Jennie stopped and stared at him. "We're not speaking French, are we?"

"I wondered how good your German was. Miss Belle, is it true you have a head for numbers?"

Jennie's eyes hardened. Men were all the same. All of them wanted her to perform a trick. "I think I'd best check on our guests. Now, if you'll excuse me."

He took her hand. "Jennie, please . . . ."

She looked at where their hands came together and asked that he release her. What would people think? The music had started, but they weren't dancing, just standing in the middle of the dance floor.

"I'm sorry," Burke said, and he escorted her off the floor, making sure they didn't collide with other guests.

Jennie's father met them as they left the dance floor, and the older man was grinning. "Mister Randolph, if you don't mind, I'd like to meet the man who can spend more than one dance with my daughter."

"Father, please . . . ."

Burke gave a short bow. "I was just getting some punch for your daughter. May I get you a glass, sir?"

Claude held up his glass. "Just for Jennie, if you don't mind."

"Certainly." And Burke gave the half-bow again and left them for the punch bowl.

"Who is that young man?" asked her father.

"You were introduced to him in line, Papa."

"I don't think I had cause to remember until now." He watched Burke have two glasses filled by one of the servants. "Hmm. Doesn't seem the least bit skittish. What is it? His age? How old is he?"

"Papa, please don't do this. I'm trying to enjoy Franklin's party."

Claude looked at his nephew on the dance floor. "I wish Franklin looked like he was enjoying it."

Jennie saw how stiffly her cousin approached his bride as they performed the quadrille, and remembered the time she'd entered their bedroom before Franklin's pallet had been taken up from the floor. "I think he's worried about leaving Rachel in Charleston."

"Oh, everything is going to be just fine. Rachel and I aren't going to fight every day."

"Mother doesn't like for you to fight at all. Papa, I

don't understand everything Rachel says, but I don't raise those issues. Franklin said that's why he and James remained friends during their years at West Point."

Claude smiled as he watched his nephew and his bride dance. "Perhaps it was the sister's friendship he valued more than the brother's."

Burke returned with the punch and offered a glass to Jennie. She thanked him, took the glass, and sipped the punch.

"Well, I'd best excuse myself," said Claude. "I need to spend some time with Sidney."

They looked in that direction. The crippled young man was leaning against the wall and talking in a low but animated voice with a friend of his, another face Jennie remembered from the attack on her carriage. As did Burke Randolph. Burke would never forget that red hair, those freckles, but he'd also made a promise to the magistrate to restrain from fighting.

"Sidney will have to get used to Alexis's desire to dance," her father said. "You don't turn off fun at her age."

"Mister Belle?" asked Burke. "I wondered if I might have permission to call on your daughter."

Jennie cut off any reply by her father. "I'm not some trick pony, Mister Randolph. I wasn't put here on earth to entertain you and your friends."

"Miss Belle, I did not mean to give offense. I was only asking if I could call."

"Is there some reason Mister Randolph should not call?" asked her father. To Burke, he said, "I'm sorry you have to learn this so early in life, but all married men answer to their wives and later our daughters."

"Father, you should be aware that Mister Randolph is a gambler and almost ten years my senior."

"Oh," asked her father, now understanding, "and which of these do you object to, my dear, his age or his bad habit?"

"Both."

"Well, there you have it, Mister Randolph. I guess you'd best find another girl to call on."

Jennie nodded, but inside her heart was breaking. Still, she would not be someone's plaything.

"I'm sorry for the offense, Miss Belle, but I was fascinated by the idea of teaching someone such as you the rules of poker."

"Poker's a man's game. No proper lady would ever play cards."

"What's this?" asked Claude, amused. "You're not interested in this young man, but you're having your first fight?"

Jennie looked away as her sister whirled by, laughing and dancing. Life was being especially cruel tonight. "Mister Randolph, I can see there's no meeting of the minds here, and even if there were, I'm certainly not going to have my daughter taught how to play poker."

Burke reached out and turned Jennie's chin so he could see her face again. Jennie was horrified, and her face instantly colored; still, she could not pull away. The man's touch was electric, and for a moment she thought it might not be so bad to be this man's trick pony.

"Mister Randolph," said her father, seizing Burke's arm, "you forget yourself!"

Jennie felt her legs weaken when the hand was pulled

away. Punch spilled from her cup and dribbled down her hand.

"I apologize, sir, and I'm sorry I won't be allowed to call on your daughter. Everyone knows the best poker players are in Charleston, and someone with your daughter's ability—"

"I'm not some freak!"

People turned and stared.

"No," said Burke with a generous smile, "there's no way anyone who met you would ever receive that impression."

Claude took Burke's glass and handed off both glasses to a passing servant. "Mister Randolph, if you don't leave this house immediately, you may never play another game of poker in Charleston. I'm very close to asking for satisfaction."

Burke gave another half-bow to Jennie but addressed his remarks to her father. "I apologize once again, sir, and I apologize to your daughter, but I doubt either of you could understand a gambler's heart."

"That, sir, is quite possibly true." To his daughter, Claude said, "I'm sorry, my dear, but I'm going to have to personally escort Mister Randolph from this house. People are beginning to stare."

Sick and tired of being bullied about her impairment, Jennie jutted out her chin. "You'd teach me all the rules of the game? You wouldn't hold anything back . . . to make fun of me . . . later?"

"And run the risk of never seeing you again, Miss Belle, why in the world would I do that?"

"And I'd never be asked to play poker in public?"

"Miss Belle, your cards, your rules."

Jennie stuck out her hand. "Then it's a deal."

They shook hands as her father protested. "Jennie, please, people are staring."

"Then," said Jennie, the young man's hand still holding hers, "I think Mister Randolph should return us to the dance floor."

"For my final dance of the evening?" asked Burke, smiling. Truly, this girl knew no fear.

"Endless dances," said Jennie as they returned to the dance floor. "That's what you've just cursed yourself with, Mister Randolph, endless games of poker and endless dances."

About the Author

Steve Brown is the author of the popular Susan Chase mysteries (set at Myrtle Beach), and several historical novels, including *Of Love & War* (Pearl Harbor), *Fallen Stars* (Vietnam), and *Black Fire* (church burnings in South Georgia). Contact Steve at www.chicksprings.com.

To learn more about Charleston:

A Short History of Charleston
Robert Rosen

An Antebellum Plantation Household
Anne Sinkler Whaley LeClercq

Bowing to Necessities: A History of Manners
C. Dallett Hemphill

Charleston! Charleston!
Walter J. Fraser

Charleston in the Age of the Pinckneys
George C. Rogers, Jr.

Mary Boykin Chestnut: A Biography
Elisabeth Muhlenfeld

The Grimké Sisters from South Carolina
Gerda Lerner

History of the South Carolina Military Academy 1783-1892
John Peyre Thomas

Honor & Slavery
Kenneth S. Greenberg

Mary's World
Richard N. Côté

Motherhood in the Old South
Sally G. McMillen

South Carolina: A History
Walter B. Edgar

Within the Plantation Household
Elizabeth Fox-Genovese

DEC   2008

F
BRO

Brown, Steve.

The Belles of
    Charleston.

$15.95

DATE			

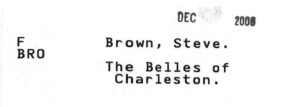

WITHDRAWN

BAKER & TAYLOR